Palestine Minus One

First published in Great Britain in 2025 by Comma Press.
www.commapress.co.uk

Copyright © remains with the authors, editors, translators and Comma Press, 2025
All rights reserved.

The moral rights of the authors to be identified as the author of this Work have been asserted in accordance with the Copyright Designs and Patents Act 1988.

A CIP catalogue record of this book is available from the British Library.

ISBN-10: 1917093020
ISBN-13: 978-1917093026

This book has been selected to receive financial assistance from English PEN's 'PEN Translates' programme.

The publisher gratefully acknowledges the support of Arts Council England.

Printed and bound by CPI Group (UK) Ltd, Croydon, CR0 4YY

PALESTINE MINUS ONE

STORIES FROM THE EVE OF THE NAKBA

EDITED BY
BASMA GHALAYINI

Contents

INTRODUCTION Basma Ghalayini	vii
THE FOREST OF SAFFOURYEH Yara El-Ghadban Translated by Helen Constantine	1
ISMAIL AL-LYDDAWI Ibtisam Azem Translated by Rana Asfour	7
TRAPPED Anwar Hamed Translated by Andrew Leber	25
KATAMON Selma Dabbagh	45
A CHRONICLE OF GRANDAD'S LAST DAYS ASLEEP Mazen Maarouf Translated by Jonathan Wright	57
THE SLEEPLESS SPRING Ahmed Jaber Translated by Adam Talib	89

CONTENTS

AL-SHATAAT Lina Meruane Translated by Andrea Rosenberg	101
THE DRAGON Sonia Sulaiman	109
MY MOTHER IN CHANGING TIMES Mahmoud Shukair Translated by Raph Cormack	119
EASTWARDS Abdalmuti Maqboul Translated by Mohammed Ghalayini	131
I SWEAR, ALL THIS HAPPENED Liana Badr Translated by Maisa Almanasreh	175
FLOOD G. Abraham	197
Glossary	229
About the Contributors	231

Introduction

PALESTINIANS HAVE THIS JOKE (it's not very funny): A Gazan is running frantically down the street. Someone grabs him and asks: 'What's going on? Has something happened?' 'No,' the man replies, 'but it might.'

Through 77 years of occupation, violence, displacement, and repeated collective punishment, Palestinians have never stopped running. Not just from the soldiers on their streets, the drones and F35s in their skies, the warships in their seas, the informants in their midst, or the world's most technologically-advanced, politically-impervious military state bearing down on all sides, but from an idea, a century-old myth, a fantasy: that you can spread a map out on a table somewhere and simply invent a country, regardless of what already exists there. It's a European fantasy, of course. This particular one being the brainchild of Theodor Herzl, an atheist Jewish journalist from Budapest, who sought to heal 'the wound' of antisemitism in Europe by creating a completely new Jewish homeland. Through a lifetime of lobbying and organising, Herzl put various proposals for such a state – including Lord Chamberlain's later-abandoned 'Uganda Scheme' – onto the European political agenda, that is to say, onto politicians' tables. Herzl wasn't the only European to indulge in table-top fantasies, of course. In late 1915, when British and French diplomats Mark Sykes and François Georges-Picot sat down at tables in London

INTRODUCTION

and Paris and secretly drew straight lines through lands that didn't belong to them, and through lives that they would never know, dividing the spoils of the Ottoman empire between three other empires, they too were indulging in a fantasy: one that would soon (if briefly) cohere with Herzl's. The new British colony of Mandatory Palestine would need partners on the ground, proxies to eventually take on the dirty work; and two years after the Sykes-Picot agreement was ratified, the British found their proxy, their co-fantasists, in the Zionists. When Lord Balfour scribbled his famous 1917 'declaration' – a document with no legal or moral basis – green-lighting the creation of a new country for a community that at that time only made up five per cent of the population on the ground, it was yet another exercise in fantasy world-building.

Five years later, in 1922, this fantasy acquired a veneer of legitimacy when the newly-formed League of Nations voted to include Balfour's terms as part of the British Mandate. There then followed waves of Jewish immigrants arriving in Palestine, resulting in a series of uprisings and strikes among Palestinians, which culminated in the so-called Arab Revolt (1936-39), a three-year-long rebellion demanding independence from the British and an end to the Zionist plan. During the Revolt, the British government's Peel Commission visited Palestine and concluded that a partition between the newcomers and the indigenous people was in order. Ultimately, the Arab Revolt was unsuccessful and was suppressed by the British Military with the support of emerging Zionist paramilitary gangs, like the Hagana and Irgun. In response to the Revolt, the British government issued a White Paper in 1939 allowing for the establishment of a Jewish 'national home' in an independent Palestinian state, but limiting further Jewish immigration and restricting the Jewish incomers' ability to buy land, overriding the Peel Commission which had called for a simple partition.

But different peoples' fantasies can only coexist for so long. In 1946, in the immediate aftermath of the Second World War,

INTRODUCTION

the Hagana, Lehi and Irgun Zionist militias turned on the British, launching several attacks against them, including the bombing of King David Hotel where the British were headquartered, killing 91. The following year, Zionist delegations to the newly-formed United Nations and intense lobbying of Truman's White House led to the 'Partition Plan', aka Resolution 181, being adopted by the UN in New York in November 1947. Perhaps the table this plan was drawn up on was slightly wider than the one Sykes and Picot had used, but the thinking was just as detached. Resolution 181 called for the end of the British Mandate and the division of the country into two halves, giving much of the Mediterranean coast, the North East and the Southern tip to the Jews, and establishing Jerusalem as an extraterritorial, international zone. As a result, clashes erupted between Palestinians and the incomers, continuing until the British disengaged from Palestine altogether in 1948. Despite the Zionists having lobbied the UN and US intensely, the year before, for the Partition Plan's map, by March 1948 the Zionists in Palestine had adopted a whole new plan that went far beyond 181's proposed borders: the infamous *Plan Dalet*. Wherever this plan was drawn up, on whatever table, it had no arbitrary divisions, no unnatural straight lines. It simply wanted everything – all of Palestine. This was a fantasy dripping with blood.

Headed by David Ben Gurion, Plan Dalet's tactics included laying siege to Palestinian villages, bombing Palestinian neighbourhoods, forcibly expelling inhabitants, setting fields and houses on fire, and detonating TNT in the rubble of already-destroyed buildings to prevent people from returning. Using detailed inventories of Palestinian villages' families, assets, power structures and allegiances, that the Zionists had meticulously gathered over many years, the militias – led by the Hagenah and including the Irgun and Stern (or Lehi) gangs – launched a campaign of terror that ultimately displaced 750,000 Palestinians from their homes, secured 80 per cent of

INTRODUCTION

historic Palestine for the Jewish incomers, emptied eleven cities, ransacked 531 villages, committed over 70 massacres, and killed at least 15,000 Palestinians. Israelis may refer to this war by other names; to Palestinians, it has only ever been called one thing: the 'Nakba', the catastrophe.

But Palestinians haven't just been running their whole lives from violent, Western fantasies.

They've also been running from their own trauma – private, collective and intergenerational trauma. And the route you take to escape trauma isn't always clear. Trauma doesn't follow any rules. It is fundamentally dreamlike in its nature: indeed the word 'dream' and 'trauma' stem from the same root (the ancient Greek root word: τραῦμα, meaning 'wound').

The two years of genocide we've all just witnessed constitute yet another dreamlike trauma that Palestinians will always be running from. A living nightmare, live-streamed on social media, making us see things that we can never unsee. As with all dreams, it has collapsed our sense of space (for us in the diaspora, bringing 'back home' closer to us than where we now live) as well as collapsing our sense of time. The past has telescoped into the present. Horror stories our grandparents once told us, from 77 years ago, have played out once more in our reels. The Nakba then has become the Nakba now.

Just one example: on the wall of a flat in Manchester, a new key hangs – a modern, Yale latch key: the key to my mum's apartment in Shalihat in Gaza which, after being bombed and repurposed as a watchtower by IDF snipers, was then reduced to rubble. The key on the wall echoes the classic symbol of Palestinian identity: the old, bulky, rusty keys that all Palestinian families kept as heirlooms, passing them down from one generation to the next: keys to our grandparents' homes, that they hoped their descendents would one day return to.

Sometimes we have to stop running. It's unsustainable. When fantasy and trauma are the cause and effect of the Zionist

INTRODUCTION

project, one way to turn and face it might be to engage with the two Nakbas - the current and the original – by fighting these living nightmares with created ones: fighting one fantasy with others, fighting dreams with more dreams.

This was the thinking behind the book you now hold in your hands: not just a prequel to *Palestine + 100* (which projected the pre-genocide trauma of Palestinians onto possible futures), but also an outlet for twelve Palestinian writers to try to process the magnitude of what has been happening, offering them an alternative, more distant iteration of the same thing: the old Nakba, in place of the new.

In the stories that follow, a recurring theme is that this nightmare is itself recurring. In Anwar Hamed's story, 'Trapped', a character inspired by Hind Rajab – the five-year-old girl, targeted and shot by the IDF in her family's car, along with six members of her family and the two paramedics coming to her aid – becomes a time traveller, portalling into other women's lives, and metamorphosing into them at other, pivotal moments in Palestinian suffering.

While some characters fuse, others split and divide. In Sonia Sulaiman's 'The Dragon', the narrator finds his identity cleaving into two, just at the moment he decides to flee, leaving a version of himself, and the life he was meant to have, forever behind. In Mazen Maarouf's 'A Chronicle of Grandad's Last Days Asleep', the narrator reflects, 'It's like there are two of me: one here and another over there', before being rendered a ghost, who along with other ghost children, starts a new life as a house servant to the foreigners who've moved into his home. In Liana Badr's 'I Swear, All this Happened', schoolgirls discuss the myth of the Qareena – a djinni-like twin or shadow that follows your every move in the underworld, guiding or misguiding you. Even buildings and institutions have a dark doppelganger that eventually replaces them: a Palestinian agricultural college, for instance, gets repurposed by the invaders as a mental institution.

INTRODUCTION

Other strange recurrences echo through the book, internally and metatextually. Reading Badr's descriptions of her beloved Dar al-Tifel al-Arabi school, founded by the formidable Hind al-Husseini, I was reminded of a group of children I'd known in my teens in Gaza, the 'Abna'a al Sumud' (children of resilience) – orphans of the 1982 Sabra and Shatilla massacres in Lebanon, brought to Gaza in the early 90s, and taken under Yasser Arafat's wing personally.

Some of the most haunting ghosts in these stories are the settings - villages and neighbourhoods wiped from the map, their names contorted and disfigured or replaced completely. We can pay tribute to these original places (and their people), or we can be haunted by them. It's up to us, all of us. It is no coincidence that the annihilation of these towns and villages provided the origin stories for countless political movements: George Habash, the founder of the Marxist PFLP, came from Al-Lydd ('Lod'), the setting of Ibtisam Azem's haunting story; two of the founders of Fateh – Salah Khalaf and Khalil El Wazir – were born in Yaffa and Ramle, respectively; Ahmed Yassine, the founder of Hamas, was born in Asqalan ('Ashkelon'); all these places were obliterated by the Nakba, stolen, repurposed. If we don't honour their original form, if we don't remember their names, or the names of the massacres – Balad al-Sheikh, Sa'sa', Deir Yassin, Tantara, al-Lydd, Saliha – they have no choice but to haunt us.

The speculative fiction devices used by the writers aren't limited to horror. Abdalmuti Maqboul's 'Eastwards' uses the superhero genre - that quintessentially American canon - to critique America's role in the multiple Nakbas. Thus, 'Vetoman' (a nod to America's decades-old protection of Israel at the UN) becomes an active participant in the al-Dawayima massacre, reminding us of America's role in the development of this plan. The Biltmore Program, a stepping stone towards Plan Dalet, that openly proposed violence as the way forward for Zionism, was devised on a table somewhere in the

INTRODUCTION

Biltmore Hotel, New York, in 1942. And, to remind us that Israel's formation had very little to do with the Holocaust, except in retroactive justification, Selma Dabbagh's story, 'Katamon', echoes the assassination of Count Folke Bernadotte, a man who had been a hero to the Scandinavian Jewish community, having saved 450 Danish Jews from the Theresienstadt concentration camp, and who was, on being appointed the UN mediator for the Palestine-Israeli conflict, promptly assassinated by the Zionist Lehi militia.

These stories are all fictions, of course. But they raise a question that could and should be asked: if a new country is conjured out of thin air and made flesh through massacres and atrocities, should we be surprised by the violence it's prepared to engage in to sustain itself? Should we be surprised by the ferocity of the 2014 onslaught on Gaza, for instance, or the 2012 bombardment, or the 2008-9 bombardment, or the violence inflicted during the two intifadas, or the everyday brutality of settlers and occupying forces in the West Bank, or the massacres of Sabra and Shatilla, or the violence of 1967, and so on, and so on? Perhaps, if we knew anything about 1948, we wouldn't be surprised at all. Perhaps we would be wary of the country's geopolitical intentions. Perhaps we could even help it face the monster of its past.

There is a story from the early days of the Zionist movement: that Herzl or his colleagues sent two rabbis to Palestine, in the late 19th century, to investigate the viability of building a Jewish state there. They reported back with the message: 'The bride is beautiful, but she is married to another man.' Even in the early days, Zionists knew that Palestine was indeed a beautiful land, but that it belonged to others. As for these stories, they should leave you in no doubt: the bride *is* beautiful, and she has been, and always will be, married to another man.

Basma Ghalayini,
October 2025

SAFFOURYEH

The Forest of Saffouryeh

Yara El-Ghadban

Translated from the French by Helen Constantine

IF YOU TAKE THE road to the north from Jaffa to the Galilee, after two hours' journey, you'll arrive at the entrance to the Tzipori National Park. Then you buy your ticket with shekels decorated with the face of Ben Gurion, founding father of the state of Israel, and scrupulously follow the signs that eventually lead you to the archaeological site you've heard so much about: Zippori, the ancient commercial metropolis of the Roman Empire, capital of the Galilee. The town where a young Jesus Christ is said to have worked as a carpenter by day, and returned to Nazareth each night.

The guide tells you the history of Zippori Tsipori Sepphoris (you choose the language), ticking off one by one the impressive mosaics at your feet. They are indeed so fine, you can scarcely take your eyes off them. Until a breath of air, a voice, *something* whispers a word in your ear. You raise your eyes to the hill overlooking the site. There in the distance, a vast forest of pine trees covers the hillside. All the same height. All the same colour. A carefully manicured green carpet that looks out of place in the rest of the landscape.

The guide, who has noticed what you are looking at, is quick to warn you not to stray from the marked path. If you do, you will endanger the precious ruins and the native flora in the National Park. Especially not to go near the forest, even if it looks tempting. Whispered rumours go through the group of visitors. Some say the forest is haunted by an evil spirit. Others tell of misadventures that have befallen walkers who have vanished there and of others who have emerged muttering incomprehensible words.

Nobody will tell you the truth. No one will tell you what this carpet of dark green is hiding. Nobody will mention the stones buried under the moss, nor the broken buckets lying around where there was previously a well. Nor the baskets that were used to carry provisions. No one will explain how these pine trees, which are not native to this soil, have spread over the hillside. No one will admit that the forest which was planted so rapidly in 1948 concealed a crime. No one will tell you it's in that place, under those trunks, all of the same thickness, that I am buried.

Me, Saffouryeh. The guide will not mention my name and he will not mention my language. Me, Saffouryeh, I come from a country that has been wiped from the map. Me, Saffouryeh, my revolutionary people known for their green eyes, who defied the British. Me, Saffouryeh from Palestine, I existed.

Once upon a time, I was a village. Lovers, rebels, poets came forth from my womb. A garden of languages breathed in my lungs. My skin told an epic tale of fragile and devouring myths. Beneath my feet geography folded, unfolded, layer upon layer of sand, rocks, rivers, hills, mountains, valleys. History has deposited the world's dust upon my body. The desert mingling with the meadow's dew, the salt-sweet breath of the Dead Sea and the Sea of Galilee, the rusty corals of the Red Sea and the inlets of the White Sea – the Arabic name for the Mediterranean.

Fruit trees pushed up through my tresses, peasants and warriors huddled together between my breasts, I have nurtured missionaries and crusaders. On one shoulder I bore a convent, on the other a fortress. On the back of my neck the villagers built their dwellings, coloured my hair with their grass and corn and made love by the springs that gushed from between my lips.

When I tell you the rest of my story, do me a favour and remember love. Remember I was neither victor nor villain. I was Saffouryeh. I slept at night, lulled to sleep by the voices of those who dwelled there. The news was about the young bride already with child, about the shepherd who lost one of his flock the other day, about the season of figs, the cheese marinating in water, salt and spices, the sick donkey and straw panniers that must be sold in Nazareth for a good price.

On quieter days, the forest of pines covering me stretches out my branches to the *shamali,* the north wind. And then I can hear the girls' and boys' footsteps echoing as they hurried to the ruins in the meadow. Their feet brushed the ground, uncovering the mosaics of the old Roman emperors. The children played, and with their dancing muddied the imprint of history. Empires came, empires went, along with their commands, their massacres and their arms. The children and the children's children, they never left me. They were a part of me, like water in the sea. Each time power laid its hands on my neck to strangle me, the dwellers in the village rebelled.

If I were no longer a ghost, a corpse or a scream, I would tell you about the rebellion in the 1930s. I would speak of Ahmed al-Toubeh, a rebel from Saffouryeh who belonged to Izz ad-Din al-Qassam's forces. Izz ad-Din al-Qassam, hero of the Palestine Resistance, Terrorist Number One to the British and later to the Israelis. You were wondering why the Palestinian home-made rockets bore the name Qassam? Now you know.

If I were no longer a ghost, a corpse or a scream, I would tell you how Ahmed and three comrades assassinated the British District Commissioner for the Galilee, one Lewis

Yelland Andrews, depriving the British regime of one of its most fervent lieutenant colonels. Me Saffouryeh, I always had something to say about history. Remember that those who bore me were not victims or villains. They were peasants fighting for their freedom against an empire, an empire whose tentacles reached to the farthest corners of our planet, one which wanted to root them out from me, their village, their cradle, me Saffrouryeh, I who have seen so many conquerors come and go. To root them out and fill my belly with other lives, stories transplanted from cold lands abroad, lands of snow and pines.

If I were no longer a ghost, a corpse, or a scream, I would tell you about the hunt for the man which then took place. The British commander who had dared to walk on my land and threaten the villagers, thinking he would find amongst these green-eyed, fair-skinned Arabs collaborators who would be prepared to betray one of their own. The people in the village suffered interrogations, aggression, humiliation. And my skin absorbed their blood and their tears.

That was in 1937. How could I have known that in less than ten years everything would collapse? The Catastrophe, the Catastrophe… So why had the sky, the earth, the wind not given warning of the *nakba* that would sweep everything away?

They came in the night, the giant millipedes. One moonless night in 1948. Millipedes with a thousand arms carrying a thousand guns. Millipedes with a thousand eyes swarming through the streets, targeting someone's head, or a heart beating too loud. Millipedes who spat out foreign words from a thousand loudspeakers. And after the millipedes came the salamanders, secreting poison from their lizard skins, corroding my hills with their fire, suffocating my trees with their breath. A warm, viscous liquid ran out on to my belly - a river of blood, a garden of heads, arms, legs. Some were small, others big. Some were sleeping, others working when the salamanders arrived.

THE FOREST OF SAFFOURYEH

I screamed. I screamed when their boots with biting teeth sank into my thighs. I screamed while they were tearing my muscles and breaking my bones. I screamed and my cry echoed from one hill to the other. I could hear the thunder taunting me, the sirens whistling, the *dum dum dum* of vengeful fists, drumming out death against the walls, doors and windows of the houses that were covering me. The grasses that coloured my cheeks were dying, my tresses were exploding in flames. The monsters invaded every corner of my body. The monsters devoured everything.

It was the silence woke me. Not a whisper, not a song. Not the squeak of a door or the crackle of a fire. I tried to get up, to detach myself from the hill, but terrible needles pinned me to the ground. A forest of pine trees had been grafted on to my skin. Thousands of little spruce trees planted in the place where I had worn tresses of olives, pomegranates and figs. A thousand spruce trees thrust into my heart, down my throat, veiling my face, sewing my lips together with their roots. I screamed. But no sound came out.

I was buried, me, Saffouryeh, the village of good people, the village of rebels and revolutionaries, under a tombstone of evergreens. Now, the meadows where the children played have been fenced off, designated an Israeli National Park, nature reserve and archaeological site. Just the remains of the Roman town and a few monuments from the time of the Crusades have been preserved.

Now and again, the wind brings me news of the survivors of the *nakba*. The *shamali* tells me they are living in Nazareth in Haret-al-Safafreh, the district of the inhabitants of Saffouryeh. As for our hero, Ahmed al-Toubeh, who was imprisoned and then escaped thanks to the help of some brave people, he had to go into exile in Syria. Ahmed died stateless.

I know this because the pine trees, jailors in spite of themselves, told me so. I know this because they refuse to be complicit in the crime. I know this because the pine trees whisper their secrets to me. I know this because their roots which are preventing me from crying out, also quench my thirst and feed me.

Buried under trees for decades now, I've learned to listen. To read the souls of strangers. Hear the secret language of the eyes. Rivers of blood spurting into the pure white. The silent drowning. From my tomb, I can decode faces. Like a gypsy reading the lines in your hand. Each wrinkle, each dimple displaced, eyelids that hide secrets, lips pursed on account of wounds, nostrils that spit out the ash from an ancient fire. I capture the very smell of their hearts. Like a silkworm, I clothe myself with the waves that saturate space. Simply by sniffing the air, I can detect vampires, stalking among the game. Me, Saffouryeh. Me, the village buried under the pine forest, I haunt the monsters in the hills of the Galilee.

Ghost, corpse, stifled scream, I still live. Violated by the feet of tourists who dream of the Roman conquests of the Promised Land, I live. I have set a trap with their fantasies and desires. From time to time comes a visitor more curious than the others for adventure. It may be a soldier taking a break from genocide or an official who is tired of signing demolition, expropriation or detention orders. Drawn by the murmuring of the pine trees, they wander off the beaten track in the National Park. Thinking they might discover a secret garden, they enter my tomb.

And they never get out.

AL-LYDD

Ismail al-Lyddawi

Ibtisam Azem

Translated by Rana Asfour

1.

I SQUEEZED ISMAIL'S HAND and, with the mosque behind us, we ran home to avoid being caught. His slender fingers trembled in my tight grip as his legs fought to support his delicate frame. I tugged him closer, worried his clammy hand might slip from mine. Was the steady stream of sweat due to fear, or the sweltering heat of July – a heat the likes of which I'd never experienced before? When my mother remarked that this July felt hotter than hell, my father had laughed and said, 'How would you know? Have you ever been?' But my mother was right. We had unwittingly found ourselves in al-Lydd's hell, the Hell of Palestine, without even realising it.

My mother always says that prayers offered with the first drops of rain are sure to be granted. And so it was that eight months prior, on the eve of the feast of St. George al-Khader[1] – the revered patron of al-Lydd – as the first gentle drops of rain fell, I stood gazing up at the sky, pleading with al-Khader to watch over us and keep us safe in al-Lydd. And he did. Yet, nothing within us has remained unscathed. I asked Ismail whether al-Khader was hard of hearing. Otherwise, how could he keep us in al-Lydd, but allow everything in and around us to be destroyed?

Ismail and I hastened, keeping pace with our terror. The streets were now traps where hunters hungered for our flesh, aiming their guns at anything that moved. That day has remained etched in my memory, alongside the haunting absence of Ismail's voice. I had assumed this silence would be temporary, just a reaction to the present moment. I never imagined it would take decades before I would hear him speak again – today, for the first time, more than seventy years after he seemingly swallowed his voice whole on 11 July, 1948.

Ismail was always singing, revelling in the Ataaba and the Mejana, performing them at weddings, as he flitted between the guests like a vibrant Palestinian sunbird. His small stature and youth belied the powerful sound that flowed from his throat, reminiscent of water gushing from the ground after a heavy downpour – abundant and captivating, drawing its audience into a reverent silence. His slight build seemed at odds with the powerful sound that emerged from deep within him, as if it were breaking free from a deep well.

2.

Ismail and I were born in the same year, but I entered the world six months before him. He's my soulmate, a brother not born of my mother. We spent most of our time together since our fathers were business partners. Despite his slender and delicate constitution, his features were handsome, and he was renowned for the beauty of his voice. He inherited his fair skin, green eyes, and chestnut hair from his mother, whereas I had my mother's dark complexion. My strong, sturdy build and brown eyes were my father's.

Early that morning, my father had retired to one of the innermost rooms of our house to catch up on sleep after being up all night. He, along with the neighbours – including Abu Ismail – and a group of local men and some refugees, had stood watch over the vineyard and the homes in our area.

News had been pouring in about the intensifying clashes in the nearby villages, compounded by the influx of displaced people arriving in al-Lydd from Jaffa and the sleepy towns in between. Ismail and his mother had spent the night at our place, and when we woke up that morning, we found she had left, leaving him behind. My mother told us she had gone to collect her mother, who lived near the Dahmash Mosque. In the meantime, Ismail's father had gone to check on their home, hoping to retrieve some of their belongings.

The week before, I had celebrated my tenth birthday. That night, sleep had eluded me, as it had on many previous nights, gripped as I was by an intense fear, fuelled by listening to the chilling tales of the displaced who had found refuge in al-Lydd. Sleep abandoned us all, so that our nights became long and gloomy. Even the moon, which only a week ago had ravished the sky, was now swallowed up by the dark. I had cherished al-Lydd's oil-lit lamps that shimmered in the streets like fallen stars, their glow brighter on nights when the moon retired and left us in darkness. At that time, the British had denied our request to build a local power station after we refused electricity from the Zionist Rotberg Electricity Company.

The previous week, a man who had taken refuge in the orange groves died mid-sentence. Although I was uncertain of the years he carried on his shoulders, it felt as if he had left an entire lifetime at the border of the village he had just fled from. As if he had survived only to share the story of a life that had been confiscated when he was expelled from his home. To give us his incomplete life so we would carry another body with us. He passed away as he was telling us how the Haganah invaded his village, tearing through homes, and stripping the residents of money and jewellery. He dwelled on his wife's bracelet, a treasured piece he had given her after saving up from the orange harvest. He appeared tanned, and despite his gaunt face, his bulging eyes still retained their radiance. He described in detail the intricate engraving on his wife's bracelet and the brown stone set at its centre. He recalled how they had travelled to Jaffa to buy it. He was describing the look in his wife's eyes when they stripped her of it. He suddenly paused, choked back tears that were still unborn, and drew his last breath right there in front of us. Just like that, the man died in the middle of the tale he was telling, giving us his incomplete life to carry.

3.

My father owned a large vineyard and worked as a merchant, trading with many orchard and vineyard owners from nearby villages. People were expelled from Yazur, Beit Dajan, al-Safiriyya, Kafr 'Ana, Sarafand al-Amar, Sarafand al-Kharab, and Saqiyah, and flocked to al-Lydd, with many deciding to set up camp in our vineyard. I often used to accompany my father on his business trips, delighting in the sight of the villagers' smiling, radiant faces – a cheerfulness long vanished since they arrived in our town as refugees.

Ismail loved to sing. He learnt it alongside his father, an oud player, who held nightly gatherings in the orange groves, where we would gather around to hear him play. Ismail also learned the Tajweed, and his smooth, melodious recital had impressed the mosque's muezzin enough to let him lead the Eid celebration the previous year. I remember the pride radiating from his father's face and his broad smile as he listened intently. Ismail's voice rang out like the sweet, unmistakable melody of the Palestinian Tamir, as if Ismail had inherited its captivating sound and shape. The town singer loved Ismail's voice and would take him along to sing at weddings, where he would become another person. He would stand between two rows of men, who leaned forward and backward in dance, their palms coming together in a steady rhythm of clapping as they echoed the lyrics of 'Ya Halali, Ya Mali,' exchanging smiles of disbelief at the voice booming from such a slender frame. No matter the place or the occasion, Ismail always wrapped up his performance with 'Ya Zareef al-Tool':

> *Oh, pleasant one, far away from the homeland,*
> *Your absence has filled the heart with sorrows.*
> *Return to your people, return to tenderness,*
> *You'll find none except in our land.*

What I didn't grasp on the morning of 11 July, 1948, was that what I was about to witness would deprive me of Ismail's sweet voice for decades, and of the 'Pleasant One' he might have otherwise grown into. With this loss, it felt as if a part of him had vanished, even though he remained right there with us.

Just days before, Ramadan had arrived in al-Lydd, bringing with it an intense heat that hadn't been experienced in July for decades. During the day, the sun hung, unyielding, in the sky, and the heavy evening breeze weighed down on our chests. My father was resolute in his decision to stay at home and vowed he wouldn't leave his town except for the grave. He stayed put in the house with a rifle he had purchased some time ago, insisting he would defend both his home and al-Lydd until his last breath. He coughed after finishing that sentence, dragging greedily on his cigarette, which seemed to blaze more fiercely as the fighting and siege intensified. Amidst his fit, he glanced our way, catching us off guard, our shock laid bare at the intensity of his cough. He appeared as if startled to see us there, even though he had just been addressing us. He got to his feet and rushed into the kitchen, soon returning with three knives that he handed to me, my brother Samuel, and our mother. He made it clear that we might need to use them to defend ourselves if we were ever attacked.

4.

That morning, Ismail was filled with questions about his mother, even though he typically didn't give much thought to her absence when he stayed with us. He was eager to find her and pleaded with me to let him go without my mother knowing. He promised to return if he didn't find her at his grandmother's house, which was located a short distance from the Dahmash Mosque.

Our house sat just a few streets behind the mosque, only a short walk away – perhaps a couple of minutes if I hurried across the road, which was what I usually did. I knew that road like the back of my hand, and it knew me just as well. Sometimes, I would wager with Ismail on who could walk it the farthest with their eyes closed, without tripping along the way. I was familiar with the small pit beside Abu Jaber's house, which, despite his wife's every effort to repair it, stubbornly seemed to get wider after each attempt. I was enchanted by the stunning purple blossoms of the Jacaranda trees near Abu Khamis's place. Numerous stories have been shared about Jacaranda and Abu Khamis, who left al-Lydd during a year plagued by locusts and famine to one of the Latin American countries, where he spent over a decade. Ultimately, his longing for home prevailed, and he returned to al-Lydd with his son, Khamis, and their family. It is said that because he still missed those foreign lands, he ordered Jacaranda trees, which he planted in rows at the front of his home, and inside it.

Ismail urged me to stay behind, worried that my mother might notice our absence if she didn't hear our voices. He snuck out of the house like a crafty cat, leaving my mother completely unaware of his departure, being so preoccupied with checking what little provisions we had left. By now, a siege had coiled around al-Lydd like a long, speckled snake, tightening its grip around our throats.

I deliberately made some noise every now and then to give my mother the impression that I was chatting with Ismail. However, she suddenly peeked her head through the door and

I jumped out of bed in surprise. Her face paled, a blend of anxiety and anger washing over her as she suddenly realised that Ismail had slipped away to his grandmother's house amid the turmoil echoing through the streets outside. I made her promise not to tell my father when he woke up. I am not sure how I convinced her, but she agreed to let me head over to Ismail's grandmother's house to look for him. Before I left, she handed me her knife to add to my own and made me promise not to linger in one place for too long, insisting I return if I sensed any danger. As she pulled me into a tight embrace, I could hear her heartbeat racing.

As I left the house and entered the eerily quiet streets of al-Lydd, a wave of fear tried to pull me back. I shook it off and held on to my resolve as I traversed the short road to the mosque, which felt longer than usual. I navigated the narrow alleys and side streets until I finally reached the peripheries of the Dahmash Mosque. Amid the constant sound of whizzing bullets in the background, I made my way to its back door, known only to the locals. As I walked in, it felt like I had stepped into the Day of Resurrection. The atmosphere was surreal, as people ran around frantically and aimlessly, as if they'd unwittingly opened the Book of Wanderings[2] and stumbled into a spell beyond their understanding. Some were deep in prayer, others were lost in thought, while a few sat weeping quietly. I wasn't sure of the exact number of people present, but it seemed to be around 200.

I scanned the room and saw Ismail's grandmother sitting alongside his mother, who was holding him securely on her lap. He sat awkwardly, his frail figure wedged between her plump thighs and sturdy arms. His tense features softened as soon as he caught sight of me. Umm Ismail sprang to her feet the moment she saw me, as if scorched by a fierce flame, all her anger migrating to her face, casting a vivid shade of red across her cheeks. She rushed towards me and seized my hand, asking how I had gotten there. As usual, she didn't wait for an answer and instead, dragged me roughly by my arm and plopped me down next to Ismail, threatening that once we got home, she was going to whack us both with a sledgehammer for wandering out during this barrage of gunfire. Though my arm throbbed with pain, I masked my discomfort with a smile for Ismail, and he returned the gesture. Neither of us said a word, eager to avoid further stoking his mother's wrath. Ismail's mother instructed his grandmother – who was in fragile health and struggling to walk on her own – that she would take us home first and then return with her husband to pick her up.

Ismail's mother approached one of the nearby women, asking her to watch over her mother until she returned. Moments later, a sudden crash rang out as one of the mosque's windows shattered, shards of glass flying in every direction. The explosion was deafening – like nothing I had ever experienced – and it felt as though my heart had leapt right out of my chest. In panic, Umm Ismail ran towards us, pushing Ismail and me down to the ground. She might have stumbled in her fright; I couldn't tell. I was too overwhelmed to grasp what was happening. I turned to the window on my right, and then everything suddenly went dark. I am not sure if I fainted. When I opened my eyes, there was a loud ringing in my ears. Blood and human remains were everywhere. Loud voices and screams mixed in with the ringing that enveloped me. I looked for Ismail and found him beside me, his face ghostly pale, as if all the blood had drained from it. His eyes were fixed on his mother, assessing whether she was still alive. I softly whispered his name, and he turned to meet my gaze, but said nothing.

The main door of the mosque suddenly burst open, and a group of men barged in. One of them shouted out, asking if any survivors needed help. I remained silent. A woman cried out for help, her voice rising from among a pile of bodies, followed by the anguished screams of a child and an elderly man struggling to stand up. The men advanced towards the wounded woman, who wore a white peasant dress embroidered crimson with her blood. As they closed in on her and on those who had stood up, they opened fire, and one by one, they all fell like pawns in a game of chess. Others shot at the lifeless bodies and the scattered remains littered across the room. I squeezed my eyes shut, certain that the next hail of bullets would find me. I could feel the shots tearing into Umm Ismail's body, which lay over us.

The guns finally fell silent. I could hear the footsteps of the shooters all around me, the unsettling chuckle of one of them ricocheting in my head. They walked out and closed the door behind them. I lay there, unable to move or open my eyes for what felt like an eternity. Perhaps I had lost consciousness; it was hard to tell. Umm Ismail's blood was seeping into my clothes. To my left, Ismail was gazing at me, and I couldn't tell if it was death's stare or if he was still alive. I whispered his name, but he didn't react.

I tried to move and soon realised that I was likely unhurt. However, I could feel blood trickling down my neck, coating my skin. Was it Ismail's blood or his mother's, I wondered. To my astonishment, as I softly called out Ismail's name once more, his hand moved from beneath his mother's body and reached out towards me. He was still alive. As I struggled to get to my feet, I reached out to help, and could hear him cry out, 'Yamma! Yamma!' We both struggled to free ourselves from beneath her, and just as we finally managed to stand up, Ismail threw himself over his mother's lifeless body, wailing, 'Yamma... Yamma,' receiving no answer. He turned to his grandmother, calling her name, but she didn't answer either. I was terrified that the men outside might hear us and return to kill us. I covered his mouth with my hand and pulled him away from his mother's body, which he fiercely held on to. I gripped his hand firmly, pulling him towards me, but he wrenched it away and threw himself back on top of her body, shaking her urgently as if to rouse her from a deep slumber. Her eyes were wide open, staring at Ismail, who continued to call out

'Yamma,' but received no answer yet again. There was no doubt in my mind, she had truly left us for good. I tugged at him one last time, emphasising the urgent need to leave.

I was terrified the soldiers would hear us and return to the mosque to finish us off. I kept my hand clamped over Ismail's mouth, fearing he might call out for his mother or sob too loudly as we scrambled to exit the mosque's back door, leaving behind the bodies and the pools of blood.

In al-Lydd, the captivating scent of oranges and lemons had always embraced me, tantalising my senses as I roamed the city every season. It was the first fragrance that shaped my childhood, even before I became aware of my mother's unique smell. Yet, on that day, the only smell was one of blood and death.

Ismail remained quiet, and with each step through streets littered with bodies, he tried to free his hand from my grip, desperate to return to his mother. We suddenly heard the blaring loudspeakers from the vehicles of the Zionist patrols roaming the city. They were calling out to the Palestinians, in Arabic, demanding they evacuate or face the same fate as those who had sheltered in the Dahmash Mosque. Ismail pushed down his anguish and swallowed his words. He no longer attempted to return to the mosque, although he would frequently glance back as if bidding farewell to his mother and grandmother. As for me, I felt as though al-Lydd had abandoned me, even though we had stood our ground for her. Ismail and I walked towards home, ageing with every step we took.

5.

I spotted my little brother, Samuel, his hair tousled and his big, black eyes peering cautiously from behind our front door as he watched the street. As soon as he spotted us, he darted inside, excitedly shouting, 'They're back, they're back!' Moments later, my father emerged looking as if he had been preparing to head out in search of us. I was worried he was angry with us for venturing out in such circumstances. Instead, he welcomed us warmly. Seeing us drenched in blood, he wrapped us in a tight embrace and carefully examined us to ensure we weren't injured. Then, without uttering a single word, he slumped into a nearby chair, and stared at us as if he couldn't believe we had survived. My mother welcomed us with eager, trembling hands. When I recounted what had happened, she broke down, slapping her cheeks and wailing as Ismail stood frozen to the spot, a shadow of the boy I knew. Gripping our hands tightly, my mother led us inside, tears streaming down her face. She gently wiped the blood from our bodies and helped us into fresh, clean clothes. She held Ismail close, her sobs escaping from her constricted throat. There was no time for us to grieve or even come to terms with what was unfolding around us.

6.

The loudspeakers mounted on the vehicles of the Palmach and Haganah gangs echoed throughout the city, blaring, 'Yalla! Yalla! Abdullah. Yalla to King Abdullah! Abdullah has bought you!' They seized control of what remained of the city, patrolling the streets in their armoured cars and shooting anyone who dared to cross their path, leaving a grim trail of bodies in their wake.

Al-Lydd was expelled from al-Lydd. Out of more than forty thousand residents, only about a thousand remained in the city. Five hundred of them were grouped in a ghetto next to al-Khader Church and the Omari Mosque, while another five hundred were kept near the railway station, because they were needed to keep it running, effectively transforming the areas into al-Lydd's two concentration camps. We endured both for over a year. Before that time, I had little to no understanding of the term 'ghetto' or its historical implications.

It was only later that I learned it was what the Zionist militias and their leaders, who established the 'New State' on the bones and ashes of our dead, had named our confinements behind barbed wire. The flies there increased daily, feasting on us as though we were expired prey. Al-Lydd was a dying body, and we, the remnants of its spirit, struggled to keep it alive.

When they first forced us all into those ghettos, I was unaware that the city was practically deserted. Each morning, the Yahoodi soldiers summoned the men to assist in the process of retrieving the bodies of dead Palestinians littering the streets, houses, and the Dahmash Mosque. When my father returned to the ghetto in the evening, it looked as though his face had run away from him. It was nearly unrecognisable, marked by the unspeakable horrors he had seen. He recounted how the soldiers forced them to search through the bodies, including the bloated ones, and strip them of gold, jewellery, and money, which they were then forced to surrender. They were forbidden to bury the dead individually; instead, they were instructed to dig mass graves, into which the bodies were collectively dumped. After several days, they were told to burn the bodies instead. Every morning before dawn, the men would set out and not return until after sunset. Yet, oddly enough, the bodies in the streets seemed to be multiplying.

My father identified his brother Khaled's body only by the watch he wore – the same one they had bought together during a trip to Istanbul years ago. He didn't recognise him, his body swollen, savaged by dogs. My father shared how he would stuff the remains he collected with other men into hessian sacks, into which what little was already in his stomach would periodically find its way to join the mix. At times, he feared that he might vomit his entire body into those same sacks. They warned him that unless he managed his reflux, he would end up like the very bodies he was gathering. He told us how he saw them loading hundreds of trucks with furniture and all sorts of valuables, which were then transported to Tel

Aviv. He often fell silent between sentences, as if his mind couldn't wrap itself around the reality of what he was saying, desperately trying to reject the truth before him. 'I don't understand why. How is what happened to them our fault?' he would say again and again. Then, he would gaze at us with bloodshot eyes, so vividly red that their whites had nearly all but disappeared. After several days, my father stopped telling us about his daily excursions and began to pull away from us. He slept in a corner of the ghetto, close enough to keep an eye on us, yet far enough to think we couldn't hear his muffled sobs in the dark.

Whenever my father returned to our ghetto near al-Khader Church, Ismail would hurriedly approach him in silence, almost as if he were seeking answers about his own father. The reality was that we were in the dark about what had happened to him back then, and it wasn't until later that we learned why he hadn't returned to us as planned, before they forcibly relocated us at gunpoint into the ghetto, under a sky heavy with bullets. It didn't take long for Ismail to stop rushing up to my father, as he finally accepted there would be no word. A year later, Ismail's uncle, Najeeb, managed to sneak back into al-Lydd, bringing back the devastating news that Ismail's father had been killed on a road paved with tears while attempting to return to the town.

7.

Najeeb informed us that he and Nofal, Ismail's father, had been forced to walk at gunpoint after being ordered to undress down to their underwear. The gunmen had set up barricades and were forcing everyone to walk in the sweltering afternoon heat of Ramadan under a scorching July sun, as if they were insects trapped in a frying pan. Their vehicles were decked with mounted machine guns, and men with firearms taking aim from every direction. At the checkpoints, they carried out exhaustive searches, confiscating everything within reach. Those who dared to resist were shot – either in the head or the back – executed publicly for everyone to witness. Those who survived the bullets, later died of thirst. They searched women, men, and children, stripping them of all their belongings. They resembled bandits dressed in military uniforms, armed with European weapons. Meanwhile, the people of al-Lydd, along with those who sought sanctuary there, walked for dozens of kilometres toward Ramallah and Jordan.

8.

Ismail withdrew into silence and became known as Ismail al-Akhras.[3] Though he wasn't truly mute, the world had silenced him. He moved back and forth between his uncle's house and ours, and, over time, I grew accustomed to his quiet presence.

Every year, on 11 July, Ismail would link his arm with mine. As we grew older, we had moved away from the childhood habit of holding hands and instead walked arm in arm to the Dahmash Mosque. It always felt like he was clinging to my arm to keep from drowning in a sea of memories. I was his crutch. Even though I was only six months older, I saw him as a much younger brother in need of protection, especially since he had lost both his parents. Every year, on 11 July, we would quietly settle into the courtyard across from the mosque, where Ismail would begin to read the Fatihah to himself. I could always tell he had started when I saw him open his palms upwards in a gesture of supplication, facing the sky. After he finished, we would once again embrace the silence together.

Ismail had no grave to visit for either his mother or grandmother. Their bodies, my father said, hadn't been among those retrieved from the mosque for burial. He suspected their bodies might have been among those they were ordered to burn. Ismail had no idea where to locate his father's grave either. All he knew was that his uncle had buried him by an almond tree on the road to Ramallah. In truth, every inch of Palestine was a graveyard.

Ismail's uncle was his complete opposite; so talkative that it could be exhausting. He would chat endlessly about everything, from plants and birds to sand, stones, flowers, and even the colour of the sky. He shared vivid stories about what he'd witnessed on the Trail of Tears. He departed from our lives just as suddenly as he had come back into them. Some believe he drowned in the well on his land, taken by one of the djinn thought to frequent the old springs. He had insisted on reopening it after the settlers from a nearby Kibbutz had sealed it off. They had seized his property, denying him access to its water. But he had crept back in under the cover of darkness to salvage what remained, watering the crops and caring for the land. After all, he insisted, even though they controlled it, it was still his land. However, there are many who swear they saw the settlers kill him and string his body from a tree in his field after he defied them and accessed water for his citrus trees. The settlers left him hanging there for days, they said, and after starving dogs had feasted on his body, they tossed his remains into the well to ensure that no one would dare to water the land after him.

9.

Ismail grew up and got married. His daughter, Bissan, bore a remarkable resemblance to his mother. When I mentioned this to him once, he gave a faint smile but quickly bit his lip, as though chomping down a sadness he'd only recently ingested. Only on a few rare occasions did I ever feel that he genuinely smiled from his heart.

In 1994, when the decision was made to reopen a section of the Dahmash Mosque, Ismail was among the first to step inside and clean the bloodstained walls. Nearly fifty years on, those walls still bore the haunting marks of the martyrs who fell on that tragic day.

The following year, when an Israeli assassin took the life of Israeli Prime Minister Yitzhak Rabin, I was sitting in a café near the Old City with Ismail. I remember clearly how he abruptly abandoned our game of backgammon, stepped outside, and stood there, trying to take a deep breath, as he looked up at the sky. In that moment, I understood what he was thinking. Rabin had been one of the military leaders behind al-Lydd's Nakba and the displacement of its people.

Ismail's condition has worsened since the latest assault on Gaza began, and I cannot deny that I am deteriorating as well. The massacres in Gaza drag me back every day to those days, which I have never been able to forget. Ismail has locked himself in his home, leaving his wife deeply worried about his declining health. She has reached out to me multiple times, hoping I can help. None of us fully understands what has happened to him. He always took great pride in his appearance, dressing sharply, keeping his beard neatly trimmed, and visiting the barbershop regularly. He now seems to have neglected all of that. The doctors suspect dementia. Yet, I can feel Ismail's pain, for I am experiencing it too. The genocide in Gaza has extinguished the last flicker of hope within us. At least, that's what I thought.

However, in late January, something none of us could have anticipated took place. Ismail frequently reached out to me with a phone call, which was his typical way of letting me know he wanted to meet. He'd dial my number, and when I answered, he'd disconnect the call. That was my signal to wait for him right by my front door. On this particular day, as I stood there, I couldn't help but notice how different he appeared. Clean-shaven, he seemed to have shed the weight of his eighty-seven years, coming towards me with the sprightliness of a ten-year-old boy with the whole world in front of him.

He carried a hammer and saw, along with a sign that featured a name written in elegant handwriting, though it was partially obscured by white gauze. Beside him, his daughter Bissan struggled to keep up with his hurried pace. He smiled whenever our eyes met, but I had no idea what was happening.

I walked beside him until we arrived at the paved square in front of Dahmash Street. He looked up at the sign that read 'Palmach Square' in Hebrew, Arabic, and English – the name of the gangsters responsible for the Dahmash Mosque massacre. For more than seventy years, we've endured walking by that blatant reminder of those who had murdered our families. Ismail neither acknowledged us nor expected anything from us, despite our barrage of questions. He swiftly tore down the old sign and raised a new one in its place, written in Arabic, beautifully inscribed with the words, *The Dahmash Mosque Martyrs' Square*. His daughter and I stared at him in shock and disbelief, unsure of what to do next. A crowd had gathered around us. Ismail's eyes locked on us, and his index finger pointed toward the mosque. Tears streamed down his cheeks, and his mouth moved as though he were trying to say something.

At first, Ismail's voice emerged scratchy and raspy, like a tracheostomy patient handed a speech device for the first time, startled to hear their voice again. He looked at the sign one more time and, before launching into a rendition of 'Ya Zareef Al Toul', he talked about the waves of Gazan refugees he had seen a few days ago leaving their temporary shelters, making their way back home, on foot, from the south to the north of the city. Unlike the masses who had evacuated al-Lydd along the Trail of Tears, Gazans were taking their first steps to return to their homes.

It was the first time Ismail and any of us had witnessed a return, even if it was to heaps of rubble.

It was the first time his daughter, Bissan, had heard his voice.

How sweet it was, and how I had longed to hear it again. And he sang…

> *Oh, pleasant one, far away from the homeland,*
> *Your absence has filled the heart with sorrows.*
> *Return to your people, return to our tenderness,*
> *You'll find none except in our land.*

Notes

1. In al-Lydd, St George's Day is celebrated by the Palestinian Orthodox Christian community on 16 November.
2. Also known as the 'The Book of Numbers', the fourth book of the Old Testament and the fourth of five books of the Torah.
2. Al Akhras – the Mute.

TANTURA

Trapped

Anwar Hamed

Translated by Andrew Leber

In memory of Hind Rajab (2018-2024)

[2023]

'Lubna, come, don't bother with that!'

The choking sound coming from the worn-out engine warned that the car might not be able to take them anywhere, even as the roar of the sorties above filled him with dread. He called out again, even more alarmed this time:

'Damn it, Lubna, come on! Bring the girls and let's go before they burn us to a crisp!'

Lubna rushed out to the car, terror on her face and each hand holding onto a child's.

'I didn't bring anything! No food or clothes!,' she said as she opened the back door of the car and pushed the two girls inside.

Hiba was her ten-year-old niece, while her own daughter Manar was not yet eight. Lubna closed the door to the back seat and headed to the passenger door. Before she could even settle into her seat, however, Mustafa was surprised by Hiba opening her door and rushing back into the house.

'Hiba!' he called after her, panicking.

Hiba entered the house as they sat and stared for a moment,

before Mustafa shook off his astonishment and rushed after her. Before he reached the front door, though, she stepped back out – embarrassed – holding something in her hand.

'What is that?' Mustafa asked, keeping his composure.

Hiba didn't answer, trying to conceal it as she got back into the car. Mustafa put it out of his mind, moving back to the driver's seat and setting off at breakneck speed.

In the back seat, Hiba looked at a plastic hairbrush, which she then placed inside her small backpack. Hiba may have only been ten years old, but her awareness of her own femininity had already begun to emerge. Her hair was the centre of her world, just as it was the centre of anyone's attention who looked at her.

Hiba's hair fell over her shoulders in waves, rather than being perfectly straight – at least on the few occasions when she let it flow freely. Most of the time, with the help of her aunt, she kept it around in two braids, enjoying the admiring looks and affectionate comments from relatives and acquaintances when she walked around at family gatherings.

Hiba had inherited her hair from her mother, alongside her slender figure and hazel-coloured eyes that always seemed to smile.

Hiba had never known her mother, though, and only knew this from her aunt Lubna's stories. Hiba's mother had passed away when Hiba was just two, of breast cancer discovered too late.

Hiba had been living with her aunt's family ever since; her father had been arrested shortly after his wife's death and sentenced to twenty years in prison.

Since then, the only family she'd known had been Aunt Lubna, Mustafa and Manar.

Right now, Mustafa was driving as fast as the car would go, despite his wife's terrified yelling.

'Slow down! Do you want us to survive the air strikes only to die in a car crash?'

He ignored her, accelerating towards an as-yet unknown destination.

'Where are we going?' Lubna asked.

'I don't know,' he said, his mind racing. 'Any place where death won't find us, I guess.'

Lubna couldn't help but laugh. They both knew that nowhere in Gaza was safe. People were fleeing from certain death to parts unknown – little better than an uncertain death. But neither wanted to sit idly by and wait for their fate. They had to do something, anything, prove to themselves they had at least *tried* to survive – had done everything they could to escape their fate.

'Slow down!' Lubna screamed, suddenly, when Mustafa seemed to lose control of the vehicle and swerved sharply to the left. 'Slow down, for God's sake!' she begged him, through tears, as the two girls in the back seat screamed.

'Can't you see what I see?' he yelled back at her, practically weeping himself.

He gestured back at where he had swerved to avoid a man's body lying in the middle of the street. The others looked behind them and began to sob even harder. Soon after, they passed the body of a woman cradling a child as well. Mustafa tried to focus on the steering wheel, with great difficulty – his hands trembled.

Meanwhile, the roar of the jets overhead continued, following them wherever they went. The whole car remained in a constant state of panic.

Mustafa had no idea where he was going, so drifted along aimlessly.

The road was lined with broken-down cars, while ahead of them other cars devoured the road in front of them – headed into the unknown as well. Not just cars - motorcycles, carts pulled by horses and donkeys, pedestrians, all hurrying towards somewhere, anywhere else.

Lubna, Mustafa and the rest had spent the night listening

to the crack of bullets and the rumble of nearby explosions, waiting for the house to come down on their heads at any moment. Then the neighboring building had come down, targeted by a missile in the middle of the night. They rushed to the car with the first rays of morning light – they couldn't spend another night in the house.

'Where are we going?' Lubna asked again.

'I don't know,' Mustafa replied, helplessly.

'What do you mean?' she asked, in disbelief.

'My God, I told you already!' he shouted at her.

The two girls were now crying hysterically. Lubna was crying too, but her tears were silent.

How did we get here? Life had plodded along in a dull, steady direction. Everything became so… ordinary that we simply adapted to it.

Barely affording the children's clothes that showed up unpredictably through the crossings, and accepting the poor quality that fetched exorbitant prices. Dealing with the travel restrictions, the poor healthcare, the blockade and the overcrowding in this small patch of land. The occasional Israeli airstrike.

Over the years, we've come to accept this as permanent, as fate. So we adapted to it and arranged our lives accordingly.

Those who had been able to emigrate did so, and those who stayed did their best to make do. Doctors in hospitals struggled to carry out their work despite a shortage of medicine and other essentials. Students completed their studies despite knowing that their futures were uncertain. Restaurant and café owners opened their businesses periodically in a semblance of ordinary life in this de facto island, serving up delicious meals from whatever ingredients were available.

Two months ago, Lubna had gone to a routine appointment with the gynaecologist. After examining her, with available equipment, the doctor told her that she had what was possibly a tumour in her uterus. Still, she would have to wait a few months, or perhaps a year or more, for an MRI. Or she could try and arrange travel to Jordan.

She had laughed bitterly. Jordan! Amman was about 300 kilometres from Gaza, a three-hour drive under normal circumstances.

But when would we be 'under normal circumstances'?

First, we would have to leave Gaza, via Israel, for the West Bank. This required a permit granted only to the lucky few, and I have never been so lucky. In any case, fate didn't give us time to worry. War broke out, and more immediate concerns distracted me from my looming anxieties.

'Ugh.' The sound tore her away from her thoughts. It had come from next to her, from her husband.

She turned, shouting, 'Mustafa, Mustafa, what happened–'

But before she could finish the question, she let out the same groan.

'Mama, Papa!'

'Uncle, Aunt Lubna!'

The two terrified girls began to wail even more hysterically.

'Mamaaaa, Papa!'

No sound came from either figure in the front, except for barely audible groans.

Then, suddenly, it was Manar's turn.

'Manar, Manaaaar!'

But Manar's head slumped over and she didn't make another sound.

Hiba, her hands trembling, began trying to look for her uncle's phone. She undid her seatbelt and reached towards the front seat, now with her whole body shaking.

'Where's your phone, Uncle? Where's your phone?' she pleaded, through her tears.

She tried every way to stretch out and check her uncle's pockets from behind his seat, to no avail.

Slowly, Hiba opened the car door, only to scream and slam it shut as bullets rained down nearby.

She tried a third time to get to Mustafa, whom she always

just called 'Uncle'. She crawled up into the front passenger seat, climbing into her aunt's arms. It felt oddly reassuring, even in the arms of a dead woman – still warmer than the car seats. She sat frozen for a moment, then reached into her uncle's jacket pocket. The feeling of warm liquid on her fingers caused her to jerk back with a shout.

Finally, wiping away tears, she saw the phone and reached for it. She wiped the blood off the screen and searched through the contact list. She found a number for an ambulance and, with unsteady fingers, pressed 'call'.

A voice from far away asked her where she was. She looked around, not knowing what to say. The voice asked her to describe the area around her. She tried as much as possible to paint a picture for the paramedics to help them reach her.

She ended the call and crawled into the back seat again. She found Manar's body slumped across the seat where it had fallen. Hiba tried to lift up Manar and get her to sit up, only for Manar's head to slump back down immediately.

The bullets and bombs were deafening. Hiba sat trembling, sometimes crying, sometimes staring silently into the distance. With every explosion she screamed in fright.

The mobile phone rang. 'Where are you?' Hiba replied, through her tears. 'Hurry up, I'm scared – the strikes are getting very close.'

'Hiba, the ambulance is on its way, my dear,' a soft female voice reassured her. 'You're being so brave, and doing great. Just half an hour and the ambulance will reach you.'

Hiba kept sobbing, silently this time.

'Hiba, are you there?'

'I'm here.'

'Did you hear what I said?'

'I heard.'

'Okay, my dear. Don't be afraid. It will be alright.' The call ended, leaving Hiba alone with her fears once again. Time passed, slow and heavy. Then came another ring, this time bringing with it a male voice.

'Hiba?'

'Where are you?' she screamed.

'We're close, we're almost there.'

An explosion nearby, and another scream from Hiba.

'Hiba.'

No reply.

'Hiba?'

The voice came to her from far away, as every part of her was shaking. Her teeth chattering, all she could murmur when she tried to speak was: 'Alhamdulilah.'

The voice sighed with relief.

'Hold tight, Hiba. Just a few minutes.'

Her teeth went on chattering, her throat making sounds without forming clear words. Her brown eyes kept staring at the place where she guessed the ambulance would arrive.

Endless gunfire as her terror grew. The phone rang. Her heart beat faster. Before she could say a single word, a warm voice said, 'Do you see us? We're very close, here in the ambulance.'

Hiba looked in every direction, but saw no ambulance. Finally, she spotted it. A deep breath. Her brown eyes tracked the vehicle as it moved towards her. Then, suddenly, the deafening sound of a powerful explosion, and the ambulance turned into a ball of fire.

She clasped her hands to her face, screaming hysterically. She tried to crawl under the car seat, but – what use was it, if the car and all its seats would become yet another fireball?

The soldiers in the nearby Israeli tank held off dealing with the stranded vehicle, waiting for others to arrive. After an hour with no sign of another ambulance, one of them decided to put an end to the waiting. Another salvo turned the car and all within it into a mound of flames, and the gunner high-fived the crewmate next to him – whooping at his latest achievement.

[1947]

'Hiba – you're here?'

It was Manar's voice, rejoicing at Hiba's presence.

'Manar? Didn't you die? Am I dreaming?'

She touched her face to make sure she was awake, that this was real.

'Come on, silly, the whole family is waiting.'

This was the voice of her uncle, but still she couldn't see anyone.

'What family, Uncle?'

'Just come.'

He took her hand and led her down a dark passageway. She still couldn't see a thing, but could hear many voices from all directions.

'Where are we going?'

'To Tantura.'[1]

She was confused. Tantura? Still, she let herself be led along by her uncle, through the gloom and along the forking passageways. The ceaseless sound of conversation accompanied them, though she couldn't pick out any of the speakers.

'It's taking a while.'

'No, we're here – at the beach.'

'The beach?'

Her uncle didn't reply, but the features of the place began to reveal themselves.

'The seeeaaaaa!' She screamed in delight, dropping her uncle's hand to run towards the water. One leap and she was surrounded by waves. She surrendered to the waves washing over her body, and the further out she went the lighter she felt, floating atop the waves…

Her head gradually filled with strange sights and scenes that were hard to understand. She was afraid of getting lost at sea, but a sense of calmness enveloped her bit by bit, as a voice whispered in her ear: 'Come back to the village. They're waiting for you there.'

She turned and swam towards the beach.

She raised her head, seawater dripping from it, and was seized by a strange feeling.

'Here's our bride! Where have you been?'

She smiled timidly at somebody who looked like her aunt.

'Fatima?'

Who was this calling? The voice was familiar, but this wasn't her name.

'Where are you? The guests are waiting.'

'Whose guests?'

'What's with you? The groom, your groom! 'Fatima! Wake up, my little one. The sun is up, and the family is out sitting in the diwan. Get up and get cleaned up.'

She closed her eyes, then opened them again to take in everything around her.

'Why do you look so confused, little one? Still asleep?' the woman — her mother — asked her tenderly.

'Get up and get ready.'

She slowly got out of the bed.

'Here, I'll pour the water for you.'

She followed her mother into the central courtyard, then held out her hands for the water that the woman poured from a metal jug. She filled her cupped palms with water and splashed it on her face...

'Where is Fayez?' she asked haltingly.

Her mother chided her.

'What do you want with Fayez? It's a little early for Fayez, let him look after his business and you after yours.'

'What do you mean, my business?'

The woman, her mother, smiled despite the bitter feelings that flashed across her face.

'All things in due course. Let's go and eat breakfast, we have a long day ahead of us.'

Fatima slipped inside and brought back a comb, which she placed in her mother's hand. Her mother smiled.

'Braids, Mother – braids!'

The woman began to comb out her daughter's long hair into strands, weaving together two braids that were Fatima's signature feature since childhood. As she did so, another woman's voice called out: 'Umm Tawfiq!'

Umm Tawfiq replied to the voice even as she sent her daughter ahead to the kitchen, where a light breakfast was set out.

'Hello, Umm Saleh.'

'Umm Tawfiq, you and your family are reasonable people, aren't you? How could you have a wedding in these circumstances?'

Umm Tawfiq tried to head her off. 'This isn't a full wedding, just the men and women of the families, a simple meal, and then the wedding night.'

Umm Saleh was unconvinced. 'Still, at a time like this? When we have no idea what will happen to us? The whole country is being turned upside down!'

At first, nothing came from the mother.

'Nothing to say?'

'Umm Saleh, God help you, the girl has been engaged for a year. War is everywhere, sure, but does this mean people can't get married? Seriously?'

But Umm Saleh interrupted. 'Fine, then, wait a few days – until we see where things stand.'

The mother laughed, replying with more than a hint of sarcasm, 'Hold off? For how many days? And what do you expect to happen in that couple of days? Leave it up to God.'

The two families celebrated the marriage, even if the usual proceedings were as truncated as much as they could be. There were all the usual songs and ululations, albeit in quiet voices, soft as if their owners were being suffocated.

The wedding night passed quietly as well. Neither the

women nor the men of the village were interested in seeing evidence of the bride's virginity, as far more valuable blood was being spilled all over the country.

After nine months exactly, Fatima brought into this world a young girl she named 'Saada,' borrowing from the Arabic word for 'happiness' – begging fate for brighter days. No happiness came, however, as the village awoke one dawn, a few days later, to the sound of gunfire. Having finally got Saada back to sleep, Fatima climbed back into bed beside her husband and was beginning to doze off, when suddenly she heard shots ringing out nearby.

She shook her husband awake frantically, only to cling to him as he arose to go outside to take stock of the situation. She was afraid for him, afraid for herself, afraid for her child who had barely spent a week in this world.

The small family stayed together, waiting for the unknown, huddling ever-closer together as the sound of the bullets drew nearer. It wasn't long until they heard a knock at the door.

'Don't open it!' screamed Fatima, terrified.

Fayez hesitated, but the knocking only grew louder, to the point where Fatima felt like they were trying to rip the door off its hinges. He finally opened the door, and a number of figures in military fatigues pushed their way in.

Fatima shrank back further, holding her newborn close to her for protection.

'You have *bay-bee*? *Mazel Tov*,' spoke an officer, smiling.

Fatima felt slightly reassured. Then she heard the officer speak in a language she didn't understand; the other soldiers grabbed Fayez and pulled him out.

She cried out in anguish, even as the officer smiled at her once again.

'Stay with *bay-bee*. Nothing will happen to you,' he said as if to calm her. But nothing could have reassured her as she saw the soldiers forcing her husband down the path.

Saada cried even louder, frightened at the sight of so many

people storming into the small home, causing such a commotion.

The soldiers left after the officer fixed a sign to the house saying, 'Moved on from here,' meaning there was no reason for others like them to enter this home…

Time passed slowly. She had no idea what was in store for her or her sleeping child…

She grew hungry, went into the kitchen and found a loaf of bread. With the bread went a piece of cheese from a metal dish nearby. She ate as her thoughts drifted elsewhere. What would she do? Where were her mother and father and siblings? What happened to them? Sporadic gunfire, unending. What were they shooting at with all this ammunition?

Night drew near, and the sound of the guns died off. Exhaustion overtook her. She nursed Saada again and then stretched out on the cot next to the child.

Fatima was lost in sleep when a violent knock shook the door. She got up in a panic, went to the door, trembled as she went. She couldn't bring herself to ask who was knocking as she drew near it. She heard a conversation with a familiar voice, however – it was the sound of her youngest brother, Hassan. She opened the door carefully and burst into tears at the sight of not just Hassan, but her mother standing behind him.

'Where is the little one?' her mother asked.
'Sleeping inside,' she replied, whispering through her sobs.
'Is it safe here?'
'They took Fayez.'
'Shhhh, lower your voice. They took all the men – your brother and I were off in the hills, so they didn't see us.'
'Where are my brothers?'
Her mother didn't reply.
'Mother, where are my brothers?'
'I don't know, dear,' her mother said, sobbing now as well.
'Like the day of judgment, nobody knows what happened

to anybody else. We wanted to come sleep at yours, and tomorrow if we're still here, we can see where we want to go. We can't stay here, it's not safe.'

Exhausted from the day's terrible events, they all fell into a deep sleep.

[2017]

'Amal, time to get up!'

She opened her eyes slowly and looked around.

'The baby has been up and crying for an hour, she wants to feed.'

She looked around her. Amal? Every time she fell asleep, would she wake up with a new name?

'What's wrong, dear? Come on, please feed her.'

She got up carefully, trying to adjust to her new life. She stood in front of the mirror in the bathroom, unbraiding her hair to leave it hanging loose over her shoulders. Today she would wash and style it at the hairdresser's.

She smiled, remembering how her mother had insisted on braiding her hair until a few years before she – Amal – had married. Since her mother passed, she had started going to the hairdresser every few months. Taking care of her hair was now a priority in her life, even if the family budget – her husband's work at al-Shifa Hospital – could only allow for it once in a while.

She hadn't gone once since the birth of their daughter, which was beginning to get on her nerves. The little girl sapped her mother's energy, waking up more than once at night to feed.

Amal felt her breasts and was overcome with sadness – how proud she had been of them! Now she felt alienated from them – pregnancy, childbirth and breastfeeding had done their work. She took advantage of her few moments alone in front of the bathroom mirror to look them over. Once they had been firm and pert – barely even needed a bra.

She hadn't even wanted to breastfeed at first, reading up on women who used pasteurised milk instead. The idea was still alien in her society, but young women had changed a lot in recent years. The internet had opened up new windows into the lives of others, and new horizons to explore.

'What have you been doing in the bathroom all this time? She's crying.' Her husband was knocking on the door, annoyed.

'Wait, I'll be right there.'

She quickly rinsed her face, dried it and went back to the motherly tasks that awaited her.

She finished feeding her little girl, put the child back in her bed and then called out to her husband.

'Hani!'

There was no reply.

'Hani, where are you? Where did you go?'

She kept calling for her husband, but still no answer. After a while, she saw him draw near in a white nurse's uniform.

'What's wrong? Why are you dressed up like that? Didn't you tell me you had the day off?'

The nurse looked at her, concerned. 'Do you need something, Umm Hiba? Are you in pain, my dear? We don't have any morphine left and we're waiting for the shipment – it could arrive any time, hopefully soon.'

'What do you mean? Hani, what's going on? I'm Amal, your wife. What are you talking about with the morphine?'

Concern turned to pity as another young female nurse joined him. The nurse said sadly:

'She's hallucinating again, God help her. It looks like her days may be numbered.'

The younger nurse leaned over her.

'Can we get you anything?'

'Oh. Could you braid my hair?'

The nurse looked sadly at Amal's head, and what the chemotherapy had done with her hair.

'Don't worry. I have some work to do, but as soon as I'm done, I'll come back to braid your hair.'

Amal tried to yell as the nurse left: 'What work do you mean? Come back and braid my hair now! Come back, pleeeease.'

She shouted for nothing. Why were they ignoring her? She continued to shout for a moment and then closed her exhausted eyes.

'Mum, don't worry, I'll braid your hair.'

She opened her eyes in disbelief:

'Hiba? My dearest, when did you grow up to be a young woman!'

Hiba smiled.

'Come on, Mum, they're all waiting for us: my aunt, your grandmother, everyone. Give me your hand.'

Hiba took Amal's hand and they set off walking down a long, dark corridor, with others joining them every now and then.

'Where are we going?' Amal asked.

Everyone in the corridor answered, in one excited voice: 'To Tantura!'

'To Tantura!' she yelled with them, laughing.

Then she asked: 'Are you returning?'

'We are all returning!' the chorus replied.

As they continued walking in the corridor, Amal suddenly asked: 'Where is Hani?'

'Dad can't return to Tantura.'

'Why?' asked Amal, surprised.

'Because he's still alive,' Hiba replied.

Amal nodded, starting to understand.

They continued walking down the passageway, which suddenly ended in waves.

Hiba shouted with delight: 'The sea! The sea!'

Everyone shouted in a childish voice. 'The sea, the sea! Our sea!'

They were hopping lightly through the waves, laughing with delight.

They turned towards the shore, led by Hiba, and walked up onto the beach. As soon as she set foot on the dry sand, however, she found men armed with Uzis in front of her.

'Where are you going?' they challenged.

Hiba panicked and froze in place, one foot still in the sea and the other on land, while the other family members stopped in place in the water.

'To Tantura,' she answered, her voice gathering confidence.

The men stood together on the beach, barring the way; the returnees stayed in the water.

Then Hiba tried to get past the men, the others following. But none made it onto the shore.

'What are you doing?' she protested.

'No entry to the Great-Grandparent's land except with our permission.'

The returnees raised their voices, protesting.

'These are the orders of the Great-Grandparent, and we carry out those orders.'

Grandma Fatima yelled from the back: 'Even here?'

'Even here,' one of them replied, sneering.

'And what do we do now?' Amal asked. 'We are dead, we cannot go back across the barrier.'

'And you can't go into the garden,' replied the guard.

'Where will we go then?' said one.

'We will ask this Great-Grandparent!' piped up another. 'Follow me.'

The guards stepped forward in unison, brandishing their Uzis, moving away from the beach and entering the garden.

'Tantura is so different in this other world!' exclaimed Grandma Fatima. 'But are there barriers and barbed wire even in paradise?'

'There must be some mistake,' Amal told her. 'We'll ask the Great-Grandparent when we meet him.'

'You won't meet him,' said one of the armed guards, confidently.

The crowd started to grumble loudly, only for the guard to shout back at them and fire his Uzi into the air.

The people of Tantura cowered in fear.

'Why were we allowed to die, then? They could have acted out this play when we were still alive,' Grandma Fatima said.

'We want to see the Great-Grandparent,' called out Grandpa Imran from the crowd.

'We told you – it's not possible. He doesn't meet or talk to anyone but us.'

'And how can you be sure of that?' Grandpa Imran asked skeptically.

The man with the Uzi gloated, the sarcasm obvious. 'You idiots, haven't you read his book? It explains everything. Everything!'

Suddenly, Grandad Imran darted through the Uzi-toting guards, followed by Imran's sons, daughters, grandsons, and granddaughters.

The men began firing frantically, yelling at the crowd to stop, but the crowd continued running forwards.

'Where are you, Grandfather?' came a cry from the family.

The armed men shot wildly into the crowd, but nothing happened. Every one of them had already died, and it seemed they could only die one death.

'The bullets don't work, then?' one of the guards wondered aloud.

A few of the armed men tried to form a physical barrier against the returning dead, but it did nothing to stop the crowd from advancing.

'Where are you going, you crazy people?'

'We want to meet the Great-Grandparent. We'll ask him to tell us our fate.'

'That's not possible – we already told you. He doesn't meet with anyone but us.'

'We'll see,' said Grandma Fatima.

And so the grandmothers, grandfathers, mothers, fathers, sons, and daughters continued their confident advance, while the Uzi-carrying men began to retreat slightly in the face of the crowd's resolve. The Uzis fired, but their bullets bounced off the already-dead as they trudged toward the unknown.

All of the returnees wanted to meet this Great-Grandparent, claimed by these Uzi-carrying men as the source of their authority and the books they referred to between each hail of gunfire.

The returnees wanted to ask the Great-Grandparent if they, too, were his grandchildren – just like those carrying machine guns. If so, why did the Great-Grandparent authorise the guards to map out their relatives' lives, restrict their movements, and keep the returnees from seeing him?

They continued onward past the Uzi-wielding men, who kept falling back to new positions. Finally they all reached a seemingly endless wall, covered in inscriptions resembling spells. The armed guards stood in front of it, an impenetrable barrier, and continued firing.

One of the grandfathers let out a shout that shook the wall; the other returnees followed suit. The Uzi-carrying guards panicked, but still tried desperately to keep the returnees from reaching the inscriptions written on the wall – to no avail.

Finally, the family reached the wall. They tried to decipher the spells, to understand their meaning, but it was no use. They attacked the wall, seized with fury, scratching at the inscriptions with their fingernails. The more the returnees wiped the spells from the wall, the more panicked the Uzi-wielding guards looked – tough men realising that their guns were now useless.

Suddenly, a light burned through the darkness, sending the tough men and their machine guns fleeing. The returnees covered their eyes at first, protecting them from the glare. Then one of them called out, 'Uncover your eyes and you'll see what's behind it!' Soon they could see that the light had revealed another layer of inscriptions.

One of the crowd said, annoyed, 'What is this? Didn't we scratch out those talismans?'

But the little girl, Hiba, cried out, 'Don't scratch them! We need to read them.'

Hiba, her cousin Manar, and several other children their age or slightly older stepped forward and began deciphering the writing on the wall.

One of their ancestors asked, 'When did you learn to read these spells?'

The girls and boys just smiled, continuing to translate and write down the words. The more they spelled out, the further the giant guards retreated until they were lost to the crowd's sight. Suddenly, doors opened all along the wall, as the older generations looked on in astonishment.

'Head in' said the children exultantly.

Generations old and new streamed in, finding themselves at the start of a series of paths stretching into the distance.

One of the older ones shouted: 'Where are you, Great-Grandparent? Our Great-Grandparent?'

The vast space echoed with his call, but no one answered.

The crowd continued onwards for countless hours, days, months, even years. They ate, slept, married, and had children, never stopping. Each path led them to another – no sign of the Great-Grandparent here, no sign there. Had he thrown his descendants into a maze, leaving no sign of the way forward except for blood?

Note

1. Tantara - a seaside village, and site of a massacre of 200+ Palestinian villagers by the Alexandroni brigade of the Haganah militia, 22–23 May 1948.

Katamon

Selma Dabbagh

MR. BUNCHE HAD CALLED me on the telephone to inform me that my husband, André, had been shot. He was now injured and at the hospital. He gave the name of a hospital. I said I did not know the hospital. It had a name like a monastery. He told me not to worry. That a car would collect me. Mr. Ralph Bunche worked with my husband André Serot and a man called Folke Bernadotte. They were professional men whose positions required them to be reassuring at all times. Mr. Bunche was being professional when he reassured me. I did not ask if André was dead. I was looking at my slippers which would need to be changed before the car came. 'Dead' was not a word either of us used.

At the hospital, two nurses guided me and two men flanked them. The men left us in a high-ceilinged white hall with archways that opened onto a courtyard. It was a perspective-rich setting, like being in an Italian Renaissance painting by Piero della Francesca or Fra Angelico or a mosque in North Africa. I didn't care, really, which one.

A nurse asked me if I knew the date and I told her that it was 1948 quick as a flash and did not let on that I could see winged dragons perched on the ledges, primed to pick out my heart. The nurses said, 'Calmez vous.' The English ones: 'Tea? There, there.' Tea? There what? There where? I am the last one to make a fuss, but I knew in my bones that my André was being neglected! I sensed it like a fever! They encouraged me to lower my voice, saying it may make it clearer to comprehend what I was saying. They said Mr. Bunche would arrive soon.

I kept telling them what needed to be done if there were wounds in André's vital organs. They kept talking about hopes for the Count. They seemed to think that that too would be reassuring. I said the Count likes to be called Folke. He is beyond his title. He was an exceptional man. He had to be, as he was, you understand, the first United Nations Organisation Mediator between Arabs and Jews. A critical and dangerous position if ever there was one. A role that required much courage and humilité.

The men who came and went wore the uniforms of doctors, soldiers, diplomats; white, khaki, navy. Colour-coded. Their uniforms encouraged them to call Folke 'the Count'. They were not open to being corrected. I imagined it was easier for them to designate him in that way. Folke being a person striding around with energy, hope and great good humour. 'Count', on the other hand, is an inherited title, Le Comte we say in France. We need to be rid of those if we are to build a new global order filled with energy, hope and great good humour, which was Folke's way; to make available to all, some of that which he had inherited by birthright.

See André? I wanted to say. *I did get out today.* That morning he had encouraged me to take a few steps outside. 'A little more each day,' he said. I had gone all the way to the hospital in an armoured vehicle. All arranged by Mr. Bunche himself.

There were journalists outside. Everyone seemed terrified of the journalists. The colour-coded men became very energised, as if action to appease the journalists would make up for their previous omissions. Questions were being asked. Which one of them had allowed the convoy carrying Folke to drive straight into a death trap manned by criminal gang members pretending to be a part of the new country's army? That was the question.

The Count would not wear a bullet-proof vest, they whined.

He would not have bodyguards, they protested. He told the officer to get rid of his Hillman automatic. Asked the men to remove their guns. 'We are protected by our United Nations flag,' he had said. 'We are on a humanitarian mission,' he insisted.

The men kept flying around the corridors, peering into the corners for someone to blame. And the killers? They were probably being patted on the back. Being given a hearty supper. Paid for by their ramshackle government, no doubt.

Personally, I blame women and bars. The men are all prone to bragging. It is the spies who give the crooks their power. They are trying to take over everything. *Loose Tongues Cost Lives.* André saw that slogan printed on an affiche in the London metro. We needed those posters in the bars of the old King David Hotel, in the sporting clubs. Their drunken flirtations have cost me.

They think the war is over. That it is only tiny little Palestine and not so much to worry about, an afterthought compared to the great American, Soviet, Japanese, African, European wars. *War weary* would be a sympathetic way of putting it, but I say they are not professional at all. The men try to remember to be compassionate with me, but they also come armed with these questions. Why had they been in Katamon? Why had they changed the route? Why had he, my husband, not been in his allocated place in the vehicle and the vehicle on its allocated route on the map? Why had it veered into Ka-ta-mon?

That neighbourhood, Katamon, had little significance to me. Leafy streets, quiet mansions, the zone of a rich élite far grander than anything we had in my city in France. I could never understand the need for such large houses, but the Arabs of Palestine liked all the generations living together, they were close like that. Our doctor friend lived in Katamon. He was the doctor I kept requesting be brought to treat my André. I was telling all of them that he was altogether a marvellous man. That he had taken a short trip to Beirut in April as the fighting was disrupting his ability to study a cluster of respiratory diseases he had found in the new immigrants. He might be back in Jerusalem as it was calmer now. The month of May had been very bad. Nightmarish. I had stayed inside our apartment. It had been quite fine in there. I lived on tinned food and refused the radio and the newspapers. André said whatever you need to feel safe, ma coeur.

The uniformed men pointed out that a trip from April until September 17, 1948, was five months, which was not a short trip by any measure and that those months in these lands had been particularly long and eventful. They said that short trips could not be taken to Beirut anymore unless you had diplomatic permissions, like Count Folke Bernadotte and my husband André Serot, who was a Colonel in the United Nations. Besides, my favourite doctor sounded like he was an Arab, which meant that for him to attempt to return would be an act of infiltration. He could be shot at the border on sight. I said this was madness and they said I was in shock. They had a point. The past falls through my body like a gust of gastric infection. My husband says it is because I survived the terrible place I was put in during the war and there is no shame in that, no shame at all.

Folke Bernadotte saved me. His white buses got us out. I want to tell the men about Folke saving me from a German concentration camp that I do not like to name. I would tell Folke if they let me see him, but he saved 10,000 Jews alone on top of the others, the Communists and Danes and homosexuals.

As Folke was there in the hospital, I could show my gratitude in person, I thought. But I worried as the men were implying that the moving around of passengers to do with thank yous could have resulted in the shooting. Mr. Bunche, Ralph, would arrive soon, they tell me again. I couldn't see what he could know that would interest me if he wasn't at the scene, or here in the hospital.

André and I called Mr. Bunche *Monsieur Bouquet*. We thought of him as a manifestation of fragrance, colour and largesse. *Super!* We both said when we spoke of Bunche, Folke's Number Two at the U.N.O., I expect he will step into those Number One shoes now. As a Negro gentleman he has to be twice as good. And he was. Is. He will carry out Folke's agenda for peace.

Nonsense about a bullet in the brain. Seventeen in the body. This reporting is the talk of hysterics. My André says it is *no wonder that the plants respond to your touch as you have such fine fingers.* I became complètement fixé on the idea that these men in uniforms were going to blame me for the Count being shot when he was needed to negotiate, bring peace to the region and allow the refugees to come home and reunite with their families. Instant damnation had happened to me before. I had been punished very severely during the long war. That incarceration had merely been for what I am, which is Jewish. I had not been brought up to think much about Jewishness. There were more interesting things to concern myself with at the time, like altering dresses for dances and finding menus for my new husband. Reading romantic novels in paperback volumes too. André liked to tease me about those.

Just that afternoon, I had been sitting at the kitchen table darning André's chausettes de soi when a large bird of prey came down from the North, over the mountains of Haifa swooping in across the rooftops and low clouds to my window. The bird was enormous: grey with a white underbelly and tail. He held himself as a messenger of stature would, knocking his beak on the pane, and was close enough for me to see the determination in his eyes. A desire for a seat at my table no less. I pricked mon annulaire, my ring finger, as I held the sock and I stayed still waiting for the bird to make his announcement and then KA KA – KA KA the telephone rang in the hallway, and it was Mr. Bunche. Monsieur Bouquet soi-même.

In the hospital, I could not stop touching the bracelet my husband had given me which, if I positioned it on my wrist in a certain way, hid the blue number that I disliked very much. The weather was too hot in Palestine for long sleeves. In the camps, we had all kinds of bugs and rashes and no sleeves. At night, your skin and your stomach itched. I realised on the day of Katamon, that we had only been given three tenuous years, between the white bus and the white hospital. Three years to start to be a man and wife again; a normal, nice couple who worried about cut flowers and fresh cows' milk. What to eat for breakfast. We were not in France and the bakeries were really very Polish with the dark bread that was good for you, but not a croissant and more of a crust.

Most couples were separated during the war. It was not polite to go on about it if you were alive and well and in Palestine. People did not speak of the past. They liked to talk of new futures and empty lands and the life of pioneers. I did not understand these proclamations. I was just a grateful guest, lying low and trying to learn the local customs. The war had forced us out of the habit of trust. One word wrong and *Buf!* the *boîte de Pandore* would pop its lid. These hatreds were best left to fester in Europe with its centuries of pogroms, invasions, religious wars and other feuds. It was best that we did not speak each other's languages in Palestine or Israel or whatever they wanted to call it. It was too late for someone like me to animate the dead tongues: Arabic, Hebrew. 'I'm surprised they're not trying to resurrect Aramaic,' I said to my husband André, who laughed his gentle laugh. 'We are living history,' he said, with his arms spread to the window, as though that was consolation for the bombs, the rifles and the criminal gangs. I hated those thugs. The Arabs could give you a fright, but the Jewish ones were the worst; Hagannah, The Stern and Lehi they called themselves. Petty criminals of the gutter; brought up with no culture other than knife fights in alleyways, made more bloodthirsty by the war, they were desperate, mean. Nothing grew from the hard lands they came from. I had sharpened sensibilities to this type. In the camps, men like them would steal a cup of water from a child. They reminded me of the Germans in France, the way they behaved in bars, on the streets, as if they could have whatever they wanted because they had guns and we didn't. Man is nothing without manners my father used to say, but it all gets boulversé when rifles come into the equation. Manners and trust became liabilities. Our young doctor friend had beautiful manners. André was awfully soft on our doctor, treated him as a nephew – a son – lent him books of poetry. Apollinaire I believe it was. Le Pont Mirabeau:

L'amour s'en va Love goes. All of it *comme cette eau courante* like water into the sea. *L'amour s'en va* It all goes, love. Gone. *Rah.*

Comme la vie est lente How stupefying life can be. *Vie est lente. Lente.* Slow. Stupefyingly slow. How stupefying slow life can be.

We were happy being incommunicative, my husband André and I. *Non, c'est pas exacte.* We read each other all the time, together or apart. We just did not need to talk about everything. He had enough action and words at work. The last thing he sought out at home was more happenings. He liked quiche lorraine, savoury soufflés preferably with spinach and salty cheese, and oh how he loved light wines from Bordeaux that reminded him of the countryside. My life was as quiet as I could make it, with all alterations to my routine being deliberated upon for extended periods of time, back and forth like tennis for ladies with a soft ball, or badminton with a coq de navette. 'It is a luxury not to have change. It is the sweetness of peace.' My husband André had taken my hand when I said that. I was picking at crumbs off the bleached linen on our formica table. It was a constant battle to deter the ants from eating more of it. 'You have such a pretty way of describing things,' my André liked to say.

The uniformed men's heels clacked on the hospital's limestone. They liked change; they went where change could be made and then they moved on. Shuttle diplomacy was the height of their ambition with its planes, jeeps and useless soldiers who did not carry guns. Their footsteps were too much for me in the hospital on a day which had had such a soft afternoon light, an insultingly quotidian light, which had no right to continue when that ruptured city had witnessed what it had. Why were the heavens not halting, stalling, crashing down with floods of locusts and storms of waters and pestilence? How dare it all just continue when those who had machine-gunned into the torsos of the most heroic of men, as though dumb pheasants tied on a cart, when they still walked this earth? May the earth damn their quests for peace in this life and may their lives be short and torturous.

Brown nurses in white uniforms fussing around me. If I were Fra Angelico, I would give them pink wings tipped with blue. I am surrounded by arches wide enough to let in angels of death. They have the bodies of eagles and the heads of gargoyles. My city in France was connu for its black cathedral made from volcanic rock that was sinister enough sans gargouilles. My friends went there on Sundays and said it was better inside, vaulted and light, but that the black-robed priests did drone on so. 'About what?' I had asked. 'Piety and repentence,' they answered. They envied me for skipping Cathedral. That was before the war. My fortune at being alive does not make me religious. It makes me ponderous. 'You have such a fascination with the inanimate,' says André.

There was 'a lot to absorb in Palestine,' he assured me, taking me to a little concert of Fauré performed by German musicians. I liked to hear them play, but when they spoke, I asked to leave and waited for my dear husband outside. He had come out with the young doctor, who also enjoyed a concert. The Doctor was interested in the new European cultures arriving in Palestine. To him, the German language had no significance and he'd found the precision of the concert's organisation calming. This must have been in 1946, when my husband and I had looked forward to the patterns of normal, nice living that we would make in our apartment with the friendly gecko and the little clock of Grandmother's that the neighbour had saved and the family furniture of my husband's, that he had never lost.

For several years, we had been entertaining the idea of buying a bird — a canary or a parrot - from the Arab bird seller who was called Abu Dina because he had no sons, but a daughter called Dina who was worth a thousand sons he declared. Dina had taken a short trip to Jericho with her mother and her siblings in the Spring. Abu Dina had stayed on to protect the shop which was his livelihood after all, and he managed to hold onto it even with planes and gunmen going door to door in May it must have been. Not our door that time, because this time being Jewish was the right thing to be.

Oh yes, I remember now, when I asked our young doctor friend why he had chosen to specialise in children — paediatrics — he told me of a child he had treated when he was a student in the American missionary university in Beirut. That she had leant up to him from her hospital bed and stroked the hair on his head and giggled. He had found such tenderness in the gesture. She had looked into his eyes with such love, he said, that he knew he had found his calling. He had not been able to save her. Madness that such a man could be shot for infiltration. Besides, I am pretty sure he mentioned that he was a Christian.

André told me that the leader of the Lehi or The Stern, Yitzhak Shamir, once proved his strength to his men by walking down the beach with a friend and co-fighter and coming back alone. His friend, also a murderer no doubt, was never seen again. 'Such an initiation test says a lot about their values,' was my André's comment on this.

I decided to confess. I tell the men that it was my fault. My husband had told me he was going to request permission to change his place in the vehicle with that of Mr. Lundström to sit next to Folke Bernadotte. They ask me why. I say white buses. Count Bernadotte had organised the white buses and I had ridden in one out of the concentration camp. I wanted my husband André Serot to say thank you to the good man Folke Bernadotte in person. The murderers at the fake checkpoint had wanted to shoot Mr. Lundström, but Mr. Lundström is now walking around and talking right as rain, with no more than little sprays of my husband's blood on his trouser leg.

There was another war in 1948. Relatively short. Nobody removed me from my home. I stepped aside. I was told I should be happy. They said it was a special war of liberation. I was not happy, but could not say that because as a Jewish person that would be ungrateful. I find this attitude enervating. My husband is not a Jew. Our parrot, which by then we had decided was to be an African Grey, was not going to be a Jew. We wanted him to be a vegetarian Hindoo, but not mystical because then he would escape through the bars like Houdini. I had strong feelings about a cage. Abu Dina had said we should consider the option of a perch. As I believe I mentioned, Abu Dina had not left for Lebanon, Egypt, Syria, Jordan for a short trip in the Spring, unlike my young doctor friend and many of the other people of Palestine around us. He had not even gone to Jericho to be with his family. Now it was too late. He got agitated when I suggested a one-way trip out of Jerusalem. Abu Dina said that it was impossible to get an African Grey now that the routes to Syria were closed and the Egyptian border was sealed and Lebanon was out of bounds and Jerusalem and Jericho cut off by the Mandelbaum Gate. What liberation did we have if the only way of getting an African Grey was if he were to swoop down from the skies on a migratory route across the seas to Africa or India or Ceylon and on that route say, 'Let me stop and become your parrot Madame Serot?' That is what my husband had said could happen. I must say that is what I thought was happening when that bull-headed eagle arrived at my kitchen window.

Our so-called liberation was cloaked in much vulgarity. I did not blame Abu Dina for losing interest in selling exotic birds and for not stocking up on his boxes of coloured baby chicks like fluffy bonbons. He just said it was all gone. *Rah rah* he said in Arabic and with his hands. He shuttered up his shop far more than he opened it. We assumed he was under curfew, although the curfew hours for Arabs were more sunrise to sunset, he liked to extend it to stay behind his shutters throughout the night. There can't have been enough light in there to sustain a fungus. When the spring fighting spread and they kept saying *Deir Yassin, Deir Yassin* and *Abu Dina* and the Doctor were speaking of women's bellies being cut open by men in trucks, of killing and raping, it must have been the Stern or Lehi or whatever those crooks called themselves. His Dina and the family had gone for a short trip to the winter house in Jericho which is now on the other side of the Gate. My husband had told Abu Dina that he should not worry so much about Hagannah, Stern and Lehi. That the British would catch them with their best detectives and punish them for being murderers and then we could get on with living our nice, normal lives and consider again whether to get an African Grey who could say short words or phrases. A parrot would probably find Ka-ta-mon very easy to repeat. The way I hear the word in my head is much like the call of a parrot.

My husband said that it was understandable that my nerves were fragile, there was no embarrassment to be had, but I should not dwell on those terrible minutes, hours, days, weeks, months, years in the camp, although he would encourage me to speak of it if I tried. At night, I would sometimes wake bolt upright with an invisible ball of a scream caught in my mouth saying 'no' to the guard, '*NO!*' And then I would find myself awake in Palestine with the pausing gecko above the window, my dear husband André asleep on his back, a small electric light on my bedside and the clock of my grandmother's and *ça va. Tranquille* I would tell myself and have a little wash of my face in the bathroom with the cool water that flowed from the tap and turned on and off so very neatly.

My husband cannot tell me very much of what he did during the war. I am allowed to be told that he was a senior intelligence officer in North Africa, *tout a fait* the commanding one. If it hadn't been for him, we may not have won the war on that front. That would have meant staying in those despicable camps for far longer or dying there before the white bus came and took me out to France, which had been home to me, before it was made strange to me.

A large hand on my shoulder. 'Don't worry,' Mr. Bunche says. 'We'll find the murderers behind this,' he assures me, although I had been told my André was just badly injured. 'We know who they are. They have already issued a statement. They have apologised for shooting Colonel Serot.'

'But seventeen bullets and one in the head,' I say, 'that is quite deliberate.'

'They wanted to kill Mr. Lundström,' Mr. Bunche says. 'They call Lundström an antisemite. The government of Mr. Ben-Gurion however condemns the attack in the strongest possible terms,' Mr. Bunche assures me. 'The Israeli government says it had differences with Folke Bernadotte, but they respected the Count and the United Nations tremendously, that is what Prime Minister Ben Gurion says.'

'But then why are they feeding the killers their supper?' I ask.

'They will catch the men and try them,' Mr. Bunche says again. 'We will ensure it is a fair trial and that justice is done,' Monsieur Bouquet assures me. 'I am sorry for the loss of your husband,' he says, although until then no one had told me he had gone anywhere.

'And Mr. Folke's resolutions for the return of the refugees?' my widowed self asks. 'Will you ensure that they can come home?'

'Of course,' says Mr. Bunche. 'There is global outrage,' he assures me, 'the United Nations will guarantee their return, or if not, compensation to them for their losses. These camps are temporary and unfit for long term purpose,' he says.

'Thank you, Mr. Bunche,' I say. He holds my right hand with two of his. 'Folke and my husband André will be very pleased about that,' I say. 'As will our friend the young doctor and the other refugees. Most grateful indeed.'

DEIR AL-QASI

A Chronicle of Grandad's Last Days Asleep

Mazen Maarouf

Translated by Jonathan Wright

I

Azmi

THE LAST THING WE did in the village was wait for the body. What the smugglers told Grandad was that my father's legs had been cut off and they would bring him in a box because it was a long way. And that would protect him from the hyenas. Then I would help him attach his stumps to two pieces of wood and we would walk back home together. Grandad made the wooden legs out of two dry branches. As my father's father, he could estimate how much weight my father would have put on, even though he hadn't seen him for years. We waited for the body every day at noon. First Grandad and me, then me alone. Luckily I wouldn't have to carry the pieces of wood by myself. I would put them on Azmi's back and wait on the limestone hills. Up there, the sun would fry my brain like an omelette. And since my father was going to come back in a box, I called him 'the corpse'. Grandad liked the name, though, of course, it would last only till the moment the village saw my father walking alongside me. But the smugglers never arrived and Grandma's view was that they had tricked us. And my father had died fighting in the hills.

It wasn't any better at night. Members of the National Committee would come every few days to take the donkey. Grandad would scowl because the smugglers had promised to bring my father back but they still hadn't come. Maybe they'd been killed by members of the National Committee. They had many suspicions and no one understood anything. Our donkey seemed to be of a breed the spotted hyenas were frightened of. The members would move by night, heads covered, with few weapons. So, taking the donkey when the gangs came close seemed a reasonable solution because then they could cut it up and distribute the meat around the village, along with the meat of other animals, such as cows and sheep. As then the hyenas would arrive ahead of the coming of the gangs, and there would be enough chaos to repel the attack with simple rifles. That's why Grandad would scowl whenever the committee members knocked on our door. He wanted to have the donkey mate and produce little donkeys with the same qualities, because that would help us earn money. That's why Grandad gave the donkey a name: Azmi. But in the final days, Grandad just lay in the courtyard and no longer listened to anything. Or maybe he was pretending so that he could stand up and bear arms after we were gone. We kept shaking his body for three days. And I felt afraid when Grandma did that. So I would leave the house because the gangs had closed the roads and we had no idea what could be done. Only on the fourth day did Grandad speak. He opened his eyes and said he just wanted to give his back a rest. Then he closed them again.

I didn't know that people die. In fact, I sat at the far end of the courtyard holding a stick of sugarcane. Grandad had split the end of the cane for me lengthwise. But Grandma Narjis says I'm good for nothing. I always ruin things and I can't tell the difference between lizards and frogs. Grandad calls it 'the lizard-hunting stick' but I feel that that expression is too exclusive, and I add frogs so that the lizards have some friends. Even though Grandma thinks I'm no good at telling the difference between a lizard and a frog, I will learn if I follow the right steps. All I have to do is aim the stick straight and not think about whether what appears in front of me is a lizard or a frog. I can't remember which of them is long and which can puff itself up and has a tail. Or the other way around. It's like there are two of me: one here and another over there. And when other people speak to me, the words go into the ear of the person that's me, but that's over there. I don't understand it myself. And every evening I'm ready when we dunk bread in black tea together. Usually I sit next to Grandma, with Grandad opposite us. I look at the cow and the two sheep and the rabbits that stick together in fear at sunset. Grandad has drawn up a plan that requires us to split up when attack time comes. My brother, Narjis and I will have to go to one of the rocky holes, stay several days, then come back when the gangs are finished. I'm practising escaping every day. I say I'm going to find an abandoned house on the edges. And if anyone stops me, I'll hold up the stick and say I'm practising hunting. Hunting frogs and lizards. As if I were really good at telling them apart.

Grandma's Sandals

I might have lost my way to the water pump. Grandad said a hundred paces and I'd be there. As soon as I haul up the bucket, frogs and lizards appear between the weeds. But Grandma's sandals slipped off my feet twice and when the hundred paces were done, I found no trace of any pump. I don't know whether Grandad was taking into account the shoes dragging along the ground, or the bits when I walked back a step. But I was in a hurry and thinking about the donkey and how it collapsed in front of the door, with flies hovering around its beautiful eyes. And on the way, I also started brushing off the ants that jumped onto my legs as I was counting the hundred paces and trying to keep Grandma's sandals on. It was as if there was something in my feet that the ants could feed on. And so I took another route. Then a bald man appeared, driving a military vehicle with a machine gun at the front. He saw me stamping the ground with my foot, listening, and raising the stick, then stamping the ground again. I thought that in this way I could lure out the reptiles. He stopped and looked at me. Maybe he asked me: 'What are you looking for?' Because I didn't look at him at first. I was trying to stop myself crying at hearing a human voice. Then he said, 'What are you carrying?' He was speaking a language I didn't know, but when he used his hands, I understood. 'A stick to hunt lizards and frogs,' I said, and my thinking was that I had never before seen a person who was as bald as a devil, like this guy. 'Show me,' he said. In the village, we don't refuse a request from a friend, or even an enemy. I stood there watching the soldier, with my hands over my face so that the sun wouldn't fry my brain like an omelette. But, as I was about to add an explanation along the lines of 'the stick only works once and then you have to...', he cocked the machine gun and opened fire at random towards me, then drove off with the stick.

II

Straw

The sound of gunfire from the guy with the bald head kept ringing in my ears: 'Yang, yang, yang' until it was replaced by a voice saying, 'You almost ruined the grass that Grandma needs to make mats'.

'I was looking for the well,' I explained in an aggressive tone, 'and I lay down on the ground. I'm practising that to avoid the bullets.'

A CHRONICLE OF GRANDAD'S LAST DAYS ASLEEP

'You've been on the ground for three days. I thought you'd never wake up,' he replied rudely. 'In any case, ranting like that is better than nothing. Get up!' He was wearing a straw hat. A big one. It slipped and he swore profusely. He's my brother. And there's a crack in his head from behind. It's clear they've executed him but he doesn't know it yet. The thing that hasn't been affected is his fiery nature. If you make a noise with your slippers when he's fast asleep, he opens his eyes and looks at you with hate. He can't bear us doing that to check that he's still alive. But the next morning, he hugs you warmly. And you feel he's giving you a lesson in how to live for the rest of your life.

'I've finished gathering straw. You can check. Didn't Grandad send you to do that?' he said. I looked around. It was morning. And there was no trace of any wheat stalks. But the air was stifling. Like a grave. And the place was full of the grasses we were used to seeing. We know my brother is weak. Work exhausts him. He was once found unconscious in the field, and since then I've been walking behind him. Or that's what I tell Grandad. Because my brother's caused many problems since my father's departure. 'I'm sorry,' I said. 'I can help now.' He took a stone from his pocket and put it in my hand. 'Good, take this, sharpen your teeth with it,' he said, and I started rubbing my teeth with the stone as he had done.

We cut the straw with our teeth. We made two enormous bundles and picked them up. The sun was lethal as we walked along the lanes and streets towards Grandad's house. But my brother was in a hurry and sometimes stumbled, and then he would curse and swear. Azmi was clumsy too and often stumbled. That meant they wanted to take him and feed him to the hyenas. Other than Azmi, there wasn't a donkey that stumbled in all the villages of Galilee. He'd stumble even when he was standing in the courtyard without moving. And sometimes the kids would sit on the courtyard wall and laugh. But Grandad didn't want to give him up because the stumbling had only started to happen to him since my father left.

A Toy Plane

The other half of the village was full of strangers now. You felt your eyes tearing up but when you tried to wipe the tears away with your finger, you didn't find anything there. We passed a house and I saw a woman and a young man with quizzical looks on their faces, and a child wearing a helmet and swinging a toy plane around in spirals on the end of a stick. I was fascinated by the sight of the toy and the child. The young man was hefting a rifle in his hand and the woman was browsing through a newspaper. There was a girl nearby picking flowers to put in a cup. My brother pushed me with a slap on the back of my head and said, 'They came on a ship. They gave the children toys as soon as they set foot in our country. Don't look at them like an idiot.'

But there was something the boy didn't like. He threw the plane towards us aggressively, saying, 'Take it.' His plane glided higher and almost landed in the pile of straw on my back. But I avoided it by stepping to the right and it fell on a stone and turned over twice. My brother said, 'Don't take anything. They're expecting that!' At that moment, another young man rushed out of the house. His eyes were lifeless and we couldn't tell what he was feeling. I recognised him immediately. He was Fayez, the butcher's son. I waited till he came over and then kicked the plane with my foot. It broke in two halves, and my brother began to laugh. Fayez pushed me and I fell to the ground. My brother attacked him with his fist, which looked like a crazy arrangement of bones. After an exchange of feeble curses, my brother fell silent and I noticed a crack behind Fayez's ear. Fayez turned to me and said boastfully: 'That was from a fall from the roof. Three floors. But the impact was more like just being hit with a stick. Anything else?'

'No,' said my brother.

'Then get the hell out of here!' whispered Fayez, gnashing

his teeth. Then he lifted the plane into the air and addressed the boy in the helmet uncertainly, saying 'It's broken. I'll fix it.'

As we watched Fayez go back to the family with unnaturally athletic leaps, my brother said, 'Do you know him?'

'Yes, he's the butcher's son,' I said. 'That's their house. He now works for the family of strangers that lives in it. He looks after the garden and fixes things. He's the only person I've ever wanted to see shot in the arse with a bullet, and I hope the bullet keeps moving without them finding it. But it turned out he's smarter than I expected.' It's clear they also executed Fayez but he doesn't know it. I wanted to say that out loud with gleeful pleasure, but it would break my brother's heart and he wouldn't laugh. He touched the crack in his own head and brooded on it as we walked along. 'Are there new people living in our house?' I asked him.

'Not yet, but they'll come. We'll try to work for them too, without them knowing the house belongs to us,' he replied.

'And Grandad?' I asked.

'Maybe he's making tea and waiting for us.'

'The gunman took the stick from me, the stick for hunting lizards and frogs. And I have to find it,' I said.

'For Azmi?'

'Yes,' I said.

'Ha! Don't think about it. They killed him and spread the meat on the hills around the village. But the poor donkey managed to come back. You'll laugh when you see him!'

Water

The man who received us wasn't Grandad. And the woman wasn't the grandma I remembered. Maybe it was one of Grandad's jokes for me being three days late. But the old people welcomed us warmly. Before we arrived, they had even prepared za'atar, olive oil and some bread. My brother kissed their hands and I followed his example. He was calling them Grandad and Grandma. What the three had in common, I thought, was that they didn't know they had all been executed. But the courtyard looked nicer now, with woven straw trays hanging on the walls. Nor was there any sign of the kids who used to sit on the edge of the courtyard to throw stones at Azmi. They were real bastards, but I miss them. 'Fayez didn't manage to get a single straw from us, did he?' my brother said enthusiastically as we put our bundles of straw down in the courtyard.

'No,' I replied in confusion. Sometimes the village kids used to harass my brother when he brought straw back to the house. One of them would sneak up on him, pull out a straw and run away. When Grandad couldn't find the straw that enabled him to have the right dreams, my brother would get upset and say it had been in the bundle but the kids had stolen it. Because of that, he feared, the gangs would now come and steal the houses.

'There's no need to bring more,' said the old woman. 'Now we need water to soak it in.'

'There's a tap in one of the houses in the village. The tap handle can be taken off,' I said.

'Where?' my brother asked, rubbing his eyes indifferently. I closed my eyes to remember and saw Grandma Narjis on the last day, taking the handles off the three taps in the house. We went to bury the handles under a stone in the field. She did that to push Grandad to leave with us as the gangs approached. But my brother went to gather straw. He said we should go on with our lives as usual. They would think we were simple-minded and leave us alone. Then Grandma and I waited for him and Grandad and Azmi came back.

'I don't remember,' I said.

'He tripped up,' said my brother. 'He was practising falling on the ground to avoid bullets, then he tripped up. Now look at the hole in his head.' Then he added: 'Azmi might remember.' He headed to a small area behind the courtyard and came back carrying the donkey around its belly, like a dog. Azmi was the same as the last time I saw him. Wandering eyes. His tongue hanging out. A bullet hole in the head.

'That's why I was looking for you. He doesn't obey anyone else,' said my brother, putting the donkey at my feet. Then he started speaking to him: 'Azmi, up you get, my dear. Get up now.' But the donkey didn't budge. 'You try,' he said.

I spoke to the donkey in my mind, silently, saying, 'Azmi, get up!' The donkey shook his head and tried to push his body forward until it managed to stand up like any animate beast. A shiver ran through me. 'Walk,' I said in my mind, and he walked. 'Now rise in the air,' I said, and his hooves rose in the air to the height of one finger's length, as if his body were made of rubber. But he panicked at not touching the ground and that was enough for the long marks to show on his hide like rays of light, the marks left by their knives when they cut him up.

'He needs to eat,' I said.

'Eat? I thought the food he'd eaten in the settlement would last him the rest of his life.'

'You're saying that because Grandad punished you rather than me. I'm sorry,' I said.

'Why don't you tell us where Grandma hid the handles for the taps? We need the water to soak the straw,' said my brother.

I said nothing, so my brother took me out of the house.

'Because these old people aren't Grandad and Grandma, and I don't want them in our house,' I said.

My brother said that when he got back to the house, he found the old couple turning over the soil in the courtyard to check that the tomatoes had grown enough. He said to them, 'Grandad, Grandma, I'm back.' They turned and he realised he'd made a mistake. But the old couple seemed to recognise him. In fact, the woman patted him on the shoulder and asked him if he was hungry and how long he'd had a moustache like that. 'None of that seems logical,' he continued, 'but what can be done? Maybe they really are our grandparents, but for some reason, we don't remember what they looked like.'

'Your moustache really doesn't suit you like that,' I said. 'You should shave it off. We'll go and find the tap handles that Grandma disconnected.'

Jumping

Azmi led us to the place. It wasn't easy. The stone that Grandma had left as a marker wasn't there any longer, so we went back home. We ate some food and the donkey had a little rest. The next morning, I tried again while the old couple and my brother were asleep. I carried Azmi out of the house so that I wouldn't make any noise, and he led the way. I found the tap handles and a sack tied up with papers and photos inside. I picked them up and went back to the house. I put the handles on the taps in the kitchen, the bathroom and the courtyard. I hid the sack and went back to sleep. When I woke up, all the straw was soaking in water in the courtyard. But my brother wasn't there. The old couple said, 'He shaved off his moustache and his beard and went to the school.' I dropped in on Mansour's house on the way, which is what I usually did. The road led to the school, but I found my brother along the way, jumping off a large boulder, without trying to fall safely. His face was covered in bruises, and Fayez and some of the guys were standing there, encouraging him. Fayez was giving him a thumbs-up after every jump. But before I had a chance to protest, Fayez went and took my brother's place and fell. The impact was horrific. But the others, including my brother, gave him thumbs-up signs while Fayez brushed the soil off his clothes and went to jump again. One of the guys asked me if I was going to jump. 'No,' I said. That guy took Fayez's place and jumped. By this time my brother was by my side and he said, 'At least give him a thumbs-up to encourage him. It's the right thing to do.'

The jumping took all afternoon. I left my brother with Fayez and the others and went to feed Azmi. He wouldn't stop eating. Then I passed by the school again to pick up my brother. He was exhausted and rode the donkey all the way back. But he wouldn't let a chance to harass me pass. 'Why didn't you jump? Were you too cowardly?' he said.

'And why should I jump?'

'You'll need to later.'

'I don't understand.'

'You'll understand later,' he said.

I was annoyed. 'You should try falling in a way that doesn't leave bruises.'

'Look,' my brother said. 'The bruises don't show any longer.'

'I, for example, can talk with Azmi. Isn't that miraculous?' I replied.

'You talk with Azmi in your head. Yet no one believes the donkey obeys your commands. If you could make two donkeys move together in the same way, we'd say something different,' he said.

When we got back to the house, we found the old couple packing a small bag with some clothes. The man came up, put his hand on my brother's shoulder and said, 'Sorry, we thought this was the right house.' My brother didn't make any objection. 'Things like that happen here,' he said.

The Teacher

My brother kept talking about the old couple all the following day. They weren't able to recognise us at the end of the day. You keep moving from place to place, and each time you get this sudden sense that it's not the original place, the one you never left, so you pack up your things and leave. And nonsense like that. I kept myself busy examining the papers and photos I found in the buried sack. Pointing at one picture, I said, 'Look! The old couple are the parents of the schoolteacher.'

'Maybe, but the faces are a little different,' commented my brother, without much interest.

'That's because the gangs killed the teacher, and the village has changed,' I said.

The schoolteacher never used to stop talking. People joked that he would keep talking even if they put a bullet in his forehead. When they found him dead under a tree, there was indeed a bullet hole in his forehead. People didn't say anything for a whole day. We didn't see his parents much after that. Then armed men started launching surprise attacks on the neighbouring villages. They would ask people to gather whatever they had in the way of photographs, personal documents, identity papers, title deeds, work contracts, birth certificates, anything, and they would set fire to it in front of everyone. When I asked Grandma why, as she was taking the handle off the tap in the kitchen, she said, 'Because there's nothing to be done any longer.' But she did also take the trouble to gather whatever papers and photos she could from the village and bury them in a hole. That's why she took me with her. She wanted to make sure I saw her bury the tap handles and that I would remember the place.

'Cunning Grandma operates as silently as a spy,' my brother said when I told him what had happened.

III

A Loquat Tree

We liked the schoolteacher. We used to ask him to repeat one of his favourite sayings: 'One of the biggest puzzles is how a human being can change from a child into a stream of shit!'

The children would burst out laughing. I thought he was saying that to defend my presence, and that if the saying had a relevant meaning, it was that life can turn against you at any moment. That's what was happening at school. We could hear the gangs approaching and the children would give me heartless looks. I knew what was going on in their minds. My father and Abu Shasha and all that nonsense. But after school, I would take Azmi and we would be part of the 'five donkeys' patrol to drive off the hyenas. That meant every donkey had to spread its dung along the edges of the village. Azmi had to go hungry first and then eat. One day the teacher took me aside and we made an agreement. He was writing letters to a young woman on the eastern side of the village. Lots of letters. He'd been writing them for months and now was the right time for her to start reading them.

The woman was Qamar, the judge's daughter. After the schoolteacher died, my brother fell in love with her. I never told him but I used to take her messages from the schoolteacher. That was until Grandad saw in a dream how Azmi and I would tramp the paths from one village to the next. And while the donkey was peeing, I would open the letter and try to read it. My brother heard Grandad talking about it in his sleep and started to follow me.

Qamar began to like the schoolteacher only when she started reading what he wrote. After his death, I went on delivering the letters as if the teacher were still alive. I wanted to announce his death only once the letters had ran out. Then I would say, 'The teacher's died' and I wouldn't appear again outside her beautiful house, which stood on a hill between three villages. I might describe how they found her beloved under the loquat tree and say he was still as handsome as he was when alive. I didn't see the body anyway. His parents buried him on the spot, with help from Grandad and some other men. I was organising my school books in the morning and Grandad came home saying, 'Don't go to school today.

The teacher's dead.' I sat on a stone outside the house and started to cry. I still had five or six letters left. I looked at them, then took Azmi and went to deliver one of them to Qamar.

Tobacco

That didn't happen all at once. The teacher's letters hadn't run out yet. My brother started getting to the judge's house before me. I didn't exchange words with him because I was now on the 'five donkeys' patrol. If he wanted anything, he could just say it straight out instead of all this chit-chat and rumours about what would happen to us if the gangs came. So my brother started watching me from afar, delivering the letters to Qamar. He said he'd never witnessed a love affair in his life and he only wanted to find out how it worked. But he would appear behind me and, with gestures, make Qamar believe he loved her. Later she asked me what his name was ('that young man there' she called him), and whether he was the one who had written the letters. 'Where? I can't see anyone,' I said. When I threatened to reveal the teacher's identity, my brother said, 'What's the difference? She's never seen him. You just want to break her heart because it was the judge who spread those awful rumours about our father and Abu Shasha.' Then I no longer had any letters, so he started going to the judge's house and meeting Qamar in the storeroom where they kept the harvest. She told him why some rich families would come and sign documents with strangers who didn't speak like us, and that we would be forced to leave our houses. It was only a question of time. But they would allow the judge to stay.

Our village's tobacco harvest used to be kept in a storeroom at the judge's house, along with some other crops. The farmers from three different villages used to store the crops there every season. The judge could sell them in the big towns. He knew how to bargain without giving up his pride.

But the gangs closed the roads and the tobacco was stuck in the storeroom. Then we heard that the judge was meeting some strangers who didn't speak our language. We thought this was in order to sell off the tobacco. The strangers had influence over the gangs and we wouldn't have objected to paying money to the gangs so that they wouldn't take our houses. But we didn't know that a dispute had arisen. The strangers had promised to take the tobacco harvest and sell it themselves, so that it wouldn't come to harm. In fact, they moved it to the settlement near us until the lorries could come. They even gave the judge a key to their storeroom so that he could take it back whenever he wanted. But the lorries didn't come, and then they offered to buy it directly from the judge at a pittance. Anyway, it was my brother who revealed the truth, after Qamar told him, and then he obtained the key from her. Grandad tried to stop him but my brother had every reason to get on our donkey Azmi and go around the village announcing that the judge had given the tobacco to the strangers who didn't speak like us. And when Grandad argued with him, my brother said he had taken revenge on the judge, not because revenge was the right thing to do but because it was the only way to convince other people that my father had nothing to do with the settlement.

IV

Abu Shasha

When the original Abu Shasha incident took place, my brother was just a six-year-old boy and I was in my mother's womb. The market that the village held every week, selling honey, almond brittle and other farm produce, was teeming with visitors from Acre and the nearby towns. Grandad didn't go to the market that day to sell his tomatoes, which were the reddest tomatoes in the village. He went to the stream instead.

He arranged two stones and a plank of wood and sat in silence. My father waited for him in the market, displaying some fruit and the woven straw trays that Grandma made. But Grandad wasn't in a good mood. In a dream, he had seen the villagers sitting on chairs on both sides of the river, looking at the water. That could mean only one thing: something bad was going to happen.

People from the villages passed the stream on their way to the market. Then the youngest of the children, being the most innocent, bent down and dipped his hand into the water in order to bless it. Maybe Grandad started thinking about some of the times when his dreams had revealed important information. In one dream, he had seen himself in a neighbouring village on a Wednesday and he had the impression something significant would happen. So he went there every Wednesday until one week, he met the woman who would become his wife, Grandma. On another occasion, he dreamt that a man from the village who worked abroad had recently been promoted. He told the man's mother about it and a few days later, she received some money from him and a telegram saying he had been given a salary increase. For three months, he dreamt about small things that people had lost, and he knew where they were. It annoyed him that people didn't talk about the things they lost. They believe that if they mention their loss, the things will never reappear. Asleep on his bench by the stream that day, he dreamed that someone was drowning in the water and he had to be ready to do something. A short time later, as he was explaining this to some men, a young man arrived on the scene, younger than my father. He didn't speak like us and in his hand he held a bag. He looked at Grandad, his foot slipped and he fell into the water.

The man said his name was Abu Shasha and his mother lived in a town far away and was in a wheelchair. They had a bookshop. They had heard about our country in the town they lived in, and he had come to see if the place would suit them. We called him the 'man who almost drowned' and took him to the settlement. The settlement didn't exist a few years before this incident, but strangers who don't speak like us had come by ship. They filled an empty space at the same level as our village. They marked it with wooden stakes and wires, and gave it a name. Then the houses, which were designed in a strange way, spread towards our village until they were side by side, as if the settlement was the other half of the village. A squadron of English soldiers came and built a small wall between us, a wall that any child could climb over.

Abu Shasha started climbing over the wall and we would give him bread and milk and say that he was simple-minded. But the settlement watchman didn't like this, and forced the 'man who almost drowned' to go to settlements far away to collect donations. The young man grew tired of waiting at the bus stop, so he spent time among our houses, never collecting a penny, until one night, when he went back to the watchman, he was kicked and insulted, and in the early hours rushed over to ours, his clothes covered in blood. He said he was going to go back to his own country because his mother was waiting there. Then he came and asked us for money because he wanted to send his mother a letter. We didn't know why he needed the money but we gave him the bus fare because the post office was far away. And so he started coming to us all the time, asking for money. Then his mother died and we heard him crying behind the wall. He kept visiting us, but less frequently. He started to think that if you approached him, you wanted to do him harm or that the things you said were offensive in some obscure way. But things went from bad to worse when, one day, three men went past our village with a box containing a boy no more than seventeen years old. He had gone to learn how to shoot a rifle but the gangs ambushed and captured him on the way. Grandad recognised him without him saying a word and pointed the three men to a nearby village. The 'man who almost drowned' was present and saw the coffin. He rushed off to the settlement. A few days later, they spread rumours that we had deliberately shown him the body of a young man about the same age as him, to send a message that something similar would happen to him one day.

Abu Shasha didn't come back to our village after that, and the watchman started carrying a pistol, which he used to shoot at any foxes that might approach. And when there were no longer any foxes, he started shooting at lizards. He did that when Father and our donkey Azmi were passing. Our donkey would see the little animals writhing on their backs and dying. He started to panic and when he panicked, he got hungry and ate a lot. Then the judge intervened, and the English made the wall one metre higher. Abu Shasha no longer climbed it. Sometimes we'd see him walking to the bus stop on the main road below the village, but he didn't say hello.

Five years had passed before Abu Shasha reappeared in Grandad's house. By then, at the age of five, I was a visible presence along with my brother, who was eleven. Grandad had raised the courtyard wall and added a bedroom, and we continued to live together. I remember my mother wearing a beautiful green dress. She was slim and spoke little with Grandad and Grandma. Because the gangs had killed her brother in the uprising, when she was pregnant with me, she wasn't pleased that Grandad saved Abu Shasha from drowning. Grandad kept saying he was in no danger of drowning that day anyway. He had just lost his footing and got some mud on his shoes. But my uncle was in a battle alongside a big leader, and they were winning. The gangs killed the leader and the other men laid down their rifles in the middle of the fighting and started weeping, and the gangs finished them off too.

On that night when everything changed, my father heard a noise in the courtyard and found a strong-bodied young man about the same height as him. My father recognised him immediately. It was Abu Shasha. This time too his shirt was covered in blood, and he was out of breath. He asked my father to keep his distance and said the watchman had hit him. He would rest a while in the courtyard, then leave the village and go back to his own country at last. My father couldn't think of anything to say. He suggested Abu Shasha wash his face at the tap in the courtyard, which is what Abu Shasha was doing when I called my father from inside the house. I was lying next to my mother, and my father came in to check up on me. But there was nothing wrong with me. My eyes were closed and I was dozing as usual. When my father went back to the courtyard with a towel, the 'man who almost drowned' had left by the same way he had come in, by jumping over the courtyard wall.

The next day, some fighters came on horseback. They said that a man had gone to the place where they had set up a camp for rebels in the hills and this man had killed two people, but they had wounded him. The people in the house next door said they had seen a man climbing over the wall of our courtyard. My father told them what he knew about Abu Shasha's night-time visit. My mother and father quarrelled. She had wanted revenge for her brother but my father hadn't woken her up. Abu Shasha had received good training in planning, thinking intelligently and deceiving the enemy, but he set out to kill the rebels on his own initiative, to prove a point to the watchman so that he would stop beating him.

The judge's assistants kept turning up at our house to ask my father questions. My mother would sit in the same room with a vacant expression on her face and think about what she would do. We didn't see her speak to my father. Then we started hearing that we had sheltered a murderer. A few days later, my father left the house to look for Abu Shasha. That's what Grandad told the judge's assistants. Grandad also said that he had thrown my father out himself. In fact, my father had hidden in the hills nearby. He didn't have any military training or any weapons. Grandma started cooking food for him and my mother would take Azmi the donkey to sell the woven straw trays in the villages. Then my brother and I would meet her under a tree with big leaves that hung down like a tent. Then my father turned up, with a thinner face and troubled eyes, and my brother took over the task of guarding the place. We would eat together, without much conversation. And one day, my mother took the donkey and asked us to meet her under the same tent-like tree. We waited for her, my brother and I, but she didn't come back. Azmi came back alone with the straw trays. Then we learned from Father that she had gone to join the fighters and he would follow in her footsteps in a few days.

A Ghost

Father spent days hiding in the hills and met smugglers who could help him. After school, I would take him food from Grandma. The first two days, only Azmi and I went. Then Father said he could hear hyenas making whooping noises at night, so I took my friend Mansour along without explaining why. Not just because he was my friend but because Mansour didn't have good eyesight. That's why his father went to Acre to work in a garage, to save up money to buy him a pair of glasses. Mansour also had a donkey like me, one called Thalj with red ears. After my mother left, my brother stopped going to the tree with the big leaves hanging down. He said they were watching him, and he would lie lazily in the courtyard, making fun of everyone - me, Grandad, and even Grandma, for whom he collected straw on the way home. But he spent more time on our land next to the cemetery. There he recovered his strength. He would work the land energetically. Once I saw him working so hard that tears started falling from his eyes.

Mansour would see me going under the tree and speaking to someone, so he asked me about it. I said that it was my father's ghost and that he had to close his eyes or else *his* father would also become a ghost. Father would appear suddenly, take the food and leave. I never found out where he was hiding. But Mansour didn't close his eyes the second time and he saw my father leaving with the bag of food. Of course, his father didn't turn into a ghost, but a few days later, he came back to the village in a box, claiming that he was dead. The gangs had blown up an ambulance in the garage, where they were fixing it. A piece of metal went into his back. Just a small piece, but his limbs no longer moved. After that day, Mansour no longer spoke to me. This was because, before his father arrived in the box, Grandad had seen Mansour's father in a dream, with people pouring water on his arms, as if washing a corpse. I hurried off to frighten my only friend by saying his father had turned into a ghost. As for Father, he stopped appearing under the tree. Instead he would shout at me from far off, telling me to leave the bag of food and go, and to do so quickly, because the hyenas might move in. One day, I waited for Father under the tree and I didn't hear any voice talking to me. So I put the bag of food on the ground and moved away. After that, something changed in me and I was no longer afraid of hyenas.

The Plum Plan

This is something that happened five years ago. I continued to go to school, like Mansour. We were together in the 'five donkeys' patrol, going our different ways with Azmi and Thalj. Whenever Azmi saw a lizard he was frightened and would eat and spread lots of dung, so I would spend a longer time on patrol. But I didn't exchange words with Mansour again until after the death of the schoolteacher. Mansour made a plan and suggested we carry it out together. Our harvest was in the settlement and the key to the storeroom door was in our possession. And the schoolteacher had died. We decided on the day. In two days' time they were going to open a dispensary in the settlement, along with a children's playground with a slide and equipment for climbing and adventure. I took the key and Mansour mounted Azmi and I led them by the halter. Getting into the settlement was easy, because between it and our village there was only a low, incomplete wall at the time. There was a crowd and some English people and a foreign photographer. Even the judge went to clap in the hope that the strangers would find a solution to the problem of the harvest. Just a few yards away, our houses were as silent as the grave. But on the way I started talking about the wretched state of Mansour's father and how he was condemned to be paralysed from now on and how Mansour would have to look after him. I expected he would cry. But his ears just turned red, like plums. 'At least my father isn't dead,' he said. Yet it was clear that if the watchman caught my friend, he would burst into tears, which would give me time to complete my mission.

We went into the settlement with the woven straw trays I had secretly taken from home. If we were asked we would say I had come to sell them. As for Mansour, he had come to consult the dispensary about his father, who couldn't move. Azmi had been hungry since the day before. The room where our harvest had been put was next to the watchman's house. It wasn't hard to find. The place stank of tobacco leaves, mixed with another smell that was rather unpleasant. There was no one there. I opened the door with the key and Mansour rushed inside. He filled his pockets with plums that were almost rotten now and set off to the watchman's house. Meanwhile, I pushed Azmi into the room, saying 'Eat everything', and closed the door on us.

We managed to carry out the 'plum plan' smoothly. The watchman didn't appear. Mansour said he put a chair in the middle of the large sitting room and started throwing plums at the windows and, because his eyes couldn't see well, the fruit began to hit the furniture and the curtains and burst, making a mess everywhere – on the furniture, the curtains, the walls and the floor. But he went on picking up the plums and throwing them again and again. Then he wiped his hands on the door and went back to the village. I don't know how Mansour managed to get into the watchman's house so heroically. He said that after his father came back, he discovered he could open any door and go in just by moving the handle, but I felt he was paying me back twofold for my story about ghosts.

A Box

On the evening of the next day, the judge came to our village, his veins bulging in anger. He said he hadn't gone to the settlement just for the opening, but rather because he was supposed to pay some money to the watchman and recover the harvest. They took the money and opened the door to the room, only for him to find some of the crops had been eaten. He picked up what was left and took it back to his house. We realised that the watchman had let us go into the room and the house in order to get his revenge, and that with the judge's money, he had bought furniture to replace the furniture that Mansour had ruined. The message was clear: we were condemned to defeat whatever we did. My brother asked me to say that he had devised the plum plan to atone for his failure to respect the judge's status, but he ruined everything as usual and was prepared for any punishment.

A few days later, an Arab officer arrived, with a whip at his waist and shouting so that they could hear him in the settlement. We were used to seeing Arab soldiers appearing quickly and disappearing behind the hills. But the officer stayed a whole day in our village. Waving his finger around like someone giving orders, he said, 'Nothing can be done any longer. You need a miracle.' But he took Grandad to the loquat tree, placed a chair there for him, and said, 'You're going to sleep here until you see who killed the schoolteacher.' They let us keep Azmi nearby for protection. I saw the Arab soldiers hitting Grandad on the head, and the band around his headscarf fell to the ground. The schoolteacher's mother and father were present. From that day on, they didn't speak to anyone. Grandad told me later that this was to help him have a dream and see who had killed the teacher, and he asked me not to tell my brother or Grandma. Maybe Grandad was right, because that same night he saw my father. Father came to the tree and started examining the branches. He said his feet were in a bad way and he needed something to support him.

We never found out what made the Arab soldiers suddenly leave. They didn't stay till the morning. As for Grandad, he set off along the limestone paths to talk to the smugglers. And the smugglers would bring Father in a box, as a corpse. Because the gangs had closed the roads. But they wanted Azmi in return for their services because he was one of the five donkeys that frightened hyenas.

Grandad started having dreams that revealed to him that Father would return. He would be in a box, without legs. But Grandad didn't know when. The dream frightened Grandma and she sent my brother out of the house to gather straw and look for a herb that would make Grandad have a dream that predicted when Father would return. Then Grandad went to the loquat tree and made two extraordinary pieces from the wood. I had never seen anyone use anything like them before. The legs went into them and were attached with straps. But I felt that Grandad was talking nonsense. He was confusing my father with Mansour's father. Even Mansour himself looked at the pieces of wood and said they would fit his father. You couldn't tell if Grandad had really agreed with the smugglers or not, or whether Father would return as a corpse or just without legs. But in any case, every night he wore the clothes that Father had last seen him in, and I ended up defending his rants and waiting for Father myself with the two wooden legs in the limestone hills where the smugglers were. On the way, I would pick wild lettuce for Azmi to eat, for Grandad said the smugglers would take Azmi on a long journey when they brought Father, so he needed plenty of energy. Meanwhile, my brother would come back at the end of the day carrying straw and telling us about rocky holes in the nearby valleys. It would be possible to hide in them when the attack was imminent.

Then the members of the National Committee started coming by night. They were masked and rode swift horses. That frightens you if you're asleep. One day they asked to take Azmi. Grandad said the smugglers were going to take Azmi when they brought Father and it would be better if no problems arose. But they didn't give us much time. They said they would come back in two days to take other animals. Cutting them up and spreading them around the villages would attract hyenas when the gangs attacked. This would hold up the attack until weapons arrived. Then people started putting animals in the courtyard of our house. We had a cow, two sheep and some rabbits. At night they would stick together and shy away if they saw you looking at them.

Mansour came too. He left Thalj with us. He said the smugglers wouldn't come. The gangs had closed the roads. And the corpses that came back came back. That was the end of the matter. I thought this meant he was asking for the wooden legs, so I gave them to him. But he said they were no good because you needed good arms for them to work. Even so, I was still saying that Father would come back and, when he returned, we would find out who had killed the teacher.

The Smuggler

I didn't want the members of the National Committee to take Azmi and cut him into pieces. I thought all night about what I would do. In the morning, I woke up my brother and asked him to show me the rocky holes that would make good hiding places. We pulled Azmi over hill and dale in the direction of the border. I didn't let him stop to eat wild lettuce. My heart was pounding. There, I told my brother that

Grandad had told me to break one of Azmi's legs so that the National Committee members couldn't take him. We laid him out under a tree, put a rag over his eyes and a rag on one of his front legs. My brother then tied the leg to the ground. I lifted the heaviest stone I could carry, remembering how Grandad had objected to the Arab officer, saying that if we made our way to the border, the travelling would never end. My brother took some grass and gave it to Azmi to eat. I was about to bring the stone down on Azmi's leg but at that very moment, when the stone was above my head, I saw him. 'The smuggler...' I said to my brother in a whisper as I put the stone down gently. The man was sitting behind a large almond tree with a little girl beside him on the ground. Her honey-coloured eyes glinted like a knife. They were looking at us but they didn't seem interested in what we were doing. 'The girl must be the corpse,' I added excitedly. But the word *corpse* frightened my brother. He ran off and I stayed. I took a picture of Father out of my pocket, went up to the strange man and said, 'This is my father. You know what I mean. And that's the donkey. It's healthy! My Grandad said I should give it to you.'

Grandad wasn't angry that I came back without Azmi. He just closed his eyes and didn't open them again. Sometimes Narjis would shake him, and I would be frightened and go off to find an abandoned house I could stay in. But I wouldn't go beyond the school. I would sit in the classroom. Maybe Azmi and the children and a new teacher would appear. When I went back, Grandma would hold my face to check if I had been crying. I'd show her the wild lettuce I had picked for the cow, the sheep and the rabbits. I would sit in the courtyard. I might sit there the whole day, watching the animals as they ate. I would ask Grandma why Grandad had closed his eyes. People outside were talking about what my brother said, about there being rocky holes in the surrounding valleys, and if we stayed there, the gangs might look for hours without finding us. But Grandad didn't open his eyes. Then the

National Committee members came by night. They took Thalj, and I saw one of them, a man in a mask like the others, whispering in Grandad's ear, while Grandad smiled in his sleep. Then he started touching Grandma's face and looking at my brother. I took the chance and ran to tell Mansour. Minutes later my friend was there, with a stick. We stayed silent, exchanging glances. Because the masked men had left, along with his donkey. I thought Mansour would say something, but he threw the stick away and went back to their house. He no longer spoke to me.

A Question

People continued to go about their daily business. But they spoke less. By day, we saw people from other villages going along the route that the Arab officer had taken. They reminded me of the smuggler and the girl. But they didn't stop to hear that there were rocky holes where you could hide. Then the National Committee members didn't show up. The animals stayed with us in the courtyard, sticking together and shying away whenever you looked at them. I would go and pick some wild lettuces for them, and sometimes my brother would follow me. He would gather straw and say that it was all no big deal. The people going towards the border were lost and looking for their homes but they wouldn't leave the country. Then some of the families in the village started to leave too, and we had some abandoned houses. But we stayed, because we had to wait for the National Committee members. But Grandad didn't open his eyes, and I began to see him in my dreams, carrying a bag of straw on his back. The bag would open out into two large wings, which he spread and flew over the school, making joyful noises like a child, which I found distressing, so I called him: 'Grandad, Grandad, who was that masked man who whispered in your ear?' But Grandad was too far away to hear, so I waited till he landed, with my brother beside me, and Grandma too, who said that when Grandad landed, we would all go and hide in one of the rocky holes. But Grandad was still flying high and couldn't hear me till I woke up.

A few days later, we heard a banging on the door and thought that the National Committee members had come. My brother prepared to take the animals out. Even Grandad opened his eyes a little. But it was Azmi at the door. He had come back with a bullet in his head and an unsteady gait. But he managed to recognise us. He headed straight for me, or maybe to Grandad or Narjis. He couldn't raise his leg to cross the threshold, so he collapsed outside the door. I wanted to do something so that he wouldn't die, so I took the hunting stick and set off to the water well wearing Grandma's sandals. If I caught a frog or a lizard, as I did on the 'five donkeys' patrol, Azmi would be frightened and get hungry. Then he'd eat, eat lots and regain his strength.

V

Miracles

My brother had been trying to find work for me all day. I would stand behind him and he would knock on the doors of the houses and speak to strangers in a whisper as he pointed to me behind his back. Then he would come back with a disappointed look in his eyes. I felt he was holding back his tears. But he never stopped assuring me that the hole in my head was well covered, which rather annoyed me. 'You have to stop stamping your foot on the ground. It doesn't help,' he said.

'Azmi hasn't eaten anything today,' I would say.

'That's - because - he's - not - hungry. By the way, who told you the well's over there?'

'Grandad! He said a hundred steps and I'd be there.'

'When?' he asked me.

I didn't remember.

'You were frightened. That's all there is to it,' he said.

Then we went past the school. Part of it had been removed now. We could make out Fayez among a handful of young men. He had a pencil behind his ear, and from time to time he would write things on a piece of paper. Some of the young men were describing how they managed to find work in their original houses. I noticed a young man with a hole near his ear, and it was hard to tell if the others were dead or alive. Fayez was boasting about how gang members had shot him while he was asleep. At close range, otherwise he would have resisted. 'Sure, Fayez, we believe you,' joked the young men, who may have been dead or alive, it was impossible to be sure. My brother and I also laughed. One of the young men said, 'No one can tell if the bullet went from back to front or the other way round.'

'Either way, they shafted you, Fayez,' commented one enormous young man.

We laughed again while Fayez counted things on a piece of paper with his finger and then, addressing my brother aggressively, said, 'And you lot? What did you all do?'

My brother took a breath and said, 'Nothing! We - literally - did - nothing. Grandad just closed his eyes. He knew nothing could be done, so he closed his eyes and said he was going to find the donkey. That's all we could do - recover Azmi. Look!' The men began to examine Azmi as if they were seeing him for the first time. On the way back, I told my brother that maybe we were rude to Fayez. He treated us kindly when I broke the plane of the strangers' son. My brother explained to me that this was the right thing to do. Whether it was Fayez or the others. That we should laugh, because the strangers don't like you to show other kinds of feelings. Sadness especially makes them emotional, which makes you liable to various kinds of harassment.

We always laughed at someone in the group. It's not just that the bullet holes hurt at the slightest laugh, it also makes you feel more insignificant. When it was our turn, my brother and I didn't have any desire to speak. Little by little, the young men secretly introduced stories they had heard. In a nearby village, people woke up to the gangs attacking and found that each of them came in two versions; one that was able to survive, and one that wasn't. One here and one over there. In one town, the hands of the municipal clock always go back to the position they were in when the people had been driven out. That happens three or four times a day. When people look at the clock tower, they often find it shows ten minutes after noon. Since the residents left, the furniture in some of the houses doesn't like to be moved around. In one beautiful house, the strangers wake up every morning to find that the furniture has rearranged itself the way it was when the owners left the house... Various stories like these, that brought about a warm feeling inside for a while. Your ribs seemed to have moved. Maybe a miracle had also taken place here, one that drew people in to work in the original houses or with the strangers. Was it possible they heard something coming from the old houses and didn't tell anyone? In my enthusiasm I asked my brother: 'Do you think that masked man was Father?'

'Which masked man?'

'The one who whispered to Grandad?' I said.

'What does it matter now?' he replied.

Wings

Sometimes we don't come to laugh, however. On the contrary, everyone starts by opening something they have brought. A bag or a packet. Each of them has two wings with straps. Something that can be attached to one's back like a backpack. People used cardboard, cloth, cotton or tree branches. Or even materials I've never seen before. Fayez wrote them down earlier and bought them for the guys. My wings and my brother's wings are made of straw. They open and close like the wings of a sparrow. The old woman left them in the courtyard in two old bags. I didn't pay any attention to them because I thought there were woven straw trays in them. We each check that our wings are working. They open, they close, there are no holes in them. Then we run and jump in the air in the school yard, one after another, and take off. You're bound to feel scared at first. But you see the others and follow them. It's like it's the most natural thing in the world. Then we hover and do acrobatic stunts and climb and descend. Our clothes are rather old. Some of us are wearing sandals and dishdashas and scarves with headbands. But they move their wings with extreme agility. Then we stay in the air, waiting to be shot at from the ground. We might stay like this for hours, but you have to be prepared because the bullets are aimed at the wings, and we fall one after another and are bruised. Then we fold up the wings and go home. When a bullet goes through your wing, it feels like someone's tickling you. You laugh but tears pour from your eyes, pour out as if you're crying, really crying. When you're flying as high as you possibly can. Without anyone knowing.

It doesn't take me long to discover that I'm using my wings with more agility than the others. One day, my brother's doing a somersault in the air and he looks at me, so I do a somersault like him and I like it. I go on somersaulting and spinning backwards and forwards. I don't know how much time has passed, but when I stop, I find no one around me. Not my brother, nor any of the other guys. Even Fayez - there's no trace of the awful smell of his wings, to which he's added real cow and sheep bones. So I realise that I've managed to escape. But I go back the next day and wait for hours. I keep flapping my wings in the hope that the others will start appearing in the sky.

Every day, I flap my wings above the school yard and wait for hours, without anyone turning up. Even our house, there's no trace of it, or of Azmi. High in the air, with tears pouring from my eyes, I hope he didn't see me escaping and think I had left him. Other than that, not much happens, except that I land in many villages and towns and perform a miracle here or there. Yesterday, for example, I ended up going into a show under the ground in a beautiful town on the sea. The air was harsh and there were blue lights and smoke and people sitting all over the place and smoking. Then someone came forward pushing a door and two windows, attached by a frame to a wooden wall. He announced that the door and the windows were pieces taken from one of the original houses and they were unlocked. Then a large man came forward and turned the door handle, trying to open it. But he couldn't. He tried the windows and neither of them was locked, but the man couldn't open them either. He even started panicking and cursing in the language of the people who don't speak like us. Then I stood up from among the audience and walked up on to the stage. It seemed the most natural thing in the world. I don't know what motivated me to volunteer, but I tell you, I'm the only person who could open the door and the windows.

EIN KAREM

The Sleepless Spring

Ahmed Jaber

Translated by Adam Talib

A Maze

ONCE MORE AS THE sun reached the horizon, a gold-orange glow bathed the village, marking the moment when Amira went out for her daily walk. She felt the crisp breeze against her cheek, and the chirping of small birds returning to their nests filled the air. Just then, the sky looked like a painting. The village was calm and quiet, which was to be expected but also quite strange. Slowly but confidently, Amira walked along the dirt tracks she'd known since childhood, past trees and rocks so familiar they felt like old friends. Everything in the village reminded her of something from her past.

To her right, the boughs of the old olive trees pointed towards the ground as though they were prostrating. They'd witnessed everything that had happened here, Amira thought to herself. Her grandfather had once told her that his father had planted two olive trees, which he'd bought in Jerusalem, on level ground behind the family house one autumn morning. Whenever Amira walked past them, she would reach out to touch a branch and inevitably feel a prickle that she couldn't explain. To her left, all she could see were fields in bloom; the fields that gave village life its rhythm. In the spring, poppies and clover painted the fields in red and yellow, but at the moment, they were blank, summer having transformed them into dry stalks. Amira could remember how she used to run through the fields in search of the prettiest flowers, but as she plodded along now, those memories seemed very distant. As distant as another life, or another world. She stopped for a moment beside her grandfather's old house and looked at the window where her grandmother used to sit in the evenings, spinning wool and singing. The memory overpowered her and suddenly she saw herself as a child, loved and indulged, sitting at her grandmother's side, listening to her never-ending stories.

Amira carried on walking, feeling simultaneously calmer and more fearful. The massive fig tree and its broad green leaves swaying in the wind reminded her of how she and the neighbours' kids used to climb it, competing to find the biggest fig. When she eventually reached the spring, she froze stiff as though she'd never seen it before, even though this was her home. Ein Karem, the spring, had been there forever and it had witnessed all the people who'd come and gone. Wildflowers grew around it and a mighty willow hung down overhead as though protecting it from time. To Amira, the Karem spring looked like the serene holy place she'd always known.

On the water's surface, Amira could see the reflections of clouds and trees, but deep down she knew there was something more to this place than mere reflections. She moved closer to the spring and sat at the edge of the stone basin. When she dipped her hand into the cold water, she felt the tickle of the gentle current. Memories from childhood flashed before her: she was sitting at the spring's edge, not even eight yet, dangling her feet in the clear chilly water, which sent a shiver right through her body. In the reflection on the water's surface, she saw things she couldn't understand and people she didn't know. The first time it happened, she thought she'd been daydreaming.

Amira saw men and women dressed in clothes that no one in her village wore. Theirs were made of coarse fabrics in earth tones and they had leather straps across their waists and chests. They spoke a language she couldn't understand – their voices sounding like distorted echoes – but she could still sense what they meant. She caught sight of a man in a military uniform standing where she often did. He had a cruel face and a rifle hung from his shoulder. Buildings, massive and soulless, appeared behind him, causing Amira to gasp. She couldn't make sense of what she was seeing. Leaning back against a large tree, Amira could hear a faint, undecipherable conversation somewhere deep down. Laughter, followed by shouting. Her whole body trembled as though she'd been electrocuted. She tried to escape the hallucinations, but afterwards she couldn't shake off those voices.

A Fork in the Road

Over time, Amira grew more attached to the spring and the trees around it, despite the trepidation caused by her visions. The surface of the water continued to reveal events from her own life and the lives of other villagers. She saw herself running through the fields as a child, and then as a young woman standing beside the spring, trying to comprehend what was happening. The most frightening visions were the ones containing people she couldn't recognise. In one, blood stained the ground. Children screamed. Women scattered. Smoke rose. Men dropped. Amira struggled to move or even to breathe; her eyes bulged out of her head in fear and impotence. On another visit, she could hear women singing while men discussed harvests and rainfall. Then the voice of a mother searching for her child cut through. Or a gunshot. Over time, the voices began speaking a different language. An unfamiliar one with a lot of Arabic-sounding words. Towards the end, Amira decided to visit the spring one last time. There was a heaviness in her heart and she knew that everything was about to change. She didn't see the familiar bucolic scenes reflected on the surface of the water. She saw a massacre taking place nearby. Soldiers firing their rifles ruthlessly and heedlessly. She knew what she had to do. She decided to run away, even though she knew that she could never escape the pain. She knew that Ein Karem would be lost, and that everything she'd ever known would be lost with it.

She walked until she reached a large olive tree, where she sat, leaning against the tree, cross-legged, and shut her eyes. She tried to shut out every sound but the sound of her own breath, desperate to find a moment of peace in the midst of all that noise and all those memories. Without her even realising it, one of her feet had become submerged in a tiny stream beside the tree, so, as she was trying to gather her thoughts, a new vision took form. She saw her grandfather as a young man; he was sneaking up on a woman as she filled clay jars with water from the spring. The woman was dressed in a traditional embroidered thobe and her long black hair hung over her shoulders. Amira's grandfather approached her carefully; a mixture of excitement and hesitation plain in his look. Amira watched the scene with rapt attention, and she even spotted the coquettish smile on the woman's face when she realised he was there. The pair looked at each other for a long time, exchanging countless unspoken words. Amira's grandfather took a step forward and whispered something in the woman's ear. Amira may not have been able to hear him, but the woman's reddening cheeks were impossible to miss. She looked around to make sure no one was there before smiling bashfully and nodding. The pair drew closer together, their hands touching tenderly, as the air grew charged with a feeling that was hard to describe: a mixture of passion, fear, and defiance. Amira could feel their racing heartbeats as though she'd been right there with them. Wind trembled the branches surrounding them and it felt like nature itself was in on their little secret. When the woman tried to pull her hand back out of shyness, something in Amira's grandfather's look made her stop and it was only then that Amira realised that the woman was her grandmother. It was an intimate moment. One full of love and worry, as though they'd come to a precipice and were unable to turn back, as though this thing they shared would shatter, if discovered. Amira returned to reality and slowly opened her eyes. She felt a warmth coursing through her heart like she'd uncovered some unknown chapter in her family's history. She understood that love had always been a key part of village life. She smiled and rose to her feet, determined to protect that precious memory.

The Abyss

It was a full moon that night, but in the sky over Ein Karem, the moonlight was wan and eerie. The air itself oppressive and unnerving. A few days earlier, rumours had begun to spread among people in the village about the Zionist forces nearby, the neighbouring villages they'd seized and the massacres they'd perpetrated at Deir Yassin and elsewhere.[1] Everyone in the village could feel the danger approaching, but none of them had any clue just how bad it would get. When Amira woke up in a fright, the ground was shaking, but it wasn't any natural tremor. It was the din of heavy boots, shaking the earth and heralding devastation. Instantly realising what was happening, she leapt out of bed, her heart beating wildly, and looked out the window. Smoke rose up in the distance.

'Oh, God. They're here,' she whispered to herself before running over to her parents' bedroom, where she found her father trying to wake her mother and siblings. There was tumult and panic in the house as the screaming outside grew louder. The family tried to gather up a few of their possessions, but there was hardly any time. The gunshots grew nearer, followed by the shrieks of women and children as night gave way to nightmare.

'We have to get out of here now!' Amira's father shouted, as he took her by the hand and led her out of the house. It was pitch black outside and the road was chaotic. All their neighbours were running; some even carried their children. For generations, they'd lived in those old stone-built houses, which were beginning to light up as the fire spread.

Amira spotted her neighbour, an old woman who lived on her own, sitting on her doorstep because she couldn't walk. People were running all around her, but no one stopped to help. The old woman was whispering to herself, and while Amira couldn't make out what she was saying, it appeared that she was trying to settle her nerves in the midst of that pandemonium. When Amira turned towards the neighbour, her father pulled her back. 'There isn't time. We have to get out of here before they come.'

As Amira followed her family out of the village, she took note of every detail along the way. Details that disappeared before her eyes, her every memory reduced to ash. The smoke nearly choked them as they struggled to reach the hills surrounding the village. Amira could feel her tiny hands shaking as she walked in line behind her father and she turned to take a final look at their house, which was beginning to collapse in the flames. The stones that had long protected them were falling. Everything was falling. As her childhood home burned before her eyes, even her memories were extinguished by the flames.

'No! No, this can't be happening!' Amira raged in a whisper, although she knew that the spring had shown it to her. She'd heard those cries before and she'd seen the destruction and panic on the surface of the water. It was the universe trying to warn her. She thought she'd be ready – ready to face the onslaught with valour – but here she was, living through it, and only then did she realise that the visions could never have prepared her for the terror of it. She could never have imagined the soul-crushing violence. In her dreams, the cries were faint and distant, but in reality, they tore through the stillness of the night. Time seemed to stop and even the air was too thick to breathe. She'd never imagined how desperate, and frightened, and powerless she'd feel in the moment. In her visions, when she ran away, it was just a form of movement, but here she was fleeing for her life, the weight of the world on her shoulders, and there was nowhere she could escape to.

Anticipation

There are secrets everywhere and in every village, there are stories that people don't tell. They just slip out between the old stones and trees and fade into the air. The past lived on in Ein Karem once, a village comprising stones, trees, and souls. Secluded in every corner of that village were the faint whispers of those who'd lived there centuries before, but only a few had the ability to hear them.

Itzhak's family wanted to move to a quiet village far away from the hustle and bustle of the city, and the stone houses they took over had simply belonged to some other people's history. Not that that was how Itzhak saw things. From the moment he set foot in the village, he felt that the air was full of stories he wasn't permitted to hear. He saw the spring for the first time one cold morning as the sun was rising and the stones surrounding it glistened with dew. As he sat down beside the spring, muddy images appeared on its surface, and he thought he was just imagining things, but over time they became sharper. He could see faces. The faces of men, women, and children he didn't recognise. He saw people smiling and playing, but above all, he saw people who belonged to the land. Among all those images, he saw a young woman approaching the spring slowly with a look of inscrutable sadness in her eyes. He watched her as she stared at the surface of the water, until suddenly she looked up and they locked eyes. It was the first time he'd had that vision and it was one that he'd never forget.

Itzhak felt himself drawn to the spring, so he used to go there every day and sit for hours, watching the water's surface, waiting for another vision. The young woman appeared to him rarely, so he'd only seen her a few times in total, but each time he did, it felt like something important was about to happen. She always looked at him in anger, but sometimes there was pity in her eyes and at others, there was indifference.

As the years passed, Itzhak became obsessed with these visions, so much so that he spent hours sitting by the spring, unable to tear himself away from it. He knew there was something important about that young woman and that one day something momentous would happen. He could see himself sitting by the spring as an old man, waiting for her to arrive. He knew she'd come. He felt it deep in his heart. His family and the neighbours gave him looks of concern and wondered amongst themselves why he was so attached to the spring. He didn't care, though. He understood that the power of the spring was great, that it controlled him and drew him to it. With each day, he grew more and more anxious. What if the young woman he'd seen was real? What if she was coming to take back everything that had been stolen from her?

Return

As sunset neared, the sky took on a greyish gloom as if the sun no longer cared to illuminate the world. Memory-burdened footfall. The earth groaning under the weight of old miseries.

The stranger took note of the trees, which had fruited proudly in all the stories she'd heard, as they shook in the breeze as though pleading for life. She stopped outside a house that resembled one she'd pictured and her eyes began to fill with tears. The walls seemed to cry. The stones wanted to extract themselves and rush over to her. The open windows stared into the void just as she had so long ago. She stood there, thronged by the ghosts of her grandmother's stories, her heart heavy with a sadness that could only be explained by the place where she found herself. She took a deep breath and as she released it, she was overcome with the need to speak to her grandmother. Everything around her spoke the language of the past, but she wanted to hear a living voice. Someone who had a different take on the stories than that of the earth and the silent trees.

With shaky hands, she took out her mobile and video-called her grandmother Amira. When she appeared on screen, it was like time had been flipped on its axis. Amira's wrinkled face appeared vivacious in the midst of that desolate setting. She smiled at her granddaughter, a smile that expressed years of painful memories and happy ones. 'You finally made it!' she said. The stranger was at a loss for words. She was still trying to get her head around it all. She looked back and forth between the old house in front of her and her grandmother's face on the screen, trying to forge a connection between past and present.

'I'm here, Grandma. Just like I promised.'

Amira sounded calm, as though she'd always known this day would come. 'Tell me. What's it like there now?' She knew the answer already, but she forced some cheer into her voice when she asked the question. 'Let's walk over to the spring,' she said, without even waiting for a response.

Amira's granddaughter couldn't stop crying. Talking to her grandmother while standing in that place was like magic. Two timelines suddenly intersecting. She looked into her grandmother's eyes and that was when she realised that it wasn't the loss of a place that caused all that suffering. It was the loss of the soul that had given that place life. When she reached the spring, she saw a young woman who looked like her, but who wasn't her, staring at the surface of the water with that same look in her eye, and she understood that nothing here ever died.

Silent Confrontation

Amira's granddaughter walked towards the spring slowly as though the past was weighing her down. She knew that it was the home of all her grandmother's memories, all her family's suffering. A mysterious charge ran through her body when she laid eyes on the spring, as though her soul was connected to the earth somehow. As she drew nearer, she saw someone who looked like a local, sitting beside the spring. He was old. His hair was grey and his eyes were sunken, but when he looked up at her, it was as though they'd known each other for years. She could feel the disgust and anger rising within, so she stopped with just a few feet separating them and examined his sad, fearful face. She couldn't understand why he felt he had the right to sit here in this spot, which had witnessed so much suffering. She knew that this land didn't belong to him and Itzhak knew it, too.

There was fear in his eyes as he looked back at her, but he knew it was her. The young woman he'd seen on the water's surface for all those years. Here she was standing before him in the flesh. Worry and hesitation had his heart beating hard and he wanted to explain himself. He wanted to tell her everything, but the words simply wouldn't come out. He knew she wouldn't understand – or maybe she would, but she'd never forgive. They stood there by the spring, neither one of them saying a word, their eyes meeting as though they could communicate without words. Anger and repudiation showed in her eyes as fear and apprehension showed in his. There was no place for him here, he thought, but he couldn't pull himself away. He worried that the young woman was going to take everything he had by insisting on her rights.

Amira's granddaughter felt that she was encountering something far larger than just this strange man. She could feel the earth speaking to her through his eyes. The earth was telling her that it belonged to her, and that it would be hers again one day, no matter how long it took. It was a tense silence and the entire scene was waiting to see what would happen. It lasted for seconds, which then became minutes. Itzhak stood still, as did Amira's granddaughter. They were both stuck in that moment, in that silent confrontation between justice and violation, between the past and the present. Despite the peaceful surroundings, there was an unease in the air.

Itzhak eventually realised that this was the moment he'd been waiting for his entire life, and there was nothing to say or do. The young woman wasn't here to talk or get to know him; she came here to take back what was hers. She knew the land was still rightfully hers, and that time would restore everything. But as for Amira's granddaughter, the silent confrontation was more than enough. She didn't need to say a word. Itzhak's eyes had told her everything she needed to know. He knew the land didn't belong to him. He was scared and ashamed that he was somewhere he had no right to be. Nonetheless, she stood her ground and she didn't say a word. That moment would stay with her for the rest of her life. The moment she'd felt that she'd got back just a fraction of what had been stolen from her family.

After a long while, Amira's granddaughter turned around and walked away. Itzhak stayed there, sitting beside the spring, staring at the surface. She left Ein Karem, and left the stranger where she'd found him. She knew that the land, and the spring, and the trees would preserve the stories of the past, present, and future; knew that Ein Karem would live on in her heart, no matter where she went, just as it lived on in Amira's heart, even though she'd never go back. No one would ever be able to take away the memories she carried with her.

Note

1. On 9 April, 1948, Zionist paramilitaries attacked the village of Deir Yassin near Jerusalem, killing at least 107 Palestinian Arab villagers, including women and children. The attack was conducted primarily by the Irgun and Lehi militias, who were supported by the Haganah and Palmach Zionist armies. The massacre was carried out despite the village having agreed to a non-aggression pact.

BEIT LEHEM

Al-Shataat

Lina Meruane

Translated from the Spanish by Andrea Rosenberg

> *There, on a land, we were told, was not our land,*
> *under a sky, we were told, was not our sky,*
> *my people live their death.*
> *We don't know how we got here,*
> *and there's nowhere else to go.*
> *At the peak of despair,*
> *we implore the gods of diaspora:*
> *Help us understand this dilemma,*
> *we say.*
> Samer Abu Hawwash

AWAY IN THE DISTANCE, our land was beginning to sink.

To sink almost imperceptibly beneath the rubble of houses stripped of their stones, exposing their mangled iron skeletons, or beneath buildings razed to the ground. Beneath shattered windows, their dust settling on broken streets or dissipating in the air that we recalled as sometimes briny, sometimes perfumed with orange blossoms. That air now stank of death and seemed thick with our enemy's incessant bombings that persisted in our absence.

We thought, from afar, that the slow sinking was an effect

produced by the screen itself, but no, no, our land was cracking and yawning open, overwhelmed by the fire that fell scorching from the sky. From planes and from drones. From warships, their bombs peppering the sea. From tanks that flattened everything in their path.

These weren't nuclear attacks, no, no, the journalists behind the cameras assured us every time a bomb exploded, one after another, by the hundreds of thousands, but they also said each one weighed thirty tons and there were lots and lots of bombs, many thousands of pounds of iron and steel and plastic, of explosives – in other words, they said, the bombs had sown deep holes with great success in such a tiny area. And they said every bomb, every precisely aimed missile, was inflicting indiscriminate, indescribable damage on that land that was still ours.

We did not understand why, but they were still hurting our land as if we were still there, as if somebody still lurked beneath it, hidden in tunnels, even though no, no, nobody was left, not there nor anywhere else in Palestine. But as if each stone, each clod of earth embodied us, they kept destroying everything that lived and grew there.

Destruction had turned the aubergines and tomatoes in our gardens, our ravaged almond and lemon and apricot trees grey with ash; it had slashed at the ancient olive trees whose leafless trunks and branches we mourned before gathering them up and burning them for warmth, since we no longer had walls or roofs or blankets. Before we were expelled, we barely had clothing. Or food beyond the fodder for the livestock that had also been killed. We were forced to set alight our beloved olive trees and any other fallen trunks, along with the evacuation letters the enemy planes tossed down at us, which we diligently collected every morning for fuel, and sometimes, as our hunger intensified, kneaded with water to make bread.

*

It wasn't on screens that we first watched the *sabra* burn, but on the mountains themselves; now, day and night on our devices from the remote distance where we'd ended up, we saw those same rocky crags crumbling like embers. And behind the mountains we saw the horizon feverishly trembling and writhing, and the sea, deader and oilier than ever, beginning to rise to lick at the sand on our beaches. That sea where we used to bathe was devouring what were once our stone houses, our thrumming markets, our narrow streets, which were, they told us, now only the memory of houses, markets, streets. We watched in amazement, rapt, as the waves climbed the wall of our sorrows, so tall, sturdy, and grey, and it started to wobble, its foundations gnawed away. That corpse-strewn sea was dragging up thousands of bones into the concrete prisons where we'd spent the worst years of our childhood, accused of something or possibly not accused of anything, those prisons where, under the pressure of beatings and shouts, we'd learned their tongue. But the water didn't stop, no, it kept advancing over their red-roofed houses with cameras and white flags with sad sky-blue stripes, their souvenir-stuffed shops, their brightly lit avenues, depositing waves of rotten fish and yellowy, sulfurous foam. It crushed the settlements with the settlers inside them, bowed heads covered by yarmulkes, wigs of plastic hair that looked real, and mouths invoking Jehovah's mercy in those cities that were ours.

*

We had never imagined a catastrophe like the one we were now watching from thousands of kilometres away. We had lived so many catastrophes already, in the flesh, both our own and those of our ancestors. We had survived so many. We continued to suffer them even after there were none of us left, there in our *ilabad,* our *al-balad,* which was homeland and land, depending on the pronunciation. And *eleblad* was the word we used because the true name, the historical name of our land, so long forbidden, made our tongues burn; uttering it reminded us that they had emptied our houses and destroyed them, and that, not satisfied with dispossessing and displacing us over and over again, and yet again, indignant because we continued to resist (no, we wouldn't flee as our grandparents had, refused to leave even though they demolished our houses, the streets serving us as cots and the rubble as pillows; no, we weren't going to go of our own accord), they had stuffed us with bullets and emptied our bodies with hunger. They wouldn't allow those of us who survived to die in our own land; unknown soldiers rounded us up at gunpoint, put us in trucks blindfolded and with apples in our teeth, drove us to their boats, and pushed us out to sea on our own, alive but desperate on the ocean's murky waters.

*

The oldest and frailest among us pulled a device from his tattered pocket. It was a cell phone, glinting in the sun. Closing his eyes, he raised it towards the smoke-orange sky as if offering a sacrifice to the gods of diaspora. But he wasn't making an offering at all; he was looking for a signal that might serve as a compass. His trembling hand, still uplifted, succeeded, and his clumsy fingers typed *pa*, then *les*, then *tine*, and his screen lit up with innumerable Palestinian points across the globe.

Palestine! he exclaimed.

Palestine! we cried, confused but excited.

There were countless Palestines scattered over the planet, and we were able to name them, rejoice in them, even though among ourselves the name was *falestin*. That name had been stifled in our mouths; we had silenced it on our lips and in our bones. Our children had never heard us whisper it, and now we could pronounce every letter; now we saw it twinkling like innumerable stars on a virtual map.

Even our hunger faded as we studied them, bending over the shoulders of the old man who could barely remain upright under our weight. Hunched, he directed our curiosity with his finger, telling us that on the coast of one nation that for centuries had been a caliphate, there was a Palestine Street. But one street wasn't big enough for all of us to settle there, we said, and he agreed, and moved his finger, adding that another city, also in *isbaniya*, had a Palestine Garden that, rather than a green space brimming with bushes and flowers, rather than vineyards clustered with grapes, was a small concrete plaza with a monument memorialising our misfortune. There was no way we were going there, we said emphatically, and the old man again agreed.

He consoled us by saying there were many more Palestines on the far side of the ocean we were drifting on, about fifteen of them scattered across northern *amreeka* in places like *texas*, *memphis* and *dallas*, *ohio* and *illinois*, and in a state called *arkansas*; even in the cities of *west-virginia* and *north-carolina*. Asking him to slide the screen open with his fingers, we saw there was even a cemetery with that name, one we had no interest in visiting since we had only just left one. The old man agreed with us; we had even been driven out of our cemetery, and we refused to settle in another one that rejected us too, since that continent would never recognise us as refugees, much less as human beings, he said, wiping his forehead, adding that that country had also actively aided in our extermination.

We weren't going to risk our lives in those northern *amreekan* Palestines, absolutely not.

The old man slid his finger southward to the tropics, and there we saw a sweltering, mosquito-plagued *eleblad* that didn't rouse much enthusiasm either. And an airport among coffee groves, or maybe coconut palms, not yet completed, atop a remote mountain, equally unappealing. The next place was La Palestina, a narrow, inaccessible patch of green that, according to the search engine results that the old man read out to us, his tongue stumbling and halting, had been the gathering place for cousins of ours, distant Christian cousins who drove there every weekend in yellow Peugeots to commemorate and celebrate our culinary traditions.

Descending through southern *amreeka*, there appeared entire towns with our demonym, and streets too, one in particular, a sad, cramped Palestine Street engulfed by a broad State of Israel Avenue that we discarded immediately, and so the old man's finger crossed a snow-covered mountain range and alit upon a desert railway crossing, a now-defunct Palestine Station beside the Atacaman Dead Sea salt flat. He didn't stop there; he kept going down, kept reading. That desert was at the end of the world in a country called Chile, he explained, and further south there was only ice. We were surprised to see the old man smile (his dry lips cracked and a bit of blood bloomed on them) because we had no intention of leaving the fire just to plunge into the cold, but no, no, he said, we won't go that far, we'll stop halfway down and be welcome. He told us we had lots of cousins scattered throughout Chile and especially in the most prosperous areas of the country, cousins from an age-old *shataat*, Palestinians who left during the Ottoman Turkish empire's brutal rule of *beit-lehem* and neighbouring *beit-jala*, *beit-sahur*, and *beit-safafa*, and that we had siblings there as well who had come not from *beits*, which in the other language meant *houses*, the old man explained without looking up from his device, but from the catastrophes of the successive *nakbas* of the previous century.

The sea breeze tousled our long hair that clung to our skin, like the skin that clung to our bones, like the memories that clung to our recollection. We held hands to invoke those murdered in 1948, those who fled their homes in terror after *deir yassin*, after *dawayimah*, after *tantura,* carrying their house keys in their hands or hanging around their necks, believing the violence would end and they'd be able to return, and we commemorated successive attacks on *khan yunis* and on *rafah* and on the thousands who died in 1967, on those exiled in 1968 who crammed into camps as if they were Limbo, praying it would be a temporary arrangement, and we recalled the massacre in the Lebanese camps of Sabra and Shatila, under the watch of the historic enemy army, and the Gaza siege of 2006 followed by the attacks of 2008, 2012, 2014, 2021 that now seemed like mere practice runs for the genocide from which we'd been forced to flee. We were alive but living our deaths and those of all our friends who now lay under the rubble, of our families felled by firing squad, of our children dead or mutilated or orphaned, of our famished siblings, of our mother without milk to give them; there we still were, lugging those losses on our backs, full of tears we could not weep, surrounded by vast waters that we did not dare to drink and fish that offered themselves as food.

Still in the boat, still adrift, we imagined that a white dove with red feet and a green twig in its black beak came to us, a biblical, benevolent dove announcing that we had nearly arrived in another land.

*

That land was not, no, was not our land and never would be. That sky was not our sky, but we would not be forced to live our death there. The gods of *al-shataat* helped us settle there as they had done with the cousins and siblings that preceded us. No matter what it took, like the rest of them before us, we were determined to establish another Palestine of sorts from which to resist our people's annihilation as we waited, waving our flag from the windows of our homes. We wanted to believe it, eventually even convinced ourselves of it, but to the catastrophe that had started with the buildings we dwelled in and the hospitals that succoured us, the universities and schools where we studied, the mosques where we washed hands and feet before prayer, the churches where we crossed ourselves to worship, the museums of our memories, the bridges we crossed, the streets where we fell in love – to the cataclysm that had been unleashed on our Palestinian bodies in every possible form of homicide, all of that had not been enough; the unbridled destruction was bent on disappearing even the land beyond our Palestine.

*

The entire land was sinking before our eyes.

Unequivocally sinking beneath the waters that now engulfed it.

We watched from our armchairs, staring at large screens, as they cried out to be saved. It was too late; the gods of diaspora told us so. But they didn't tell us whether we should rejoice in their debacle, which was indisputably our debacle since we would no longer have a land to return to. No, we weren't certain whether it grieved us or not, that land disappearing to the bottom of the sea.

DEIR YASSIN

The Dragon

Sonia Sulaiman

THE LITTLE BOY KILLED the kittens with a stone, not out of malice, but curiosity. A part of him didn't believe that the stone would crush them, even as he let go of it out of the first floor window of his home. He immediately regretted what he had done as an image of Judgement Day swam in front of him, between him and the carnage he had brought into the world.

His mother walked in, noticed him hanging out the window. And, of course, she knew what had happened. She looked at him, a strange light in her eyes, a tightness in her mouth as she said 'Go play outside.' He promptly grabbed his ball and left his room. His father and strangers were talking together as he passed them by in the hall.

'What will become of the orphans?' his father was saying, looking up just in time to see his son. 'Be back before dark, Ahmed.' He and the strangers watched silently until he was gone out the front door.

Outside, the world exploded with colour; tinted greens, pinks, and blue dappling the yellow-red earth. Ahmed didn't notice that the streets of the village were unusually silent. He was consumed by his feet as they deftly moved the ball in front of him. He followed its rhythm perfectly, attempting tricks and ignoring the world around him until he found the old mulberry tree. It grew beside the village mosque. He caught his ball and sat in the tree's shade, like he used to do when his father was there to visit with his brother, the imam, whose name was also Ahmed.

Here, the music of Mary's Spring which flowed beneath the mosque made the boy thirsty. But, first, he grabbed a handful of the bright red fruits hanging above him, and ate until his mouth was red with their juice. He swatted away the bees which hovered near him, and approached the spring to wash and to drink.

He cupped his hands into the clear, pure stream that flowed out from a dark, narrow channel striking into the very stone of the mountain. It was the very same spring that had nourished Maryam when she was pregnant with the prophet Isa. Ahmed didn't know that; only that the water was so cool and good.

Ahmed had the feeling that he was being watched. He turned around to see a dark man on a white horse. The horse and rider were beautiful, and indistinct with the light behind them. Ahmed couldn't tell if the man was Black or if his eyes were adjusting to the glare. In a commanding tone, the stranger said: 'Give my horse a drink of water from that spring!'

Ahmed turned sulkily. 'My father is a rich man, and my uncle is the imam! I come from a good family! Don't you talk to me like that!'

'For your lack of compassion,' said the stranger and then Ahmed reeled, falling to the ground as if struck across the face. 'I leave you with half the blessing. Shall I take away more?' Ahmed felt his face. It was hot to the touch, but there was no wound.

'What are you talking about? What blessing?'

'I am sent to bless you,' said the stranger.

Ahmed, for once, was silent.

'A warning: a great trouble is upon the land, and will be for a very long time. You will be spared, and your family. But you must be corrected before it is too late… So, for you, it will be difficult. You will have the Blessing of John, the prophet born in this place, but without the mercy of sleep.'

Ahmed remembered one of his friends, Elias, a Christian boy, who told him that a king once tried to kill many children, and how a famous prophet born in their village had been spared when God hid him inside a stone.

'Are you a ghost?' Ahmed could make out now that the man wore a red-crossed tabard, with a long scabbard at his waist. Was the man a crusader knight?

'I am an ally of the One.'

The spring made a wet, bubbling sound. Ahmed turned. The clear water was transformed. It ran a dark red, and moved slowly over the side of the stones in long, thick, slimy clumps. He quickly covered his nose as the foetid stench washed over him.

'It has come,' said the stranger. 'You had better hide.' Before Ahmed's eyes, a splinter of light blazed in the stranger's hand. It coalesced into a lance. The light around him faded, but his face still shone – it shone with its own light. Now he could see the man's handsome, dark eyes, the black curls of his hair. 'They are coming,' he said. So, Ahmed ran.

He pulled up short on the way home. He ducked into an alleyway, and watched as a stream of neighbours, his teacher among them, ran down the street. They were carrying bags, hauling furniture, all kinds of things behind them, on their shoulders. Even little children were hauling things. Every few minutes, a gunshot volley would ring out, and his neighbours and friends would run just that little bit faster. Ahmed prepared to run with them.

A man ran by, carrying a mattress on his back. The volley sounded again, and the man fell, disappearing into the crowd as they all broke into a panicked stampede westward. Ahmed's breath caught. He clenched his hands around the ball he still carried.

'What happened to him?' wondered Ahmed as time slowed around him. The gunshots were distant, though louder somehow, leaving his ears ringing. He could make out the embroidery on the robes of his neighbours as they ran.

The street was filled with dust. Particles of limestone, or that yellow-red earth, drifted through the alleyway where Ahmed was standing, staring. Like rain, they landed on him, speckling his form. Then they hit with the force of hail. The punches kept coming, all over his body. Larger and larger stones rolled down the alley, enfolding him, burying him alive. He struggled, of course. His mind was screaming for him to move, somewhere, anywhere else. When his breath gave out, he gasped and inhaled the rubble dust and stones. His mind went blank with terror. But that wasn't the end. His flesh had become tight, his limbs heavy and clumsy. He dropped his ball, but it didn't fall from his hands. It had become part of them, a limestone sphere. Before long, the transformation was complete. Ahmed could move only his glossy, shell-like eyes from the mound of stones his body had become.

Darkness rolled over the village, blotting out all colour and life. A blood-red haze replaced the sun. Ahmed tried to scream, but nothing would come out but a puff of gravel and dust.

Strange sounds replaced the bird song. Metallic, grinding and screeching sounds in all registers and tones bellowed and screamed in chorus. As the din rose and fell, the small noise of footsteps on gravel caught Ahmed's attention. They were unlike any footsteps he could have imagined. When the being walked in front of him, he knew why. For this being had not feet but clawed paws, talons like sickles farmers use for harvesting wheat. Ahmed blinked his dry, shimmering shell eyes. They clinked as the shell met stone. And the creature approached, curious.

The boy frantically tried to turn away, but his limbs were heavy and distant as if he were a puppeteer and not the owner of his own body. When he shut his mind and clawed his way to a hunched and protective shape, he opened his eyes again. The creature was still stalking the alleyway, climbing along the walls, like a lizard basking in the sun. In the middle of the path, between Ahmed and the creature was a small boy of ten. He looked exactly like Ahmed, and he was staring straight ahead, looking past or through Ahmed.

Pained and silenced, he watched as his double slowly walked past him, past the creature. There was an unnatural calmness about this other self. It didn't see the monster? Couldn't hear the cries of terror that filled the air? The other Ahmed stooped and picked up a soccer ball, like the soccer ball which was fused to Ahmed's stony hands. Ahmed watched as his double paced the alley, casually playing with the ball as he had done that morning.

The creature opened its maw and a black, oily ooze poured out. It drenched the wall it was clinging to, and pooled in the spaces between the stones. All was red and black. The most natural thing in the world happened. A soldier, one of the Zionist militiamen, rounded the corner with his rifle and pulled up short. He slowly panned the alleyway and when he saw the creature, he fired. The sound of the shot went on and on. The entire world was consumed by the echo of that bullet as it rang in the alley, as it pierced the beast's side.

The beast slid off the wall, peeling itself free of it, and grew tall and thin, standing on its hind claws like a man. The unspeakable head elongated and teeth sprang from the upper and lower jaws. The beast was smiling at the soldier. It held out a clawed paw and offered him something. It was hard for Ahmed to see what it was in the red glare, but when the soldier took it and placed it to his lips, he knew it was a cigarette.

The soldier took a drag, letting the smoke billow out, blood-red in the glare of the dying or blighted sun. It looked like fire. Fire from a dragon. Then the beast swung its tail back and grasped the soldier by his legs, it twisted and heaved and its crocodile-like body wound around him until the man was hanging upside down from that scaly tail. Ahmed heard the man's bones. The beast was extracting them, one by one, leaving the soldier a limp, wet casing that made a horrible sound when that impossible beast let it fall. *What did it do with the bones?* Ahmed wondered.

A small hand tapped the creature, half-crocodile, half-man on the shoulder. It was the Other Ahmed. 'Sobek,' said the other Ahmed. 'You forgot about the game.' The monster turned to Ahmed's double. It was clad in a suit now, with a pair of glasses on its snout.

'My dear boy,' said the monster, its lips speckled with black foam. 'I was just getting to it.' It produced a map from its suit pocket. Together, the other Ahmed and the creature sat in the middle of the alleyway and looked over the map. Ahmed could not recognise it, except by the coastline. The sea was always the sea. But what were these terrible twisting, treacherous lines snaking across the land? Now here, now there, sharper than a knife.

Ahmed's eyes were raked by light, the force of the sun breaking through clouds nearly blinded him. It took his breath away and he felt himself sag. 'Ahmed!' He heard a familiar voice coming to him as if through miles of water. 'Ahmed? Ahmed! What are you doing? Boy, you cannot stay here!'

Ahmed looked around him, at the blue sky, the weathered sandstone of the alley, free of oily taint. The monster was nowhere to be seen. Instead, Salma – who owned the orchard – was shaking him gently, steering him away from the wall. Where were his hands? He looked down and saw the flesh of them, still clutching his soccer ball.

'Ahmed,' Salma nestled his head on her shoulder and quickened her steps to the east. 'Come, your family will be waiting for you.'

'Where, Aunt?'

THE DRAGON

'In Bethlehem,' faster still. Salma did not look behind as they briskly covered the ground between them and the road to Bethlehem. She did not ask why he was so grave, so silent. How could she? Not like that, with the village dying around them. Behind them, the Other Ahmed walked idly along, performing tricks with his football.

Ahmed had the sudden idea that this other him was a part of his soul, that he had lost this sliver of his spirit. It was all because of that saint. Wasn't it? It was some kind of curse. A double-curse, instead of a blessing.

As Ahmed watched his doppelganger play, he felt more and more sure that this estrangement was never going to end. He would always be ten years old and playing in the village with his football. No matter where he went or how long he lived. There was a hollowness to his existence now, he felt numb and cold, so very cold. He scrubbed at his face, trying to awaken the vigour of life to it, to comfort himself.

'You are not injured?' asked Salma as they hurried along the road to Bethlehem.

Ahmed nodded. 'I'm fine,' and he meant it too. His inner thoughts said: *No, you have died! You are the walking dead!* But the detachment he felt extended to his tongue. It was strange, a nested existence where he could feel and see himself responding to Salma and even approving of what he said, all the while screaming inwardly. It made no sense.

He would have been bothered by this, only he was still made of stone and shell. 'Do you know anything about dragons?' He asked just to change the topic from whether or not he was alive, and what being alive would mean for him to the end of his days.

Salma replied casually. 'Of course, Mar George defeated the dragon.'

'Yes, but what is a dragon exactly? Do they exist? Are they real things you can see and fear?'

'There are two types of dragons,' said Salma after a

moment. 'And while they are real, I don't want you to get the idea that they are to be feared; for they can be defeated too. They look like reptiles, or snakes. Some say they look like lizards, some have wings and others walk on four legs. That is less important than what they are, what a dragon truly is. It is the condensation of everything that stands against life. Wherever that spirit, or anti-spirit dwells, there is a dragon. That's the first kind of dragon, the real one. The fantasy is that dragons are creatures that lie on beds of gold and capture youths or lay waste to the countryside from their cavern-like lairs. Those exist only in the imagination.'

'And how do you defeat a dragon? A real dragon?'

Salma looked over her shoulder at the smoking village where it still shone in the morning, beautiful and at peace. 'I know only that it can be done. There is no trick to it that I can teach you, like the tricks one can play on ghouls. Ghouls are easier to defeat than the dragon.'

Ahmed shook off her arm. 'Then what's the use of your words? What good is your knowledge?'

'Ahmed,' said Salma gently in the face of his vehemence. 'The dragon grows stronger on despair. Its victims must believe that life is not worth living anymore, and that the dragon is inevitable and its victory absolute. The more you despair, the greater its appetite for your very soul.'

Ahmed looked again at his double who was listening intently to what Salma said. It angered Ahmed to see the open, honest face of his unholy brother. He lashed out again. 'But hope does nothing but hurt, it is the way of the unwise. I will not put myself into the grasp of your hope, with no means to make that hope a reality. I would rather be eaten alive!'

Salma walked on in silence for a while until Ahmed interrupted again: 'That's the way of the world: the strong do what they want to, and the weak just suffer and endure what they must.'

'Do you think the soldiers back there, the ones who bring

rifles to fight us villagers, are strong or are they weak?'

'I'm not interested,' said Ahmed.

'In what, my dear?'

'This is a trick question. The answer is so obvious, you must have prepared a riddle for me just to distract me from the fighting!'

'You are quick,' said Salma. 'But that is not what I mean; you must not confuse the dragon for a hero. You will grow up into a man someday, and not a dragon. Dragons are strong, and they do as they like, but they are always defeated by a hero.'

'I would rather get what I want,' said Ahmed. 'Like the dragon. Who cares if a hero puts an end to me after I have enjoyed life for years? I will be strong and no one will take what is mine again, no one will make me afraid.'

'You would not be like Saint George, who was a strong hero?'

Ahmed shook his head. 'He curses people.'

'What are you saying?'

'That you know nothing; everything you've said; it's pointless like a mattress is pointless when the soldier shoots you in the back.'

Salma walked on. 'I see. My dear Ahmed...' and her voice was sad. 'The little dragon you are growing into...'

The double who had been shadowing them stopped. Ahmed turned to look at him while he continued to follow Salma. The boy smiled and waved to Ahmed before turning his back and running to the village, his ball rolling faster and faster towards his childhood. Ahmed set his teeth, and inwardly was glad; he would never have to see the double again. That part of his soul was dead to him. Let it burn and be forgotten. It would burn in the breath of the dragon.

The petrification that the saint had brought down upon him, the curse and the blessing – what had it done? What did it mean to survive, when the contagious dragon would steal into him and with a sudden fierceness transform him from a boy into a monster? Did the saint snatch from him his chance to reform his life? Or was there really no alternative path for him but this one he walked?

AL-BARRIYA

My Mother in Changing Times

Mahmoud Shukair

Translated by Raph Cormack

1.

In 1935, my mother and father, along with all the members of the Abdallat family, left their homes in al-Barriyya,[1] to settle on the outskirts of Jerusalem. Two things had forced them to make this decision. The first was the drought afflicting al-Barriyya, which made life barely livable; even the sheep's udders dried out from lack of grass or anything else to eat. The second was fear: fear that the family's lands on the edges of Jerusalem would be requisitioned by one of the thousands of incomers who had been pouring into Palestine from abroad since the British took control of the country.

But my mother did not feel safe in the stone house they had built for themselves in the village that came to be known as Ras al-Naba'a. During the night, worry descended on her and enveloped her, accompanied by murmurs in the darkness. She couldn't tell if they were the sounds of men or strange creatures who would not be silent. One morning, she awoke with a start at the sound of an eerie female voice saying: 'Abdallat, arise from your slumber, get up!'

She was convinced that this was a *ghuleh* taking the form of a woman.

When we were all together at night, we begged our mother to tell us the tale of Awwad's *ghuleh*. When she was in the right mood, she would tell the story, rich in all its vivid details. When she was in a bad mood, she would summarise it as follows: 'A beautiful woman once came to Awwad's house on the edge of the village. She invited Awwad, his wife, and their daughters to take lunch in her house. Awwad's wife was suspicious of this invitation, as were his daughters, but Awwad himself did not heed their warnings. He went off with this beautiful woman. As he left, Awwad's wife grabbed his hand, trying to hold him back, but he ignored her. The *ghuleh* took Awwad far away to her house, closed the door and locked him in. At that point, Awwad felt the fear rise in him. This was followed by terror when the beautiful woman revealed her true form: a hideous-faced *ghuleh* with sharp fangs.

'The *ghuleh* asked: "Which part of you should I eat first?"

'"Start with my hand, the one that disobeyed my wife."

'The *ghuleh* devoured his hand with impressive speed. And she didn't stop, asking him which part of his body to eat next, until nothing was left but his skeleton and his skull.

'She carried his skull up to the top of a hill and threw it down, all the way down to the door of Awwad's house. When his wife and daughters saw the skull, they wept tears of grief and pain, cursing him for not heeding their advice.'

2.

My mother used to put her hand on her cheek before she opened the gates of memory onto her favourite subject: the days when she had lived in al-Barriyya. She told us that she had been born to a gentle mother and an angry, short-tempered father, who was often cruel to his wife and children. As my mother grew older, she started to notice her shadow, which followed her everywhere, from the plains to the hills, like a beloved brother. To escape the tyranny of her father, she became more and more attached to her shadow and used to play with it a lot.

When she stood on her tiptoes, it would stretch out; when she crouched down it would become smaller and she would touch it with her hand. When she lay on the ground her shadow hid underneath her. She would smile at it as it lay by her side, and when she got up and ran off, her shadow would run after her.

She taught herself to live in harmony with her world's supernatural inhabitants (later she would get to know the cruel inhabitants and see them working against us in full view of everyone). She invoked God, in an attempt to avert their harm; when she started walking, she always began with her right foot, not her left, so she would not anger them; similarly, she would never toss water aside carelessly, in case it hit some of them on their heads while they weren't paying attention, and infuriate them so much they would send one of their number to possess her and drive her mad.

3.

'Oh Lord, how much I have suffered since we moved from al-Barriyya to Ras al-Naba'a on the slopes of Jabal al-Mukabbir,' she used to say. 'Some nights, I only sleep a few hours, tossing in my bed from all the worry. As I lie beside Mannan, I hear a quiet voice coming from outside. Mannan tells me that it is just the sound of the wind. But I know that it's the sound of our forefathers slain in battle; they wake up in the night and call out for revenge. He tells me: "Wadha, go to sleep. Leave it in God's hands." And I respond that I will try to overcome my fear and close my eyes for God is noble and kind.

'In the morning, I open the windows and seek refuge in the Almighty from the wiles of Satan. Seven times I recite the name of God. Then I take a bucket of water, which I splash onto the courtyard and on the street. After that, I take a bowl of dough out to the shed where the stove and the *saj* for cooking flatbread are kept. I always enter the shed with my right leg first and recite the name of God, because I am sure the place is inhabited by spirits or djinn.

'I light the fire under the *saj* and, as flames engulf the wood, I become aware that the strange inhabitants of this shed are blowing on it to kindle the blaze. I waft it with the edge of my dress to increase the flames. Fire is female. I neither love it nor hate it, but do fear it because it is unpredictable, even though I know it gives us warmth and does all kinds of other useful things. I am also afraid of the inhabitants of that place where the fire lives. I dread the otherworldly touch of a rebellious djinni that could drive me out of my mind, yet I continue to feed the fire with wood. I take the first little ball of dough, shape it into a small, round full moon in my hand, then put it on the *saj*. I keep going until I have finished the whole bowl of dough, keep looking straight at the bread so the djinn do not eat it. I am convinced that they are constantly debating between themselves how to keep me from coming into their home, but every morning I am forced to go there (knowing there will be strangers who can't stand to see us in their homeland).'

4.

My mother told all kinds of stories at our late night gatherings. She would vary the subjects, depending on the audience and the extent of their desire to listen. If she needed to stop telling stories from her life in al-Barriyya, she went back to Ras al-Naba'a[2] and her life there. For decades after, she would recount the attack that Jabal al-Mukabbir[3] suffered in 1948. Tens of men from al-Sawahira faced it with whatever guns or rifles they could find. A number of people from Ras al-Naba'a, among them my father Mannan, rushed to their aid. Before this, Mannan used to spend his time greasing his rifle and cleaning it with oil, or doing target practice, along with other members of his wider family who had bought weapons to defend their homeland. 'I was afraid for him when he went to war,' my mother said. 'War is a wicked woman who devours men (more will come from over the seas who will continue to ignite wars and delight in the killing of women and children).'

My father went out, shot all of his bullets, put his rifle under his arm and came back home.

The events of that night formed a story that my mother never tired of repeating – when the right moment came, of course. She could not just launch into the story with no context or with no reason to tell it. Sometimes, she would prepare the ground for the 'Battle of the Jabal' by casually talking about events that were linked to it, so that everything would come in the right order and in the right place. Then she would launch into the story, full of digressions and embellishments, spinning out the narrative. She would look around to check my father was there as she began her tale. He listened attentively, always finding his attention gripped by something in her story, as if she was Scheherazade ensnaring Shahriyar with her entrancing tales.

She would say that the companions who had come from Mecca to Jerusalem with Omar ibn al-Khattab[4] and were buried at Jabal al-Mukabbir after long lives, rose up from their graves to fight the enemy that night. The men of al-Sawahira[5] who fought in that battle saw them. 'They witnessed them appear in the shape of white ghosts with swords in their hands,' she would say. My father, not intending to cast doubt on my mother's story, would say that he was so absorbed in firing his gun that he had not time to confirm that Omar's soldiers, may God be pleased with them, were present among the fighting.

Another story she often returned to was her fear of the radio that the British Mandate authorities had given to her husband because he was head of the Abdallat family.

It always sat on a table in the corner of the reception room. She believed it was possessed. Whenever she heard the voices of men or women emanating from it, she was terrified and recited the name of God, begging Him to keep the family safe from the evil plots of the radio's djinn.

Once, when she was preoccupied, cleaning the reception room and straightening out the cushions and pillows ready for guests, she dared to approach the radio and turn the dial. As incoherent mumblings emerged, she felt a deep fear, believing that she had awakened the djinn. She cursed herself and tried to silence the noises, but no sooner had she moved the dial than clear voices emerged from inside. She fled the reception room and left those voices to blare out on their own, sometimes a solitary voice and sometimes many. My father was not home that day and my mother did not dare to go back in the room until another man from our family had come and turned the radio off.

5.

'I am sure,' she once said, 'though true knowledge lies only with God, that the djinn caused the death of my daughter Aziza. What a sweet girl she was! Her hair was long and her eyes were like two small coffee cups. She was tall like her father Mannan. I gave birth to her four years after little Mohammed. When she was ten years old, she complained about her head: "Mama, I have a headache."

'I burned incense for her and asked her what had happened. I told myself that she must have been struck with the evil eye, maybe some jealous woman saw her as she came back from school. I asked her: "Honey, did you notice anyone staring at you on your way home?" She said she had seen no one. I vowed to slaughter two sheep for the sake of God almighty and fly seven white flags from my roof if Aziza recovered. Mahira, the wife of Abd al-Jabbar, mentioned to me someone called Fattah, who lived in the village of Anata, just outside Jerusalem. I went to see this Fattah, and he made a protective amulet for my daughter.

'Afterwards, I started to scrutinise the mirrors in our house.

I realised that Aziza had looked at the mirror in our room a few days before – mine and Mannan's. Now, mirrors are female, and so they are never safe from the schemes of the djinn. I remember, it was just before sundown and Aziza had gone into our room to get me a prayer mat. Oh God, she went into the room and even told me that she had looked into the mirror. Dear Lord, I'm sure that the inhabitants of that mirror possessed her and afflicted her head with some horrible ailment.'

6.

My mother became increasingly terrified of the unseen beings who lived alongside us, listening to us talk and watching us while we worked and while we rested. She said that she no longer went out at night to check on the flocks in the enclosure (we still had five of our goats from al-Barriyya, whose milk we drank) because once she saw a watcher-djinn running through the mountain paths. She could follow its movements from the light that shone out from it, until it disappeared down a well at the foot of the hill. Since that day, she had not gone out at night.

When, one evening, she was eventually forced to fetch water from the well after sunset, she repeated the name of God seven times before removing the cover. As she dropped the bucket down and pulled it up, she never stopped reciting the name of God, to keep the djinn away and prevent them grabbing hold of the bucket.

The other women in the family always accused my mother of trying to introduce her fear into their hearts. Her only ally was Uncle Abd al-Jabbar, who told people that the djinn also visited him at night. They grabbed his arms and legs and tossed his body around the empty room before returning him to his bed, to sleep soundly beside Mahira.

But the deeds of the djinn did not stop there. Sometimes Mahira woke up to find that Abd al-Jabbar was no longer beside her in the bed (Mahira was old by this point. She no longer had the same spring in her step and couldn't glide along the floor the way she used to like a dove. Instead, she limped as she walked, due to the pain in her legs). She knew that he had most likely slipped away to the bed of his other wife, Khadija. But when Mahira confronted him, he swore in stubborn oaths that the djinn had picked him up and put him in Khadija's bed. He claimed that they had then run away home without giving any explanation why. What's more, how could he ask them why they were doing it when he was asleep the whole time? It wasn't possible. And even if he had, they would never have deigned to give him a reason.

My mother took comfort in his stories, since they corroborated her own assertions, even though they risked jeopardising her friendship with Mahira. She took various precautionary steps to prevent the djinn getting to her, including covering the mirrors with thin cloth, believing that looking into them at night could turn someone insane.

She hadn't always been so obsessed with mirrors but then, one night, she saw, in the pale darkness, a ghostly figure moving inside one of them. She was struck with a deep terror and wondered why she hadn't recognised the danger that lurked in them when Mannan had bought their first mirror many years ago. At the time, she had welcomed it, even celebrated it; in fact, day and night, she used to stare at her face in that mirror.

It is not only the djinn that occupied my mother's thoughts. She was convinced that the place where Manan built our house in Ras al-Naba'a was haunted by the ghosts of forefathers who fought and died on the land many times before, pouring their blood into its soil. At night, she claimed, these spirits rose, in search of revenge or to re-enact the events of the past. My mother would hear the clashing of swords, the whinnies of horses, cries for help, screams, and moans. The sounds were so vivid that she was scared to fall asleep.

Before she went to bed, my mother splashed water across our threshold, reciting the name of God and reading the appropriate prayers to both calm the mischievous djinn that lived alongside us, as well as to quench the forefathers' thirst, cooling their desire for revenge.

She told the other women in the family about her fears, sharing only part of them. She warned them against throwing any water away in the dark without invoking the name of God; it might hit one of the djinn, who would then get angry, possess them, and send them mad. Any one of them might go crazy, just like the sister of a revolutionary whom my mother had once seen coating her dishevelled hair in dust (she had gone mad at the hands of the invaders). The war in this country was at its most intense point and she warned that the land faced grave danger (indeed, the land has continued to face the dangers of war all the way up to the current genocide that we are living through).

7.

There is one day that I still remember vividly. As my mother and father sleep, I, their twelve-year-old son, Little Mohammed, am awake all by myself. In the calm of the night, I am deep in my studies. But fear of my mother's stories stands over me like a tyrant. I imagine the djinn standing outside the window, watching me, considering my every movement, surprised that I am still awake. Of course, they do not care that I am a diligent student, working late into the night. If anything, it angers them more and makes them want to expose me to fear and suffering. I imagine the ghosts of our forefathers standing outside the same window, in an alliance with the djinn. They stroke their beards as they gaze upon me with evil intentions. They surmise that I will not be the one to take their revenge for them. No, I will forget them, concentrating instead on my school books, which will never bring them back to life, not even for a moment.

I cannot make up my mind at all: should I keep studying or go to sleep? Finally I decide. I refrain from looking out of the window to avoid some unsettling surprise and go to sleep.

I will make sure I spend enough time studying during the day so I can go to bed early and not disturb the djinn or the ghosts (not that it matters because the Nakba of 1948 forced the schools to close for several months).

My mother and father know, at this point, that the war has engulfed most of the country and is approaching Jabal al-Mukabbir.

8.

Every chance I got, I would listen to what guests were saying in our reception room about the atrocities that Zionist gangs had committed: the Deir Yassin massacre, where the bellies of pregnant women were torn open, and the Dawayima massacre, when 170 children were killed and many women were raped. I overheard talk about forced expulsion, listened to the sound of bombs from Jerusalem, and I was afraid.

One night in the summer of 1948, my mother woke me up and told me to get dressed as quickly as possible. Her sudden and unexpected instruction scared me. I asked her why. 'Don't you hear that sound of bullets and mortars?' she replied. She told me the Zionist gangs had reached Jabal al-Mukabbir and we had to flee the fighting. 'Are the djinn who inhabit this place alongside us not enough? Now these strangers are coming to attack us, kick us out of our homes and live in them instead of us.'

I listened carefully and realised that this was war; how much I hated it at that moment!

9.

We all left – my mother, my three sisters, and me. On our way out of the house, we met other women and children from our wider family. Before we could move on, our father came up to us carrying his rifle.

'We will not let our women suffer the same fate as the women of Deir Yasin. We will not let them kill our children and throw their bodies into wells.'

When we were finally able to come back to our house, after the defeat of the attack on Jabal al-Mukabbir, my mother declared, 'The fallen companions who came with Omar ibn al-Khattab determined the result of the battle.'

My father respected her opinion, even if he himself was not entirely convinced. My mother herself didn't really add any details to her assertion, nor offer any proof. Instead, she started to tell the story of the sister of one fighter, shot in his back by enemy soldiers who then snuck his body into her house while she was outside talking to her neighbours, and wrapped it in her bedclothes. When she got back home and unrolled her blankets to sleep, she found a body inside them. As she lifted the blanket up, she saw the lifeless face of her brother. The horror sent her out of her mind.

10.

One day, after the war had ended, the larger part of the country had been lost, and the newcomers from across the seas had established their state, my mother decided to go back to al-Birriyya and visit her relatives. Before she crossed the valley, my mother saw that woman – the fighter's sister – sitting on the ground, her hair dishevelled, her expression dark and terrifying. She stared at my mother like a wild animal. She might have pounced on her had some farmers, who just happened to be passing by, not protected her.

My mother fled this poor mad woman, the sister of the murdered fighter. She thanked the farmers who remained loyal to the land and walked, as quickly as she could, to her father's old place in al-Barriyya where he still tended his flocks.

It took many years after the shock of defeat for the country to stand on its feet again. But, through all this time, my mother never stopped telling her stories. This time, though, they have become the stories of a new era, its jaws dripping with the blood of the innocent.

Notes

1. Al-Barriyya – meaning 'wilderness', it was the name of a wide area to the south east of Jerusalem, inhabited by Bedouin tribes in the years before the Nakba.
2. Ras al-Naba'a – a fictional village near Jerusalem.
3. Jabal al-Mukabbir – a village south east of Jerusalem, famous for being the site where Omar ibn al-Khattab first stood and proclaimed *Allahu Akbar*, settled by members of the Bedouin Sawarha tribe at the turn of the 20th century. It is now a suburb of Jerusalem and part of the al-Sawahira suburb.
4. The second Rashidun caliph (ruling from August 634 until his assassination in 644), Omar ibn al-Khattab succeeded Abu Bakr (r.632–634) and is regarded as a senior companion and father-in-law of the Islamic prophet Muhammad.
5. Al-Sawahira – a Palestinian village situated 6 kilometres southwest of East Jerusalem, now a suburb of Jerusalem.

AL-DAWAYIMA

Eastwards

Abdalmuti Maqboul

Translated by Mohammed Ghalayini

'Yousef! There, there, can you see it?'
'Huh, see what?'
'Look! Inside the cave door, beneath the entrance to the house!'
'The only thing I see is darkness.'

Maybe I was going crazy, but I went a little closer, stepping gingerly downwards over strewn rubble. I passed through a stone entrance that retained its arch and continued my descent towards the cave opening. What was that breaking the totality of the darkness? It looked like hair framing a face? Eventually, her white dress confirmed her identity! But, what was this girl doing here?

'You, girl! What are you doing here?'

No response but Yousef said: 'There's nobody there, who are you calling to?'

'There's a girl inside the cave.'

He took a closer look for a moment, then replied, 'Ya zalameh, I'm telling you there's nobody there!'

But the girl was very much there, standing perfectly still and staring back at me. She raised her hand slowly and signalled me to come closer. I looked at Yousef before moving forward. 'Where are you going? Don't go into the cave, seriously, B'ism Allah, B'ism Allah.' The girl retreated, as if dissolving into the darkness. I said, 'B'ism Allah' and let myself follow her.

Between light and darkness, it only took one step. When we were outside, we couldn't see what was inside the cave, but inside I could see Yousef clearly, standing back there among the rubble and overgrown grass, gesticulating, speaking then shouting. I couldn't hear him.

'Istaneet*ach ch*'teer. I waited for you so long!'

The young girl's voice echoed around the empty space. As my eyes adjusted, I could see that her face was as white as the whiteness of her dress, almost lighting up the place with its brightness. Three black dots undercut the brightness - her two eyes and a mole on her right cheek. Her rosy lips parted and she spoke: 'I've been here waiting for you for 77 years!' The echo emphasised her last word: 'years, years, years.'

What on earth was she talking about? How could a girl who's barely fifteen years old have been waiting that long?

'Where are your parents? What are you doing here on your own?'

'Meen *kalatch*? Who told you I'm on my own?' she asked, then turned her face towards the depths of the cave. My gaze followed hers only to settle on what seemed like a human form. The man was crouching, kneeling perhaps and dressed as if for work, in a dark suit with a white shirt under a striped necktie, complete with a matching waistcoat. His slick black hair parted on the right. He wore black-framed glasses and was clean shaven.

'*Meen hadtha?* Who are you? What are you doing there on your knees?' I asked.

The man stayed motionless and unresponsive, as if completely frozen. I looked back to where the girl was standing. 'What's up with him? Who is he? Is he alive or dead?' My words echoed around the space.

The girl spoke: 'Help me and all your questions will be answered.'

'Help you, how?' I asked.

'Follow me,' she said as she walked towards a door in the stone wall.

'Where are you going?'

'Don't you want to know what's going on?' she replied. 'It seems this is what God wanted for you. All these years that have passed, so many people have come and gone as I've stood by the doorway and nobody saw me and I didn't allow anyone to come in. But as you saw me and came in, it means it is your fate and you must come with me.'

'OK, but tell me, are you from al-Dawayima?'[1]

She left me and walked through the dark, arched doorway. I looked at the crouched man and ran after her.

★

Suddenly, standing together in a room teeming with curious faces, we become the centre of their collective attention. The hanging lamp was hardly enough to illuminate the features of the house. Al-khityar, the elder, straightened his back till he was upright and let go of the ladle and the barley that was in it.

'Who are you?' he asked, then turning to his girl, Maryam, 'who's this?'

His wife let go of a hessian sack and addressed the girl as she stood up, 'Mahbouba, where have you been since yesterday? Who's this you've brought with you? Answer me, we really don't have time for these shenanigans!'

A small child jumped up, then another, a third boy larger than both of them sat back to assess the situation. One of the boys took Maryam's, or is it Mahbouba's, hand and said, 'Mahbouba, I still can't fall asleep without you. I'm so happy you're back.' Without showing any emotion, she stroked his head and said, 'Hamoudah, help your father and mother and make sure you and your brothers do what they tell you.'

She looked at me and signalled with her eyes and then head. I didn't understand till she started walking away and I followed her. Her father shouted, 'Where now? Where now? We need to finish collecting all the wheat, barley and corn, and we've yet to go to all the stores, which we'll need to if we're to leave the village tonight or tomorrow morning. Maryam, you mustn't go out, I'm telling you, girl.'

He looked back at me and repeated his first question, 'Who are you? Maryam, who is this man? I've never seen him before, he's not from these parts!' No answer came from me, as I was in shock, still taking in the sudden jolt to this room in an ancient house. Its walls were stone, rendered with mud, its ceiling was vaulted, and the clothes they all wore were from a different world!

'*Yalla*, come now!', that's how the girl called to me as she reached for the chunky metal key sticking out of the keyhole. She couldn't move it easily. I wanted to experience what it felt like and touched it and turned it with difficulty till the door opened, creaking loudly, and we went out into the alleyway as Mahbouba's father called after us, 'Maryam, don't be late, we need to load everything onto the camel and go with God's will.'

I was fixed to the spot outside the house. Where was I? Was this the same place I had just been visiting with Yousef? If it was, then where were the bare hills and empty valleys? Now, in the distance, I could suddenly see scattered ancient ruins here and there, remnants of a life that once was.

'What are you doing standing there, why aren't you following me?'

'Follow you where? I'm not moving till you explain what's going on!'

'You just need to come with me now. I'll explain later.'

I couldn't take it anymore and shouted at her: 'Listen to me, I am not going anywhere.' I had barely said these words when a dog shot out from behind a stone wall, and leapt up at me, knocking me down. At the last moment, Mahbouba managed to stop him from tearing into my face. She embraced him as he barked almost hysterically and stroked his neck to calm him and told him that I was a friend. All this occurred with her face quite devoid of any expression. As the dog became docile, she let him go and started to walk off. The dog and I followed.

Even though it was night, the village was bustling. None of the inhabitants of those houses were asleep; I don't think anyone was able to sleep. The sound of panicked activity came from all around, doors opening and slamming shut, familial arguments and people chivvying each other to speed up.

'Yalla ya Fatima, we need to get to our storeroom and load up so we can get going!'

'Ya Abu Mohammad, bring the feedbag so we can finish up!'

'Saffiya, go find your siblings. Where are Mahmoud and Zeinab?'

As we walked, our path rose gradually above the other roads on the hillside. We kept crossing paths with others here and there. We heard the whinnying of an approaching horse, then saw a cloud of dust as it came towards us. The horseman brought his steed to a halt and jumped off, hastily tying the horse to a tree before bounding into the village's most prominent house. 'This is where the elders are gathered,' Mahbouba tells me, 'but who cares about them, we need to get going.' This time, I ignored her and crouched by the open, arched window. The dog followed me and we sat together, listening.

The religious leaders and elders of the village had gathered to confer about recent events. Fear and trepidation filled the air as they talked with urgency. The horseman walked in and grabbed everyone's attention for he carried news. He stopped, took a few breaths and then announced, 'Beit Jibreen has fallen, so has Qubeibah. The Yahood are coming from the west. They aren't sparing stone, flora or human. You need to decide quickly what you're going to do.'

Silence prevailed. A few seconds passed and then the opinions started to fly.

'We won't leave, even if they kill us!'

'Brother, don't you understand, they're slaughtering everyone that stays, cutting off their heads. Do you want us to stay and wait for death?'

The commotion returned. Then the village mukhtar rose from his seat at the centre of the council, adjusted his *i'qaal* and *hatta* headdress, and said, 'Listen up.' He waited till everyone was silent and said, 'Understand what I am about to say to you, fleeing our homes and land like this would shame our grey beards, but we also can't tell what these dogs are going to do to our girls, our wives and our children. So, the girls and women should leave the village, whoever wants can go with them. As for me, I am staying and will not leave the village, no matter what happens.'

The cacophony of voices returned and Rummana the dog stood up and barked. I noticed Mahbouba staring at me; she seemed to be saying something to me without speaking. I asked her, 'What do you want me to understand? What could be more important than the calamity that's unfolding around us?'

'It's obvious that you've forgotten, you are here to help me!'

'No, no, it's not that I've forgotten, I just never imagined I would be here, during –'

A sudden flash of movement pierced the sky leaving a wake of dust, followed by something landing just behind the council house. From her vantage point, Mahbouba saw nothing. I got up and ran round to the other side of the house only to see a human figure with a fluttering piece of fabric fastened at the neck, fluttering as the wind caught it whooshing through the sky. Of course I was too slow to see who the supernatural figure was and as I came back round the building, I bumped into Mahbouba.

'Did you see?' I asked. 'What was that?'

'I won't wait a minute longer, we're already behind schedule. If you don't want to help me, you can stay here.'

'But…' She walked off with Rummana in tow looking back at me as it panted. I called to her, 'Isn't it time you filled me in on what we're doing exactly? Where we're going and what help you need from me?'

Without breaking her pace or looking back she said, 'We need to go to Aljroun, it's not that far from here.'

'What's Aljroun?'

'The highest point of al-Dawayma. It's where we need to pick up the first amaanah.'

'Amaanah! What's an amaanah?'

'Be patient.'

Mahbouba stopped in front of a newly constructed rock terrace and turned to me with a look of vindication, 'We're here!' She pointed at the wall, kneeled then dislodged a medium-sized rock from the base of the terrace and started digging with her hands, positively cat-like, till she reached a small wooden box. She pulled it out and blew off the remaining dirt. Her white dress may have been sullied by the dirt, but her eyes were dazzling in their brightness and her face still beamed with an innocence, despite all her scheming. 'Do you want to open it?'

I could scarcely hide my curiosity as I nodded in the affirmative, but I quickly changed my mind, saying, 'No, no, you open it! I don't even know what's inside.'

She lowered her head to inspect the box and placed her hand over its lid to open it. Her fingers were quite thick-set in contrast to her wispy body. I leaned in to have a closer look. What was it I was looking at, I wondered, as the lid came up. It looked like a wooden mask. Were we looking for a doll?

'Mahbouba, what's this?'

'What do you mean, the thing coming up behind you?'

'What, where?' I spun round but there was nobody. The villagers were still moving in and out of their houses, packing their belongings onto donkeys and camels, setting off towards safety. 'Mahbouba, there's nobody there! Mahbouba, Mahbouba, Where are you?!' I looked around me, staring at the path that had brought us here and the other way. She couldn't have run away that quickly. Where had she disappeared to?

'I'm right here, beside you'
'Where?'

There it came again, a disembodied voice, 'Over here.' I looked to the left. 'Over here.' I looked to the right. The voice seemed to move around as if it came from a surround-sound system. It moved from my left ear to my right ear and back again. It had a beautiful rhythm. Still it frightened me.

In the distance, I could hear an argument escalating.

'Offload it now, I'm telling you, we don't want your services.'

'Yaba, leave it on, we need to finish up and get out of here.'

'No, this guy is robbing us blind, I won't have it. Over my dead body will we go with him.'

Mahbouba whispered in my ear, 'Go down there and sort out this problem and then I'll tell you where I am.'

A young man was arguing with the camel driver, who was asking an exorbitant price to transport some boxes of clothes, food and drink. Before long the young man's father joined in, wanting to settle things, but the son thought that the driver was exploiting their need and profiteering off the situation. The young man jumped up in an attempt to bring their belongings down and caused the camel to buck. I approached him and offered to help. Eventually, the camel driver went off saying, 'May Allah be with you. There's a thousand other families looking for transport, you've just pissed me off and wasted my time.' The dog barked and the family resumed their argument with the boxes piled up by their front door.

'Mahbouba, where are you?' I whisper.

There was no answer, so I chased Rummana who was running towards another one of the stone terraces; maybe he had caught her scent. The dog stopped and sat down beside a wooden box and I sat next to him on a large, flat stone by the unfinished end of the terrace wall. 'You stick out like a sore thumb in this time.' I didn't answer her voice, simply stared towards the outskirts of the village, at those who were already fleeing, and then back at those who had decided to stay and face the terror. There was an eerie quiet and the sound of crickets emanated from the shrubs and the trees, accompanied by the cawing of crows and, as the night began to fall, the odd cry of an owl.

Then, as suddenly as she had disappeared, Mahbouba reappeared. There she was, sitting on the stone beside me, removing the mask from her face. I was so taken aback, I fell off my perch. What was this? Was her rematerialising from nothingness real?

'Mahbouba, where did you come from?'

'Don't worry, I'm not a djinni. Or at least, I'm not a real djinni.' I wasn't sure if that was a joke, because she wasn't smiling, just the same, expressionless face. And as if she were reading my thoughts, she added: 'Joke!! But now, seriously, this mask is one of the talismans entrusted to me by Sheikh Mahfouz. It's one of eight masks he made specially for me.'

'Who is Sheikh Mahfouz? Why has he made you masks?'

'Here's how it is, ustaaz – can you believe I don't even know your name?'

'I'm Abed.'

'So, Ustaaz Abed, when I was born, I came out of my mother's womb without crying or any tears, not even a sound. I was told that even my eyes were motionless. I remained like this, a silent child who neither cried nor laughed. It drove my parents to distraction. At first, they thought I was stillborn. But

I was alive, only to face a dozen possible deaths, due to the many hazards of being mute: one time, I was half-strangled and I couldn't protest; another time my mother swaddled me too tightly and I nearly suffocated; another I broke my wrist when my mother sat on me and I couldn't cry out. From hunger to thirst, I was forever nearing death, and no one knew anything of it. This went on for a few years, until I was five. At this stage, my mother hadn't spared a doctor, nurse or nanny trying to understand my case, but nobody knew what to do. Then one day, she decided to take me to the dervishes and the first dervish she spoke to sent her to another particularly pious and wise dervish who was also a carpenter. He lived in the hills of al-Khalil and his name was Sheikh Mahfouz. So we went to see him and he recited the Quran over me and sensed that I had a gift from God and that I would be loved, 'Mahbouba'. He said that my mother would need to learn how to manage me, and to help me communicate and express myself he would make eight wooden masks that he imbued with Quranic recitals to give them special powers, but their power would only start once I put them on. Only then would their magic flow into me.'

I listened in silence to what she said. It sounded crazy. Although, if it were true, there was a beauty to it. For this to work would be nothing less than a miracle.

'Can I try the mask on?' I asked.

'Didn't I tell you they were made for me?'

'Ok, put it on so I can see it work.' She put on the mask and simply vanished. 'Take it off,' I commanded and she reappeared.

'Off, on, off, on.' She followed my instructions like a little doll, till I felt that she was getting bored.

'And what about the seven other masks?' I asked.

'We should get some sleep, it's past midnight. I hid one of the masks at the Friday market, we should go get it from there first thing.'

'Ok, so let's sleep.' But where were we going to sleep, I wondered, before seeing Mahbouba already curling up next to the dog who had been asleep for more than an hour. I propped myself against the base of a fig tree and fell into a deep sleep.

*

I stirred from my sleep to the calls of the traders in the market. The sun was making its way towards its zenith, and everyone was dressed in traditional Palestinian attire – each man had his head covered with a hatta and i'qaal, while wearing the qumbaaz robe and baggy shirwaal trousers. As for the women, their dresses were interwoven with different colours of tatreez. The place was filled with all the animals, donkeys, cows, goats and camels, their scents intermingling with that of the za'atar and lemon and various perfumes. Whichever horizon you looked towards, the eye saw only green. The distant hillsides were planted with olive, fig and all manner of almond trees. A blue sky crowned the beauty of the scene. It was as if nothing at all happened last night.

'Ah, you're up!'

I smiled: 'I'm up, I'm up.'

'Have some.' She passed me a warm piece of bread that had just come out of the oven, followed by a round disc of white cheese. 'We need to eat before we get going. Take a good look around. I don't know if we'll see this again. Look at all the roads, this way is to Akka, and this way goes to the hills of the West Bank, and that way goes to Gaza, and this road goes to al-Khalil. Behind us is the shrine of Sheikh Ali. And here is the Souq el-Jum'aa, the Friday souq. The traders come from all those parts and others like al-Lydd and Beit Jibreen and al-Faluja.'

We finished our bread and cheese and made our way down through the Souq el-Jum'aa. I was loving being back in this time; it was a delight to hear the original dialect alive with all its quirks. This was exactly what I was researching at the time, for a piece of fiction I was writing, brought to life in every possible way. One of the sellers called as we passed, he greeted me with open arms.

'Ahleen wa sahleen, most welcome, where are you from?'
'From Nablus,' I offered.
'Ahlan wa marhab b'il ghawali, you're truly welcome here in al-Khalil district. But tell me, what's this you're wearing? Where did you buy it?'
'What I'm wearing?!'
'Yes, what's going on with you, ya zalamah, it looks very different.'
I smiled and replied, 'Ha, this is from DeFacto.'
'De-what now?'
'Ha, D E F A C T O,' I spelt out in English, forgetting where I was for a moment. 'It's, er, a shop where I get all my jackets and trousers.'
'Mashi, it seems you're a bit crazy. OK, move along now.'
We reached the stall of Abu Mahraan, another villager. Mahbouba stopped and told me that the second amaanah was here. There was a large square platform on top of his cart next to the stall.

On top of the platform there was a neat pyramid of fruit. They were orange, in a hue that was pleasing to the passing eye. Abu Mahraan was standing by the cart, yelling, 'Oranges, oranges, three for ten for the navelina oranges.'

Before I could even imagine how we were going to retrieve the second mask from inside the pyramid, Mahbouba popped up and said, 'Here's it is: mask number two!' *What? When? How?* I asked myself as I watched her kneel down with the small wooden box in front of her, taking off the first mask and putting it in the custom made box alongside the second one. The box was clearly made for all eight masks, each of them with its own special place.

'So, this second mask, what does it do?'

'This one...' Her explanation was left hanging as someone called out to the market traders: 'Two riders coming in fast!' Already we could clearly see the horsemen as they approached the market and in that moment, everyone's eyes were glued to them. The riders were not alone, slumped over the first horse's withers, just below its mane, was a body. The rider dismounted and brought the cold, lifeless body down. The dead man's clothes were covered in bright red blood.

'Friends, people of Dawayima. This is your brother Mo'tasem, son of Abu Raghib. He was martyred in the battle for Maqhaz.[2] I came quickly from Beit Jibreen to warn you to be cautious. The Yahood have not honoured the truce, and the Egyptian troops have all but collapsed and are withdrawing. This means you too are now exposed.'

The people's agitation rose like a stormy sea. Traders left their stalls instantly as if they had been waiting for this news, or secretly fearing it. They scattered in all directions like the fragments of an exploding bomb. I looked at Mahbouba who was re-opening her little box and taking out the second mask. She put it on and it seemed to dissolve through the infinitesimal pores on her skin and melt into her face. She stood up, tall and straight, her face skywards, her dark eyes glinting while her mouth set in what looked like a sarcastic grin or perhaps an expression of confidence. This was the first time that I was able to understand, through her body language, what was going on in her head.

'Don't be alarmed,' she whispered. 'This is the mask of fortitude.'

'Fortitude?!'

'Come on, this is not the time for yapping...'

Her voice changed as she bounded forward like a cheetah pursuing its prey. I wondered where the second rider had gone as I followed her, weaving effortlessly through the masses of people heading in the opposing direction, abandoning their stalls and shopping. We weren't heading for the corpse, it seemed, but the second rider. Mahbouba stopped and crouched down by the corner of a house and signalled to me to conceal myself too. I leaned forward and we watched the scene. There was a horse tied up in the midst of a clump of olive trees. The rider who had spoken at the market joined his companion. They were both masked by their hattas. The first rider reached out and took a pouch laden with coins. This could only mean one thing, and I exclaimed audibly: 'He's collaborating!'

'Hush! Keep quiet!'

The horseman who had just been paid quickly mounted his horse and whipped it to speed off. The remaining horseman looked over towards us, but we managed to duck out of sight in time.

'I need to find out who this idiot is,' Mahbouba whispered. 'Stay here, don't follow me.' As she left the sheltered corner to confront him, a strange motion swept through the sky above me. I looked up and there was the second rider, still masked with a red piece of fabric fluttering on his back, flying up, up, up. Mahbouba returned a few seconds later, 'I couldn't find him, did you see where he went?'

I wasn't sure how to answer exactly. Should I tell her that he just flew away! 'Hmm, I'm not sure,' I began. 'I have a feeling that this masked man is the same person we saw outside the village council.'

'What are you saying, are you sure?'

'I can't say for sure.' Her pupils darted left to right with obvious speed and then her eyes settled and stared at me.

'What is it Mahbouba?' I asked. 'Do you know who he is?'

'I do, but we have to be certain. Come on, we need to hurry and get to the mosque before the Jum'aa prayer.'

'I get it: the third amaanah is at the mosque and you want to retrieve it before the adthaan starts!'

'No, we need to sort it out before there's a reckoning.'

★

We just about made it to the Dervishes' Mosque in time. The village elders and notables had gathered around and inside. For once, the occasion for their meeting wasn't the Friday prayer; there were more pressing concerns, and in the disruption, no one paid us any attention as we entered. I took off my shoes, and Mahbouba her slippers, and we went in. But wait a minute! Wasn't this Mahbouba's father? I recognised him from that single glance last night. And now here he was, trying to convince what appeared to be his elderly father to leave the mosque and to go with them out of the village. He was trying to bargain or plead with him, telling him that they would return tomorrow, or the day after at the latest, after the Yahood had left al-Dawayima. But the old man was adamant, 'By God, I won't leave, even under threat of death. How can I flee to the far corners of the earth when I'm old and grey! Do you want me to leave, humiliated? I was born here and I gave my sweat and blood so my land would bloom. l won't die or be buried anywhere else. You go, may God be your support and your protector.'

At this point, Mahbouba piped in, 'Come on, Yaba, you can see there is no moving him. That's it, hurry up, go with my mother and brothers and leave quickly.'

Mahbouba's father had been unaware of her presence until this point. When he saw her, he erupted: 'Maryam? What are you doing here, you imp! Where have you been since yesterday? I have no time for you now, we need to get out quickly.' He lunged at her, grabbed her hand firmly and dragged her towards the entrance. But then suddenly, he stopped and paused, as if remembering something. He turned around to face her. Cupping her face tenderly in his hands, he said, 'Are you okay, Baba, I'm sorry, I pulled your hand. Are you ok, did it hurt? Tell me, are you're ok, tell me!'

Her face had its usual blank expression, as if she were still mute. She put her right hand on top of his left hand to remove it from her cheek and then she kissed the open palm of his hand.

'I'm okay, Yaba. I'm fine, don't worry.'

Outside, she walked a few yards to the place where we had left the wooden box. Opening it, she took out the first mask. Her father knew what was coming and tears welled up in his eyes as he watched her disappear.

'Yaba, go quickly,' her voice whsipered. 'And whatever you do, don't go to Tur al-Zagh. Yaba, please tell me you understand not to go to Tur al-Zagh.'[3]

'So that's it?' he despaired. 'My darling daughter, who cares about these masks you've been entrusted with! All that matters is you – everything else can go to hell.'

A bustle of voices grew louder outside, some were cheering. A voice called out: 'Tanks are crashing into Wadi al-Ghafr, from the direction of al-Qubeiba.' Another voice answered: 'No, guys. These are Iraqi tanks! They're our brothers coming to protect us. Don't be afraid.'

Mahbouba's voice rang out: 'Yalla Yaba, make haste, there's not much time left!'

He left, looking dejectedly towards the place her voice had come from. While the elders already in the mosque supplicated and cheered, the rest of the elders entered. Mahbouba removed her mask and put it back in its place. She shouted over the din: 'Near the mihrab, on the right there's a big closet. The mask is there wrapped in yellow embroidered cloth. Hurry! Hurry!'

The popping of a volley of bullets echoed with such force outside, it shook the building as much as our hearts. I checked the yellow bundle and opened it to make sure it was the mask. I tried it on my face, but nothing happened! 'Ya Ustaaz Abed, come on!' I ran towards Mahbouba and the door. She placed the third mask in the box. As I was slipping on my shoes, someone noticed Mahbouba. 'Where are you headed? Isn't that Maryam? Stay here in the mosque. The tanks are firing everywhere, stay in the mosque. It is a holy sanctuary, nobody will harm us here.'

As we were about to leave, we exchanged glances with the elders. These figures were the roots of the earth as well as its flowing pulse. They were its warm embrace and a symbol of all that was authentic, standing on two feet. But we had to leave them. Even though Mahbouba knew what the answer would be, she had to try anyway, 'Please don't stay. The mosque won't be safe! You still have time to escape.'

They looked at her as if she were spouting crazy talk. Silence fell only to be broken by the sound of renewed bursts of gunfire. We moved quickly out towards the daylight.

Outside, people scurried like drunkards, flailing along the road. The tanks that were creeping in from the west of the village were not Iraqi as some had thought. They were monsters sowing death in their path and making no distinction between old and young, animate or inanimate objects. A modern 1948 Chevrolet pickup moved slowly past the mosque, amid the masses of departing people. In the cab was an entire family of at least ten people. Their bodies were tightly packed, their heads close together. On the back, a group of women, children, and men were squashed together, some sitting, others standing. Many villagers pursued the vehicle, trying to climb aboard. Some managed to reach it and cling on, while others fell helplessly to the ground and were trampled underfoot. We watched as the tanks advanced through the fields on the outskirts of the village, and listened to their stuttering roar. A man stood in the middle of the road, both arms extended trying to oppose the fleeing mass, to halt their advance. He called out, his voice lost among their screams: 'Ya people, ya people. Stay here, don't leave. Die here on your land and don't abandon it...'

His words evaporated on the hot tin of their terror like drops of water. No one could hear him. 'We have to get back to my home,' Mahbouba said. 'Quickly, before the tanks arrive.'

This wasn't the time for me to suddenly find myself in a state of paralysis, trying to take in the sight of waves of people rippling past me. Then the first bullet landed. It whizzed past my head, and I heard its whistle a split-second before it pierced through the door of the mosque. I saw the lost children crying. I saw the face of Mahbouba speaking. But what I was doing was reliving the history I had always known and studied. These tanks advancing into the village from three axes – western, northern, and southern – were none other than the 89th Division of the Israeli Army. The same division, composed of the Stern Gang and the Irgun, that had already participated in several massacres, including the Deir Yassin and Kafr Qasim massacres. Here, in al-Dawayima, they became an official, organised army for the first time, during Operation Yoav. It seemed some hidden magic had allowed me to relive this history.

'Hey, hey. Ustaaz Abed! Why are you silent? Come on, ba*kollatch*, listen to me, let's get out of here before the tanks arrive.' And so we left the main street for the alleyways and all the while a flow of people oozed from their houses, while many still remained, either out of self-respect – refusing to let themselves or their children become refugees – or out of an inability to leave due to illness, infirmness or immobility. On the balcony of a house, an old woman and her granddaughter were sitting. The old woman's voice sounded worried:

'Who's there? Who's there?'

I pause and answer: 'Yes, ya hajja. What's up? What's wrong with you?'

'Who's that? You're not from around here?'

'There's no time for that, ya hajja! How can I help you?'

'Take Safiyya. Don't leave her here. They'll kill me, but they won't kill Safiyya. Her father, mother, and brothers went and left us here.'

'Who's Saf–'

'We can't,' Mahbouba interrupted. 'She will delay us. We'll

die if we take her. We have masks to collect.'

'But she's a child!'

'She's as blind as her grandmother. They're both blind. We have to go. You will see a lot of this kind of thing, we have a long road ahead of us.'

Across the way, a woman slammed the door of her house as she was leaving. In one arm she was carrying her baby, with the other she was dragging another child trailing behind her. She was running barefoot. But wait a minute... She *wasn't* carrying a baby, she was carrying a long pillow, shaped like a baby, wrapped in a short sheet.

'Mahbouba,' I stopped. 'This woman has forgotten her baby...' The sound of crying rose from the house. Did the small child know he had been forgotten? I looked to try to catch the mother, but she had disappeared into the general throng of the villagers.

Mahbouba admonished me: 'Keep going and don't even think about it.'

Watchful eyes took in every move. As we approached Mahbouba's house, I noticed a figure moving across the sky. It landed at the house of Saffeya and her grandmother and placed a red mark on the door. Mahbouba saw me looking as she opened her door and said, 'Don't be surprised. What you see is real. And before you say anything, I'm not crazy. This guy is flying in the sky.'

'He's a superhero!' I cried.

'A what?'

'A superhero! It's a type of fictional character from films and comics from my era. I didn't know they existed! They wear capes and fly around. Just like this.'

'They call him "Vetoman" and he's no hero,' Mahbouba chided. 'He's a criminal. He ruins lives. Look at him putting signs on the houses where people live so that when the Yahood arrive, they'll know who to kill. He's the one who brings them all their information firsthand. Come on, come in. We'll see what happens. Let's fortify ourselves.'

She entered her old house and I followed, locking the door tightly behind us. The boxes of wheat, barley, and clothes were still there. Mahbouba's family had left without taking any of the provisions they had prepared. Mahbouba asked me to wait, then disappeared into an inner room and emerged carrying a rolled up piece of fabric. She sat on the floor and brought the wooden box out and placed the fabric beside it. She took out a piece of cloth and a quill pen from the box, unrolled the fabric and extracted a piece of paper stuffed inside.

'Sit,' she said to me. I sat opposite her.

'This hijab is from Sheikh Mahfouz, it's also a protective shield. I will recite its spell and you will repeat it after me, then write it down on the piece of paper. You need this protective spell, ok?'

'A hijab, what for?'

'Something to surround and protect you. So that God may protect and preserve us and the house. Enough with the talk now, come on.'

And so she chanted, 'We protect ourselves in this house with God, the holy tablet, and the holy words. By the seven words that the prophet Muhammad uttered on the mountain. From the night, we seek no medicine. From the horses, we seek no seed. No creeping thing will creep upon us, nothing small or large will get close. The sun rises and prays for the beloved Muhammad.'

I repeated the strange words, in the same dialect and manner, trancelike. Then I came to and wrote them on the piece of paper. We finished and she took the piece and folded and wrapped it in the cloth and tied it to her. I made sure that I did the same with mine. 'We're ready and prepared for anything now,' she said.

The sound of gunfire outside continued, although the screams were getting quieter with each passing minute. I opened the door with the iron key left by Mahbouba's family. But the alley wasn't empty of activity. A group of foot soldiers were marching past. They stormed the house opposite with a red sign on the door. The blind old woman called from the balcony in a worried voice: 'Who's there? Who's there?' My heart nearly tore from its socket. I went back in and closed the door. The barking of a dog behind me almost gave us all away. 'It's Rummana, let him in.' The dog came in and leaped onto Mahbouba, licking her hand and face while wagging its tail. Despite her happiness at seeing him, she hushed the dog as we heard the screams of the blind old woman and her granddaughter, tearing at our hearts. We wished it were the sounds of bullets ending their lives painlessly, but it was the sound of clubs slowly deforming their bones and skin.

'They beat them and shattered their skulls. May God have mercy on them and accept them into heaven. We must get going Ustaaz Abed.' I couldn't even begin to understand this girl's heart! How could she be so calm? How could she even function with all this evil around us? Even if she had lived through it once before!

'We need to go to the carob tree.'

'The one on the edge of town? But that's where the tanks came in!'

'We put our trust in God. After the hijab, we are protected by his blessings.'

I couldn't help but question the reason for collecting these masks, these objects she's been trusted with. How are they more important than helping the bereaved? Why is she holding this above all else? I answered flatly: 'I'm ready.'

Mahbouba sensed my reluctance to carry on following her. Staring into my eyes, she said: 'Go into the inner room, back there, and you'll find yourself back in the cave. And from there, you'll emerge as if nothing had happened. No one is forcing you to come with me.'

Her words shook me deeply. Would everything end? In

two steps? I didn't think this was what my soul wanted. I knew I'd never have this chance again. Of course, I would help Mahbouba gather the masks.

'No. I want to continue,' I said. 'I'll stay till my last breath. Even if my death is the end of the road.'

'Good, then let's leave the house.'

I cracked the door to check our path. The alley was filled with soldiers. How would we make it? At this point, Rummana nosed the door open and ran towards them. They raised their machine guns in his direction but instead of firing, they called out to him, looking to play with him. That was our chance to leave. I crept out with Mahbouba behind me. We stole around the back of the orchard. Then we scurried through the weeds, the 'za'amtout',[5] and the olive trees. Looking back, I saw a red mark on Mahbouba's house. The sounds of gunfire emanated from houses here and there around the village. They entered any house with a red mark and killed whoever they found, either with clubs or bullets. Lifeless bodies lay strewn about the streets. The colours of their white scarves stained red with blood. Tiptoeing over those motionless bodies, mixed with the dust and stones of the earth, was a terrifying sight. I stopped to examine a child in his mother's lifeless arms, but he was dead, like her, his little head punctured by an enormous bullet wound. Next to them: the corpses of donkeys and sheep who hadn't been spared either. They wanted to murder the very place, so they cut short every soul that took sanctuary in it.

'We're almost there, the carob tree is just ahead of us.'

The sun was way past noon as we reached the large carob tree. But what now? What was hanging from a large branch in it? A body. The corpse of an old woman, swaying with the wind.

'This is Umm Abdullah Muslih. They took her and strung her up there. Help me up so I can get her down and retrieve the mask hidden above.'

I cupped my hands for Mahbouba to step onto, and she clambered into the branches. Reaching for the knot, she tried to untie it, but to no avail. I handed her a pointed branch. She prodded the top of the rope repeatedly until it weakened. I positioned myself under the dangling legs. The rope broke, and I caught her. But I couldn't take the weight, so we both fell together. Her blood trickled onto my face and clothes. I tried to wipe it off and got back to my feet. Mahbouba had left me to my confusion and continued climbing. Eventually she found what she was seeking and threw it down to me. She clambered down and took the mask from me. But another body was descending, much more gracefully, behind the carob tree. His arms were crossed. He smiled at Mahbouba and me as he reached the ground majestically.

'See. Superheroes are real!'

Mahbouba put on the fourth mask without the man noticing. Her features started to change. Her eyes first shone, then swivelled from right to left, closing slightly. She stuck out her tongue and licked her upper lip, saying, 'I heard that your type have a name! He calls you a superhero!' She seemed to say this with a sly look on her face or perhaps it was more cunning. The flying man couldn't hide his surprise at the word. 'Who said that?' he asked, in an thick Western accent. 'Where did you hear that word, Mahbouba? From the one with you, no doubt. Who is he, tell me! Not from here, clearly. Anyway, it doesn't matter as you're both going to die.'

He extended his right hand to the sky, and put his left hand behind his back. Suddenly he rocketed into the air, and landed near one of the stationary tanks. The faces of the soldiers on top of it turned towards us before the whole tank started coming our way. With the same cunning look, Mahbouba said, 'We'll see what happens. Come on, Ustaaz Abed.' The moment we tried to leave from behind the tree, the advancing tanks fired a volley at us. Bullets ripped into the trunk of the carob tree, behind which we'd returned for shelter, and they also ripped into Umm Abdullah's body lying on the ground. Some of them hit the rocks and bounced back in all directions. I was overcome by a mixture of emotions: I didn't know what I was afraid of most: death, or the thought of never returning to my home and my time? Or maybe I was more afraid for Mahbouba? How would she continue her mission?

'Their bullets will run out soon,' she shouted, interrupting my thoughts. 'The moment the Bren gun stops, run to Abu Samih's house.' Seconds passed. The trunk behind us continued to splinter. Then the gunfire stopped. We ran without thinking. I stumbled on a pothole and fell, and in that moment saw, hovering above us, Vetoman, delivering a crate of ammunition towards the hungry tanks. 'Come on. Get up. There's no time.' We reached Abu Samih's house, and hid behind it, pressing our backs to the wall. 'There are two masks nearby,' Mahbouba panted. 'One is in the canal, the other in the well. We have to get them before they reach us.' Mahbouba took off the fourth mask, which clearly gave her the ability to calculate the trajectories of flying bullets, and placed it in the box – the one she never let go of – then took out the first mask. She disappeared. 'Go *through* the houses,' her voice whispered. 'I'll go ahead of you to the canal. After that, we'll head straight to Bir al-Ad, the well by the mosque. Agreed?'

But we hadn't agreed! That was the first time Mahbouba really left me. She just disappeared. I don't mean she just became invisible. I mean her voice and her presence left me too. I had no choice, but to creep through the houses, one by one, toward the canal. I made sure the soldiers didn't see me. I also took care not to be seen by the looming eye of darkness that was Vetoman. All I could hear were the voices of soldiers looking for us. The sound of bullets had faded away as the afternoon went on.

I moved forward slowly and carefully. In one of the alleys, I heard an old man's voice calling: 'Wait, Hassan! Atutruchneesh!

Don't leave me, ya Hassan. Don't leave me...' He repeated it endlessly, inviting death with his own tongue. I moved away, fearing that Mahbouba would outpace me and I'd never catch up. In another alley, Israeli soldiers were chasing a group of chickens. When they caught one, they confiscated it and put it in one of their vehicles. I waited till they had finished stealing all the chickens and sheep from a house adjacent to the canal, then ran across and into it stealthily. Once inside, I made my way to a window overlooking the canal and opened it slowly. I could see the water flowing and ebbing. It seemed as if someone was swimming underwater but I could only see the transparent outline of it beneath the surface. It must have been Mahbouba. The movement stopped. 'There you are!' a voice said, as she suddenly re-materialised in the middle of the canal, removing her mask. Her white dress clung to her small frame, just as her velvety hair framed her expressionless face. That face, pulsating with life! That face, captivating you even with its silence! That face, divine in perfection, needing no modification or refinement. I thought – without realising it – that I should thank her for her presence in this world. But I preferred not to disturb her; the troubles on all sides were enough for her.

'Yes, here I am. Did you get the mask?' I asked.

'Not yet. I was waiting for you.'

She held the mask in her right hand, took a deep breath, pinched her nose with her left hand, closed her eyes, and dove in. A minute or two passed. Then she emerged, holding a mask in each hand. The new one, mask number five, was wrapped in a piece of cloth. She resumed her usual silence as she stared at me. Water streamed from her body into the canal. She drew her right hand, holding the mask of invisibility, towards her, set it back on her face and disappeared. But where had she gone this time? I called out to her, to no avail. I cast about me. Suddenly the place I had just come from seemed about to burst with soldiers! Not to mention the accumulation of their rifle barrels! All pointed at me. Vetoman stood amid them –

arms folded, commanding the crowd. Not a shot was fired. Their faces were difficult to read. I broke the silence:

'What do you want from me?' One of them tightened the grip on his weapon. '*No, wait!*' I said in English. They couldn't comprehend who this English-speaker was, dressed in such fancy-looking, if dirty, clothes, not seen before in the Arab countryside.

'I am tired of trying to work out who you are,' Vetoman said. He never got to his question. A soldier entered the building behind him, approached quickly and whispered. Vetoman's face was filled with interest. He said in Hebrew (which I understood): 'What are you saying? Okay, I will go and return quickly to explain everything.' He turned to me and before flying away, said:

'Take care of him while I'm away.'

Seconds of silence passed. 'Tie him up,' the group leader barked, as he marched out of the house. 'Bring him with us.' The soldiers looked at each other; no one had talked about arresting people. They had no experience in this. One of them found a rope in the pantry, and approached ordering me to hold my hands in front of him. He tied them so loosely, I could have untied it if I pulled on one end. We processed out of the building in silence and anticipation. We continued walking until we reached a gathering of armoured cars. The soldiers stationed there stared at us in astonishment. 'Who is this?' one of them shouted. 'Why didn't you kill him?'

'The Boss wants him alive,' the group leader replied.

Over the chatter that ensued, another group of soldiers could be seen emerging from behind a tank. They weren't ordinary soldiers. They weren't wearing traditional military fatigues, nor were they carrying any equipment or weapons. In the middle of them, perhaps unsurprisingly, was the man himself. The one-eyed monster. Moshe Dayan. His left eye having been lost in World War II. The commander of the Operation Yoav, in al-Dawayima, the man who'd go on to be

Chief of Staff of the Israeli army six years later. The same man who'd become Minister of Defence twenty years from now, then Minister of Foreign Affairs. Oh, how honoured I was to meet him! He looked like a little Putin!

He looked at me calmly, then asked them about me again. Their commander replied with the same answer. 'Wait for the Boss then,' Moshe said calmly. The group commander ordered that I be taken to the armoured personnel carrier. But at that moment, a strong gust came upon us. The soldiers and I looked up. Vetoman was returning. He flew past the mosque's minaret, which the soldiers had made one of their military outposts, watching and firing from it at anyone that moved in the streets. Vetoman landed, shouting furiously: 'There are families hiding in the Tur al-Zagh cave. Hurry up and get them.' The location was set. Everyone prepared and reloaded their weapons. I stood still in the middle of all this commotion. I hadn't yet reached the personnel carrier. Vetoman advanced towards me, a knowing smile spreading across his face. His head towered over his immense body. I almost recognised that face! I'd met him before!

'Ha. Tell me,' he said, 'where are you from, and what are you doing here?'

'I'm from 2025. I didn't come here by choice.'

'What does "from 2025" mean?'

'It means I come from the future. I come from seventy seven years after this time.'

He raised his hand and rubbed his cleft chin. He smiled and said, 'You're playing with me! You don't seem to know what's going to happen to you?'

Behind me, the military convoy had started heading off towards Tur al-Zagh. Vetoman came towards me, grabbed me tightly, and together we flew into the sky. It was a strange feeling to be in Lois Lane's shoes from that movie, *Superman 1978*! It wasn't flying I was afraid of as much as the place we were going to. When we got there, in less than a minute,

Vetoman tied me to a rock overlooking the entrance to the Tur al-Zagh cave on the other side of the hill. 'You'll see for yourself what will happen to you if you don't start talking,' he said. 'Sit back and watch. Enjoy. I'll get back to you.' Then he flew back towards the oncoming convoy, to help pull the armoured personnel carrier out of a dirt hole it had got stuck in. Half an hour passed. A tank arrived in front of the cave entrance, blocking it, followed by several infantry soldiers, who strapped on their weapons and waited for the signal to storm.

'Oh God, I hope my family aren't in there!'

'Mahbouba, is that you?'

She appeared, removing the mask, and putting down the box. She returned the first mask, then brought out the fifth – the latest in her collection of treasures. She put it on.

'By God, by God. If my family are still in the cave, I will…'

I stared at her facial features. Red. A vein protruding from the right side of her forehead. Her breathing rapid. She was chewing on her lower lip with her teeth, her mouth opening wider than usual, and the volume of her voice almost giving us both away.

I whispered. 'How about you calm down and try untying me?'

'I haven't got time for this, can't you see?'

Despite saying this angrily, she came up to me and untied me. We took cover and watched the horror unfold from a distance.

★

The soldiers entered one by one. Others took up positions on top of the tank. Still others spread out behind the stones and among the olive trees. The sounds of panicked residents rose from the heart of the cave, mixed with the shouts of the soldiers ordering them to leave. The blackness bordered by the frame of the stone entrance betrayed its temporary residents. Mothers and children emerged, carrying and being carried, dragged and pulled. They shared the tears and terror between them. Some of the men came out with one hand in the air, and the other holding up their Qumbaz, exposing their stomachs. Each carried in their raised hand their hatta. The commander preceded them, signalling them to line up in front of the stone outcrop that made up part of the cave entrance. The number of families exceeded 30 maybe 40 – more than 100 people in total. Mahbouba got to her feet. She struck the trunk of a nearby tree with her right hand. Blood gushed from her wrist.

'What's wrong?' I asked.

'There. My family is in the cave. I told them. Kultellu, my father, don't go to Tur al-Zagh. He didn't listen!' Sparks flashed from her glittering eyes. (The sparkle of her eyes was a constant through all the masks.) Her facial features seemed almost angular, especially her frown. She took a few steps to the right, then back to the left. 'What should we do, Ustaaz Abed? How can we help them?'

While I struggled for an answer, the reply came from farther off. Voices shook the fields and horizons as soldiers began firing their weapons at the people lined up outside the cave.

Countless bullets riddled their bodies, as they fell, face-down. Dozens of lives erased in a single instant. A child ran from one place in the huddle. Another girl ran from a second. There was still some spirit clinging to them. The soldiers didn't notice as the two children crept away through the long grass behind the bodies, they climbed above the cave and, from there, up the mountain. A shepherd, who was hiding like us, grabbed the first child, picked him up, and ran away. The girl chased them into the mountains. After the soldiers finished the killing, the group leader gestured. Vetoman emerged from where he'd been hiding. He hovered over the dead, moving slowly, checking for any signs of life. If he found any, he signalled to the soldiers to snuff it out. Mahbouba crouched over her injured hand, leaning against a stone. She started moving off. 'Where are you going?' I asked. She didn't answer. In a few steps, she would be exposed to the soldiers on the slopes! I ran and blocked her path. 'Where are you going?'

'Listen, get away, bakullatch,' she shouted angrily. 'I want to go down to my family and see them.'

'Okay, we'll go down when the soldiers leave. We still have to collect the rest of the valuables. If you go down now, they'll kill you. That way you won't be able to continue!'

She stared at me for a long time, her eyes blazing as her breath quickened. Reluctantly, she returned with me to our hiding place. The soldiers and their tanks retreated. I told her that we should take cover before Vetoman came back. The sun was about to set. Silence had fallen over the place, as it had over al-Dawayima, which we could see from our vantage point as we descended towards the cave. These refugees, fleeing from one death to find another, were not only from al-Dawayima, but also from al-Tina, al-Qubeiba, and al-Faluja. They had tried to flee eastwards, as if searching for a new day, for a glimpse of life. Drenched in their own blood. Bodies upon bodies. Piles of mangled flesh. Mahbouba ran towards her mother. She grabbed her by the shoulders, trying to lift her and move her. I was surprised. She tried again, but she couldn't.

'Mahbouba, what are you doing?'

'What do you think I'm doing?' she shouted, turning her angry face towards me. I want to lift her or turn her over.'

'Why?'

She looked at me with a flushed face, 'Come on, help me instead of your constant questions!'

I hurried forward between the strewn bodies. I tried not

to step on anyone. As I lifted the body of her dead mother, a child emerged from underneath, still alive. Mahbouba lunged at him. She hugged him tightly to her chest.

'Are you okay, Hamouda?' she asked frantically.

He didn't answer. She shook him by the shoulders and repeated the question with an unremitting anger: 'Answer me boy! Are you ok?' Again he didn't answer. Instead his entire body trembled. She called me over and I picked him up. 'Oh God! Where is my father? Where is he?' Given the circumstances, her anger was understandable, but the intensity of her rage was strange, as if the mask she wore amplified it. I remembered that one of the masks we needed to collect was in the Tur al-Zagh cave. I left her in her rage, searching for her father and headed to the cave entrance, carrying Hamouda. The rocky outcrops were full of gaps. Where could the mask be? I put Hamouda down and searched the area randomly, to no avail. After giving up, I went back to the child and saw him playing with a piece of wood. It was the mask! I hurried over to him and scooped both up, then left, eager to give the mask to Mahbouba, who by this point had found what she was looking for. Kneeling, she cradled her father's body. He was still fighting for breath. 'Yaba, why didn't you listen to me?' she sobbed. 'Why!? I told you not to go to the Tur el-Zagh cave! By God, I have been here before, and I knew what would happen.' Breaths came slowly to him. His chest heaved up and down painfully. He had been shot several times in different places.

'It doesn't matter,' he said with difficulty. 'Yaba. What matters is that you're okay. That's all. This was our fate, it was written, ma*tch*toob, and the eye will see what is ma*tch*toob on the forehead.'

She started sobbing again. Her face red and flushed, her eyes still sparkling: 'A forehead and an eye! We have brains that can think, you know...' I set Hamouda down and approached gently. 'Mahbouba! Take off the mask and try this one!'

Her father turned his head to me, then nodded approvingly. She looked at me as she removed the mask of anger. Her face calmed. We exchanged masks, and she put the sixth one on. No sooner had the mask melded into her skin, she burst into tears. The sparkle in her eyes turned into an endless stream. 'Don't go, Yaba' she sobbed, 'Don't leave me alone.'

He smiled faintly and raised his hand hesitantly, touching her cheek: 'Maryam, the love of my life, the light of my heart. I wish, my dear, that you could have grown up with me beside you. I wish I could have visited your house and brought you fruit and vegetables from my garden and had breakfast together. But it seems that life has no time for crying! You know why I called you Maryam? So that God would bring you someone with great knowledge. I didn't call you Maryam because I was worried about you. Don't cry, don't smile, you don't need to do anything. I named you Maryam to resemble the Virgin Mary. So that God would protect you from evil.

'Your mother only called you Mahbouba because Sheikh Mahfouz told her to. "Kallha," he said, "this girl will be Mahbouba" and it's true you are my beloved, my heart and soul.' He coughed, spitting blood.

'Enough. Enough. Don't say any more,' she said. 'The Khalili Society car will arrive soon, and Misbah will be there. I'll flag them down, and they'll take you to the hospital.'

'Come close, Yaba,' he said with great difficulty. 'Closer. Let me kiss you.' He kissed her with lips perfumed with blood, and his soul departed. Mahbouba was the last thing he saw, the last thing he touched, the last thing he smelled, and the last thing he heard. She held him to her chest and wept bitterly.

★

We returned to the place from which people fled. We returned to the alleys strewn with death. Misbah took Hamouda. They were on their way to the village of al-Koum, one of the villages of al-Khalil district (al-Dawayima being only 24 kilometres from al-Khalil). Then, after a few months, they would go to Ain al-Sultan in Jericho. Years later, they would settle in the city of Zarqa in Jordan, and await their return – like many others in different places – until this day, in 2025.

Tears never left Mahbouba's eyes. We retraced our steps toward al-Dawayima, passing the remnants of the houses' stone walls, scattered into the roads. Those that fled had demolished them to hinder their pursuers. Evening fell. The moon lit our way. Bodies lay scattered where they fell. We weren't the only ones returning. Others were creeping through the night, returning in the dark to fetch necessities left behind in stores and wells, after hearing that the Yahood had left. But the roads were mined to trap those who tried to return. Mahbouba removed her mask, satisfied with all the crying she had done, or perhaps because she was now emptied of all she had carried with her so heavily for 77 years. She couldn't return to her time through the cave except in my presence. So here she was, repeating the act, reliving the massacre for the second time. But she would complete what she had been unable to do. Mahbouba opened the box. She returned the sixth mask to it. Two more remained to complete the number.

'Ustaaz Abed. Let's go back to the well, Bir el-Ad, near the mosque. But look out for mines and there's still a Yahoodi sniper in the minaret.' I nodded, though I wasn't sure if she could see me nod in the dark. She walked, and I followed cautiously. We stopped in front of the mosque, its door now broken. I knew the fate of those who had sought refuge there, but I wanted to enter. Mahbouba raised her hand signalling it was okay. The threads of moonlight filtering through the windows revealed the horrific scene. The bodies of the elders – more than 75 in number – were piled on top of each other. Grief and silence reigned in the sanctity of the mosque. Their hopes of receiving mercy dashed; all they received was death. Their spilled blood was almost dry. It was pooled where their foreheads had touched the floor, prostrating to God, all their lives.

'Ustaaz Abed, we must act before they return. Or before Vetoman sees us.' My heart ached. But Mahbouba was right. We had to complete the journey, which would ultimately bring hope after pain. We left the mosque and continued on our way towards Bir al-Ad. When we reached it, Mahbouba said, 'Put me in the bucket and lower me down. As soon as I get the seventh, draw me back up.'

'Okay.' I held the upper end of the rope. Mahbouba put her feet into the bucket and held on to the length of the rope. I began to lower her down. Before long though, the strain disappeared.

The top of her head was still visible from where I stood. She carefully lifted one foot out of the bucket and felt around with it.

'Ustaaz Abed, there's something wrong here! I just can't see what!'

She stepped completely out of the bucket and felt around with her feet to make sure she didn't trip. She looked up to me and cried out in panic: 'It's a body! A body!'

I let go of the rope and leaned out over the well. I couldn't see anything.

'We need some fire or a lamp to see properly.'

'No need for that!' I remembered my cell phone. Taking it out of my pocket, I turned on the flashlight. Mahbouba was surprised by the brightness. I leaned over and aimed it at her feet. It was a shocking sight. Mahbouba screamed and jumped towards the wall, to escape what she was standing on. She slipped to the ground. The horror overwhelmed us. In the phone's light we could see a mass of bodies entwined together. Hands mixed with legs, tangled with heads. All crushed together at the bottom of the well.

'Ohh Mahbouba! You can't imagine the ugliness!' I cried. 'It looks like they had tried to hide their crimes by throwing people's bodies into the well! Can we not leave this precious mask?'

'What are you talking about, of course not. We need *all* the masks. My heart wants to explode with horror. But I can't express it. The mask in the well is the mask of weakness, don't forget. We need all the masks to break the spell and leave the cave!'

We had no choice. We had to exhume the dead. Oh God! I got down there and trod all over them. I removed the first body from the bottom and hoisted it up to the lip of the well, where Mahouba stood and pulled it over. The same with the second and third. But as I got deeper, it got harder. I prepared a fourth body to be lifted, tied the rope around its waist, and started to hoist it from where I stood. I called Mahbouba to help pull from her end. I could no longer make much out down there. Where was my cell phone? I wondered.

'Mahbouba,' I shouted. 'Do you have my phone with you? Can you shine the flashlight down here.'

'Phone! What phone? Ha.' She bent down and picked it up.

'Good, it's still on!' I shouted. 'Lower it down to me.' I had nearly finished hoisting the remaining bodies, when suddenly I saw the merchant from al-Khalil, the one who'd asked me about my clothes. Clothes that were now smeared with his blood. May God have mercy on him. I hoisted him as far as I could and Mahbouba pulled him over the wall. Then I reached below me where the last bodies lay in the pool of water.

'Here, Mahbouba!' I called. 'I've reached the water! What should I do?'

'The mask is in a hole in the wall somewhere near the waterline. Look closely.'

I looked around the wall, and found a cavity. I reached in and drew back a piece of cloth in the shape of a mask.

'I've found it.'

'Excellent. Put it in the bucket.'

She reattached the bucket and lowered it down to me. With the mask placed inside, she began to draw it back up but just as it reached to her, a hand appeared over the top of the wall and snatched the mask out. Then the same hand reached out again with a knife, and cut the rope, leaving the severed ends to fall towards me. The same hand grabbed the phone off Mahbouba and took it away. A pitch-black darkness enveloped me.

'Mahbouba! Mahbouba! Where are you? What's happening?' I shouted. No one answered.

★

I spent the night in the pitch-black darkness along with the dead at the bottom of the well. I tried calling out to Mahbouba to break the silence. Her name echoed upwards in the cylindrical space above me. What had happened to her? I prayed she was unhurt. Would I join the group lying in the water around me? What was contained in the fine print of my destiny? I prayed to God and surrendered myself to His will. In the morning, I woke to the sound of a huge explosion. The laughter of soldiers rose outside. One of them said: 'So what do you say, Mukhtar Mahmoud! Now we've blown up your house? Will you remain silent? No one will know what happened in your precious Dawayima. Do you understand?' I heard no response, save for the sound of scattered gunshots. I was reassured that those shots were not directed at the Mukhtar. And of course, he wouldn't die now, because he would go on to speak about the massacre, breaking the wall of silence, and exposing their atrocities 36 years later. An hour passed. Two hours. The sound of gunfire returned. One of the soldiers could be heard saying: 'Don't let any of those who returned home live. Kill them all. Let the patrols comb every alleyway, twenty-four hours a day.'

The Yahood had returned to the village. Yesterday's nightmare wasn't over. What was I to do? Call out? If they found me, that would be it! Was I to remain silent? Hunger and thirst would take me eventually! The water in the well was undrinkable, being so mixed with the blood of the corpses. I tried to climb the walls, with no success. The sound of a truck approached. It was parked on the road next to the mosque.

The soldiers' voices were incomprehensible. I could hear them carrying things and slamming them down. Were they transporting the bodies of the dead? The day passed slowly, heavily and unbearably. Each minute was marked by the sounds of explosions and scattered gunfire. A feeling of intense cold gnawed at my bones; my whole body was drenched. I felt the moment of the end was approaching. I would die here, far from my family, and yet close to home. It was a special feeling, a feeling of comfort and reassurance. Before sunset, a head appeared at the mouth of the well. The head of that flying crow, Vetoman. He smiled arrogantly. 'So you're still alive? Or maybe you're dead? Ha. It looks like you're alive. Have you learned your lesson, *k*habibi? Come on, get up. I need you to explain what this device is that lights up when I touch it!'

I didn't move. My teeth chattered and my body trembled. He threw me a rope. I tried to grab it. I struggled. With all my strength, I reached the rope and held on to it.

'Ready!' I groaned. 'Pull me up.'

I looked up. With one hand, and with a sly grin on his face, he lifted the rope, and I rose with it. But about halfway up, he let go. I plummeted back into the water, crashing through the remaining bodies. As for him, he started laughing hysterically.

'Enough. Enough,' he laughed. 'I was just kidding with you. Come on, grab hold again.' He threw the rope once more but this time I refused to take it. Vetoman boiled with rage. 'Take it!' he shouted. 'If you don't, I'll leave you down here.'

'I choose death over humiliation,' I replied.

He didn't wait, but rose into the air above the well and descended vertically towards me. Stopping just above the corpses, he paused mid-air. Reaching down, he grabbed me by the collar of my shirt. My whole weight gathered around my neck as we rose. At the opening of the well, I saw the bodies piled around it. Like a missile firing out of a silo, we then sped towards our destination. I knew where that was. Mahbouba had told me it was the highest point in the Dawayima region, an area called al-Jaroun. A vantage point on all the roads, 'ruins', villages, and towns in the distance. Vetoman landed at the Sheikh Ali shrine. I was on the verge of fainting from the chilling effect of the cold air rushing past my wet body. He threw me onto the dirt and gravel, then commanded, 'Take him in.' Four soldiers appeared and each grabbed one of my limbs.

They carried me into the shrine, which had been converted into a military barracks filled with weapons and equipment. The inner room contained tables and chairs. On the tables lay maps, and on the chairs sat the commanders of the 89th Division. There, in the far corner, Mahbouba was strung up to the ceiling on two ropes. Her feet weren't bearing her weight, which was instead concentrated through her wrists. The soldiers stood me near her, so I could look at her scarred face and bloodied body. My God! They had tortured the child!

'Mahbouba! What have the dogs done to you?'

She was unconscious. Vetoman stepped forward in his blue and red clown costume, holding my phone. 'What is this?' he asked, holding it up to me. 'It looks like a crystal pod from my home planet!'

'I won't say a word until you let her down and get me a blanket to wrap myself in.'

His face darkened. The audience seated around us also denounced my comment.

'You're going to die any minute, and you're still giving orders!'

I didn't answer, just lowered my head, and hugged myself

to preserve some warmth. Vetoman flinched and called for a soldier, ordering him to take down Mahbouba and fetch a blanket. Mahbouba's face showed the toll of her ordeal. I couldn't bear to see her like this. I wished I was the injured one. That no harm would touch her again. 'Mahbouba! I'm here,' I whispered as I approached her. 'I've come. I'm next to you. Everything is going to be OK. We need to continue with our journey.'

Seconds passed. Her lips moved, her eyes closed. She said wearily: 'Thank God, Ustaaz Abed. Thank God you're okay. And I'm okay, don't worry about me. We have to go home, with the box. Don't forget, the house is surrounded. If we can't go back, it's over for us. There's nothing left.' The soldier threw the blanket. I caught it and wrapped it around me.

Vetoman said, 'There, now I've got what you want, tell me: what is this device?'

'Sure. Sure,' I began. 'But there's just one problem. This device won't work without a charger. And the charger is at Mahbouba's house.'

'A charger? Okay, we'll send soldiers to fetch it.'

'Yeah. No. That won't work. We have to go. It only works there. Next to the charger.'

He was silent for a moment, then said, 'Okay. I'll take you, let's go.'

'Yeah. No. Mahbouba has to come with us too.'

He grew furious. 'What does the girl have to do with it? We're going for the charger and to turn on the device. She must stay for what she must answer to when she wakes up. She has to explain what this box is, and what these masks are inside it.'

'Yeah. Again, all of those masks are part of it. Their magic only works in Mahbouba's family's house. We all have to go. The box and with Mahbouba.'

The leaders looked at each other, then at the boss, who said, 'There's no harm in it. Let's give them one last chance. If they lie, they die, and who cares about the crystal device or the masks.'

They shook their heads. He ordered the soldiers to prepare the vehicles. As they travelled through the villages, the houses seemed to all be on fire. Such devastation. Vetoman flew alongside the car carrying Mahbouba and me. The military leaders rode along with us. Several other cars filled with soldiers accompanied us. At al-Dawayima, everyone disembarked, and gathered in formation in front of the house. I looked at the boss and said, 'You know, they won't all make it inside.' One of the leaders stepped forward.

'Silence,' shouted one of the captains. 'Enough of this nonsense. You don't give the orders. We're all going in.' I looked at Mahbouba, unable to fully grasp the situation. She shook her head, not knowing what to do.

'Yes, yes,' I replied. 'As you prefer, come on, Mahbouba, open the door.' I took out the large iron key from the box, inserted it into the lock, and opened it with difficulty. Then picking up the box I gestured: 'Here you go, Mahbouba.' I jumped in after her, the box in my hand, and turned to Vetoman. 'Here you go, Boss.' But before anyone could follow, I slammed the door shut and locked it. The captains and soldiers were furious. They began to beat on the door with their hands and the butts of their rifles. One of them drew his weapon and aimed it at the door, at which point I could hear Rummana pounce on him and tear into him. I looked around us. A silent Mahbouba stared at Vetoman. I joined her in her gaze. His brightly colourful costume disappeared. It had turned into a formal suit with a waistcoat and a striped necktie.

His hair was shiny and black, parted on the right. Drops of sweat trickled down his forehead. A haze descended over his eyes. He reached into his jacket pocket and pulled out a pair of heavy, black-rimmed glasses with flat lenses. It was him! The same man who'd been tied up when I entered the cave. I felt a heat radiating from the hijab.

Outside, the sounds of gunfire shook the air. Rummana barked and chased as a skirmish ensued. 'Come on,' Mahbouba said. 'Quick. The last mask is on the second shelf, behind you. Bring it.' I ran to fetch it, while she found and opened a box full of clothes. She took out an oversized white dress. The now-besuited Vetoman staggered, without any balance or strength. I found the final treasure, the eighth mask. Outside, a bullet hit Rummana, and he let out a sad, whimpering cry. The door of the house began to shake, as bullets pierced it relentlessly. Mahbouba put the dress over her shoulders and held the box out with both hands. I hurried, holding the mask in one hand and grabbing Vetoman by his sleeve with the other. We passed through the inner door, and found ourselves once more in the cave. The suited man was once again tied up. Mahbouba and I lined up in front of the entrance, the one I had passed through days before. Nothing had changed. Except for our injuries and the box – the sole outcome of our journey. I held out the eighth mask. Mahbouba put it on, and the wounds on her face disappeared. In fact, her lips blushed red. Her eyes took on captivating colours. Two dashes appeared at their ends – two dashes like two bows containing two beads.

This beauty mask was enchanting. But I preferred the natural clarity of her face – without wounds. She moved towards the suited man, who was now kneeling, and said, 'So, Vetoman, here we are... What do you think? I found the box, and now I'm going to leave the cave. I will have a life after all, despite your efforts.' She turned to me, taking off the beauty mask, returning it to the box and taking out the third – the one from the mosque – that she hadn't used yet. Perhaps its moment had come! She put it on, and a strange smile spread across her lips. A smile that, if it had the chance, could have achieved anything. A smile that breathed life and took life away. A smile that made me forget our journey, the dead, even my own name.

'I don't know how I can thank you, Ustaaz Abed! These masks aren't just wooden! These masks are what life entrusts in us. These masks are the details of hope. If one of them were to break, the job could not have been completed. And without you, I would never have been able to leave that cave.'

'No, don't say it like that, Mahbouba,' I protested. 'Now, I can say my story is finally complete. My story, the one I've been conducting research for. It was on the village of al-Dawayima and what happened there. It was only completed in and with you. So thank you.'

Her lips continued to smile, and her warmth continued to surround me.

'Turn around,' she said.

'Why?'

'I want to change into my mother's dress, may God have mercy on her.'

I smiled and turned around until she finished and said, 'Come on. Ready?'

'Ready.'

The dress was too big for her. She lifted the hem with both hands and walked, and stepped towards the mouth of the cave, the dividing line between darkness and daylight. She turned towards me and extended her hand. I raised my eyebrows, and a smile spread across my face. I approached and held her small hand, with its slender fingers. It was the first time I'd touched it. We looked at each other. Then we stepped over the edge. When we crossed the line, the sunlight blinded us. We closed our eyes, then opened them to the plush green of trees to our right and left. And yet... Mahbouba! She was no longer a little girl! But a very old woman. Over a hundred years old! The details of her pure face were lost among its wrinkles. Her back arched, though her skin was just as luminous. She said in a soft, high-pitched voice, 'Hey! Ustaaz Abed! What happened to me? What happened to you too?'

I looked at myself and I must have aged ten years myself.

Mahbouba smiled. Her smile turned into giggles that made her a child again in my eyes. The magic of her smile was a spell that the years would not fade. I laughed, and we climbed the stairs to the top. The sky was blue. The sounds of birdsong echoed in our ears. But then, somehow, the houses weren't destroyed. The fields weren't barren.

The 'Amatzia' settlement, built on the lands of al-Dawayima, no longer existed. A crowd of people stood waiting for us. My friend Yousef stepped forward. For a second, I didn't recognise him, for he'd aged like me. He embraced me, tears welling in his eyes as he said, 'I waited so long for you, hoping you'd return. When the country was liberated, I swore I would take a house here in al-Dawayima. And the descendents who returned didn't refuse me.' Mahbouba and I smiled at his words. A roar shook the sky behind us, the source of which we didn't know.

Notes

1. On Friday, 29 October, the village of al-Dawayima was subject to a series of systematic massacres of men, women and children, in different locations, including the village mosque during Friday prayers, the threshing floor of the local market, and outside the Tur al-Zagh cave. For decades it went completely unreported. According to British statistics, the number of those killed was estimated at 570. Other reports place these numbers at more than 1,000.
2. The Battle of Al-Maqhaz – a decisive victory for the Zionists, northwest of al-Dawayima, near the village of Beit Jabreen.
3. Tur al-Zagh – a cave near al-Dawayima that villagers fled to

and the site of one of the massacres (*Forensic Architecture*).
4. Khalil Society - an emergency relief charity, like the Red Cross, but specific to al-Khalil district.
5. Za'amtout – a wild plant (of the cyclamen family), used for medicinal purposes and in cooking (usually to wrap rice, live vine leaves).

SHEIKH JARRAH

I Swear, This All Happened

Liana Badr

Translated by Maisa Almanasreh

To Hanan and Maysara and Aline and Jihad and Lutfiya, and to all those who were there.

MY FRIEND FARIDA, DURING our secondary years in boarding school in Jerusalem, once told me there exists a mirror version of each of us. Whilst we live above the ground, our double, which is called the 'Qareen',[1] lives below it. Farida said that it's difficult to know anything for certain, except that we do not only exist in one form, and that we have to acknowledge this parallel existence below the earth. Her grandmother had told her this: whilst we're happy going about our lives above the ground, another identical version of us carries on at the same time beneath it. It wasn't a particularly easy topic to digest, so I tried not to dwell on it too much.

I hid my fear and trembling eyelids from Farida, as I tried to picture this identical image of every living human being. Was it possible for the above-ground version of ourselves to ever clash with the below-ground version? Would our human faces look just as beautiful in this underworld, or would they appear distorted? Do our features appear in the same way 'down there' as they do 'up here'? And who, I wondered, has ever seen both at the same time?

Every morning, Madam Subhiye stood before us with her silver hair and her military posture, scolding us for our laziness when it came to studying English vocabulary, and our minds for always wandering far from our class assignments. We worried that our teacher, Madam Subhiye, might discover that we were only pretending to be dedicated students concerned solely with the pursuit of knowledge. We were paranoid that she would see how distracted we really were by gossip about the teachers, love stories from novels or Indian films – which we very occasionally got to watch – or with our own crushes on film stars or the boys who sometimes passed by our schoolyard fences. All these whispered conversations took place quietly away from class, while during lessons, we stared intently at the floor, terrified that she might discover these preoccupations.

I never revealed the dread that overcame me after hearing Farida talk about this double-existence, because I was always competing with Farida to be top of the class. We were rivals at the end of each term, racing to see who would read the greatest number of library books each week. Would it be me, or her?

So, night after night, I quietly contemplated what Farida had said, searching for evidence of this strange phenomenon. What would be the point of having this Qareen – this spiritual double of ourselves – living in the underworld? I was gripped by the thought that this double could control every move I made. According to what I could glean, this Qareen mirrored all our thoughts and actions, tracking every move with utmost precision. That, to me, sounded dangerous. What if it made a mistake? (Some of the girls reassured me that it could not act independently.) But still, especially if it looked and sounded exactly like us, and shared the same moods and everything that was inherent to us, wouldn't it be dangerous if, for some reason, it did something wrong? Farida reassured me again that these underworld creatures, our spiritual doubles, had no will of their own, and that they only followed us and did what we do. So long as we did nothing bad, she said, there was nothing to fear, nothing they could do wrong.

Still, after dinner, I had to pretend to have a cold, when I started to tremble at the thought of my Qareena sitting at the hairdressers where my mother always took me in the school holidays. Would my Qareena also cut her hair 'á la garçonne' – as my mother used to say admiringly, to raise my morale and compensate for the hideousness of my unruly, black hair, that refused to meet the customary standards for beauty. Even during the hardest times, my mother, who had graduated from the Rosary Sisters' High School, never changed her opinion, always echoing that of my auntie's (her sister's), that my hair wasn't suited to be long like the other girls in our family, because it was too thick and impossible to tie neatly into a braid or ponytail.

My mother would say 'á la garçonne' with pride, as if she were offering me a fine piece of cake, to entice me into accepting this boy cut and spare everyone at home the trouble of having to drag a comb every day through hair so tangled it resembled a dense bird's nest. My mother's alleged admiration for this boy cut was just her attempt to assuage my disappointment about not having silky, straight hair like my sisters. Did my Qareena have the same hair as me, causing the same discomfort and misery to everyone around her?

Farida and I were standing on the basketball court, having finished our daily chores. The sunset cast its red glow on the large stone building next to our school that housed foreign pilgrims, known locally as 'The Colony', separated from our school only by a fence.

I asked Farida again, just to be sure: 'Seriously, is there *really* a Qareen for each of us living in the underworld?'

Her golden hair came loose from her braid and tumbled messily over her forehead, as she answered: 'Of course, it's true. Honestly! Parents just don't tell their children, so they don't get in a panic about it. Otherwise, they'd have to make them drink water from the 'bowl of nerves' all the time.[2] Only us orphans, who've lost our parents, know about it. That's why all the adults around us only want us to be calm and good.'

This was one of Farida's attempts to imply that I was on a similar path to orphanhood as her, and that soon she wouldn't be the only one with no family around. Over the years, the other girls often alluded to the fact that we never saw any of Farida's family, except for one brother who dropped her off at the start of each school year, who she never talked about.

She also never mentioned her late father's family, or her mother, who was of Armenian origin and had fled from a distant homeland that had shown her no mercy. So, Farida couldn't help sharing, tenderly but clearly, that she felt I was walking the same path to orphanhood as her. After all, the school we attended was a kind of orphanage, and there are many types of orphans in the world.

It was clear to us that having a seriously ill parent meant orphanhood was a natural possibility, so the orphanhood I was experiencing was only partially complete, not fully formed. My mother was so ill that we, the youngest of her children, couldn't understand the extent of it. This is why my family had sent me and my youngest sister to this school – to relieve my mother of the burden of having to care for so many children.

In the evening, we continued our conversations while embroidering in the hobby room, to earn Miss Marta's praise. After dinner, we helped clear the tables, hoping to earn extra points from the Qareena we each supposedly had. We kept this a secret just between the two of us, until the incident with Imtiyaz[3] the following month brought all these conversations back into our lives, making us wonder again if it was in fact possible to see our Qareena'a, the way Imtiyaz had seen her djinni.

Imtiyaz

Imtiyaz had a warm complexion that seemed to glow each time her eyes lit up with laughter. She was a dark-skinned twelve-year-old, on the shorter side, who always dragged herself sluggishly as if she cared about nothing in this life. Perhaps it was because she had never known anyone to call family or be called family by. Her sole talent, or 'distinction', seemed to be her ability to smuggle out extra loaves of bread, despite the strict school rules that bread was only to be eaten in the dining hall and during the three designated meal times.

She was favoured by Umm Mahmoud, the head cook who had fled the village of Deir Yassin after the massacre. Umm Mahmoud's left eye had been damaged by a shard from a grenade that exploded right beside her while she was being chased by Zionist militias under a hail of bullets, along with other villagers. They used to say that Imtiyaz was found as an infant, tucked into a stone nook behind Bab Al-Amud, the grand Damascus Gate, one of the main gates in Jerusalem's old city wall.

Eyewitnesses later said that Imtiyaz's sister had been carrying her as they fled from the snipers of the Irgun and Stern Gangs, who had stormed their home and killed both her parents and her grandmother. They said the sister had then handed baby Imtiyaz to an elderly woman who was crawling on her hands and knees under the pine trees beside the road to Jerusalem, searching for a lost sandal. After that, the sister had been forced to run back and look for her youngest brother, who, in the chaos, had disappeared between the legs of the fleeing crowds. The old woman never saw the little girl's sister again; she too was lost to the crowds.

This was the reason why the headmistress, who adopted the child, named her Imtiyaz, meaning 'distinction,' hoping that good fortune would see her grow into someone special like her name. When she was young, Imtiyaz stammered, unable to answer when asked about her name. Perhaps that's why Umm Mahmoud, as head cook, always gave her as much bread as she wanted, no questions asked. She even slipped her the soft, warm, fluffy loaves, fresh from the oven, that were reserved for the teachers who boarded at the school.

For us, getting our hands on fresh bread felt like a rare privilege; we hated the food we normally got – always the same preserved tomato-paste stews over bulgur, lentils, or dry white beans, and nothing but bone broth to go with it, if anything.

The headmistress committed all her resources to rescuing the orphans who were left behind, scattered through the old streets of Jerusalem after the Zionists had raided their towns and villages. As a result, she couldn't afford to give us anything but the bare basics. We loved her, nonetheless. Between us, we always whispered about how the grown-ups admired her determination and her tireless work in collecting donations from Jerusalemite families to keep us fed – which is why she too strictly forbade wasting bread.

But it was tough being hungry all the time.

The smell of fresh bread drew us to the back door of the kitchen, where we hovered near the vent, even though the cold draft and pigeon droppings that rained down from above made it a miserable spot to stand. We waited there for Imtiyaz to come out with her stash of bread that she got from Umm Mahmoud, so she could share it with us whenever hunger struck just before dinner time.

I still wonder if there was some kind of connection between the warm scent of bread and the strange thing that happened next with Imtiyaz. We had never noticed the name of Imtiyaz's room until the bizarre night when the djinni appeared. Each of the bedrooms upstairs in that large stone building was named after a historic Palestinian town or city from which the families, both children and their parents, had all been expelled. The names made it easier for us to remember which room belonged to whom. Mine, for instance, was named 'Yaffa' and had a small balcony overlooking the Orient House, later called Bet El-Sharq. From that balcony, on summer nights, my friends and I could hear an orchestra as Jerusalemite families danced.

Imtiyaz's room, on the other hand, was on the western

side and faced The Colony – that sombre hotel that always seemed quiet, despite being full of European pilgrims visiting 'the holy land'.

One morning, a great uproar broke out among the girls as they shared the news that a djinni had spent the night standing by Imtiyaz's bed, whispering the whole night through in a voice so low it went unnoticed by the others in the room. Before long, however, other girls from 'Tabaria' room, where Imtiyaz slept, started confessing to hearing murmurs, though none but Imtiyaz actually saw the djinni.

We all crowded around Imtiyaz before the morning bell rang but she told us to come back after the classes had ended. When we did, the older girls kept interrupting, making it impossible for us to understand exactly what the conversation with the djinni had been about. Whenever she started speaking, the girls who shared a room with her would intervene, showing off how much they also knew about what happened.

We believed the djinni was real. In fact, there was an old laundry room up on the roof, and everyone knew it was home to a yellow-horned snake and a djinni of its own, who appeared and then retreated on a whim. And although they said he was harmless, he was also unpredictable, which was why we never dared to go up there alone, always going in groups to do our laundry.

So no, we didn't find the story far-fetched. A djinni has the power to choose who it speaks to and who it wants to scorch with its fire if it doesn't want them there.

Day after day, we circled around Imtiyaz, trying to get a better understanding of what her conversation with the djinni had been about, and wondering if it was the same djinni as the one from the laundry-room. Meanwhile, the older girls smirked at our questions, refusing to answer them like it was some private joke.

According to Imtiyaz, the djinni told her that it was tired of being alone, with no family or neighbours. But now, being among the girls, it felt part of the family; so, it clipped its long, claw-like fingernails to make sure no one scratched themselves if they came too close.

It was strange how gentle this djinni was. Despite its enormous size – its head scraping on the high ceiling – it stood quietly by Imtiyaz's bed, waking her softly to talk to her, always kind, never harsh. So tender, in fact, that every girl secretly longed to get to know it. Except for me, of course. I was ashamed by my own cowardice; I was too superstitious to even say the word 'djinni', saying the phrase 'in the name of God, the most Gracious, the most Merciful' instead.

But Imtiyaz also had proof. Even the school nurses needed to question her about the large red marks that appeared on her skin – all of us had seen them. Her extremities were covered in blood-red spots, which she said came from the djinni's presence, the heat it gave off, raising the temperature of the room, even in the bitter winter cold.

Amid all this confusion, my spirits were lifted by a beautiful, surreal dream I had around the same time. A winged, ivory horse came to visit me. It stood on the open rooftop in front of the laundry room. In my dream, we became friends, and I stroked its soft mane and thanked it for the radiant rainbow colours that shimmered and reflected off its coat. It strutted proudly on the bare floor looking like the Buraq Horse[4] that artists draw in New Year calendars. Then it took off, its colours changing from sparkling silver to a sun-like glow, soaring over the rooftop, and leaving behind the clothesline and remaining pieces of laundry the older girls had yet to take down.

How I regretted not knowing if the djinni returned after that or disappeared forever. Not because *it* left, but because *I* had to leave the school. After my mother died, my family pulled me out of the school so I could care for my younger sisters back at home. My responsibilities multiplied as, all of a sudden, I was expected to cook, do the laundry, study and help my sisters. Time became so precious, I couldn't spare a moment even to pay my old school a passing visit.

Occasionally, I'd hear news that Imtiyaz was still defying her teachers and getting in trouble for refusing to do her homework. Whenever she did, she would be barred from spending the evenings with the other girls in the art room, where they embroidered, drew, and wove straw baskets.

As for the djinni? I lost all contact with anyone who could tell me what was happening in my absence.

Then came the war.

We had gone to Amman with my father to file some government paperwork, and a few days later, the war broke out, with no one expecting the outcome to be the full occupation of the West Bank. Within days, the military had bombed the Allenby Bridge – the only road connecting Jordan to the West Bank – leaving us trapped in Amman.

In the blink of an eye, and in our darkest moment, we were no longer allowed to return to our hometown. The occupiers refused to let anyone back who happened to be away during that time, even if they were only outside their villages by a few centimetres. So, this is how we got swallowed into exile, becoming the new refugees of 1967.

Following what, for some reason, they called the Six-Day War, even though it dragged on for almost two weeks, my family got scattered across the diaspora. Thanks to my high grades, I received a scholarship to study in an Arab University. And when we weren't at home when the occupiers carried out a population census, our fate was sealed once more, condemning us, and tens of thousands of others, to permanent exile.

More than two decades passed following this expulsion. Then Oslo was signed, and suddenly I was allowed back, along with the tens of thousands of other 'returnees', along with the Palestine Liberation Organization as part of the deal. At that time, I was overjoyed to be back in my homeland. My heart bloomed with hope and longing, despite the disappointment of seeing how the occupiers now ruled over every street in the West Bank and Gaza.

But one nightmare continued to haunt me; it was the last dream that I had about my school.

The dream was particularly disturbing because it first occured right after leaving to go to university. Ever since, it's continued to instil a feeling of dread that I've never fully managed to shake. A dread that I kept seeing and reliving in great detail, like I was still present inside the dream, standing there with these frightening strangers at the school gate, watching them as they prepared to break in.

In this dream, several men and women, people I've never seen before, stand at the gate, trying to storm the place. Among them, a short man dressed in a long black robe, like a priest or some kind of religious cleric, gestures to the group – made up of women dressed in old English bonnets, looking like they were straight out of the nineteenth century, and men dressed in old-fashioned suits – asking them to prepare to storm the school, despite them all being complete strangers to the place and having no business there.

The crowd hesitates momentarily, reluctant to force their way through. Then I see a crane, like one of those used in the construction sites to move bricks. Hanging from its tip are thick, white chunks of fish. Someone whispers: 'That's Imtiyaz.' Her flesh, which has now been chopped into chunks, is waiting to be devoured. The dream always breaks into fragments, but the worst part of it is the image of that huge crane with the white fish chunks dangling from its tip, and me hearing someone in the background saying Imtiyaz had been transformed into these chunks.

To this day, I still wake up trembling at this image, even though I know it's just a dream.

1994

When I returned to Palestine thanks to the treaty named after that distant European capital, which was impossible to process for the way it spoke of freedom at the same time as tightened our chains, I went to visit my friend Farida, who was now a supervisor of the teachers at our old school. I asked her about many of our old friends, and she had to apologise for not having heard from most of them since graduation. She had lost touch, she explained, not only because of the passage of time, but also because of the multiple layers of exile they'd been subjected to, and the frequent closures of Jerusalem. Many of the students ended up scattered abroad. And for those who remained in their towns and cities, movement was restricted by occupiers' demand for permits, which were almost impossible to get. And when I asked her about Imtiyaz, a flicker of tears welled in her eyes.

'Imtiyaz left for Kuwait,' she said. 'She got married and left. We never saw her again.'

'I can't imagine the mischievous Imtiyaz turning into a dutiful wife,' I giggled.

Farida fell silent, presumably overwhelmed by the rush of memories. I tried to draw her out of her silence, but I couldn't get her to speak. I felt like she was hiding something from me, but Farida insisted she knew nothing about Imtiyaz, promising that she would ask around and get back to me.

Later, Farida would confess that she had indeed known more about Imtiyaz, but she hadn't mentioned it because she didn't want to break my heart so suddenly.

Our precious friend had got married and travelled with her husband to Kuwait, where his job took him. But during the Coalition airstrikes, as hundreds of civilian cars waited at the border outside of Kuwait trying to flee the war, hunger and chaos, Imtiyaz and her husband had stepped out of the car to buy sandwiches for their children. The warplanes flew faster than any of their feet could carry them, bombing them, along with countless other civilians, leaving many of the injured to die in the desert, beyond the reach of any ambulance. Her husband, whose wounds were not fatal, survived, while she was among those who didn't make it and were hastily buried beneath the desert sands.

1995

Strangely, the occupiers had assigned a Qareen for every place in Palestine. The name of every village, city and town was either distorted or completely replaced with another word – layered on top of the real name, setting in motion the pretence that all the newly-coined names were actually the original ones.

Such was the absurdity of this rewriting of history, by simply renaming things, it began to feel like we were living in a car dealership in Los Angeles or somewhere, where each car can be give its own personalised numberplate according to the customer's fancy. The invaders wanted to transform the land itself into a mythical, ancient space that belonged only to them, as if changing the names was enough to do this. Hundreds, even thousands of places, remote, out-of-the-way corners were assigned names that had somehow been forged anew. I even saw this layering when I came across Al-Nabi Samuel, a village that hadn't been destroyed in the invasion of 1948 because the commander in charge had struck up a friendship with its mayor. At its centre was a building, which I assumed was a mosque, but which housed two shrines, one on the ground floor and one directly above it on the first.

What struck me was how identical they were, both equal in size and graced with the same thick, elegant green velvet. I was told that the upper tomb belonged to the people of the land – the Palestinians – while the lower one had been claimed by those who came later, acting like they could steal any place they wanted, even if it belonged to others, merely by expressing a desire for it.

One Morning

One morning, unexpectedly, I had to take a trip to Deir Yassin – or 'Giv'at Shaul' to use their designation. What was the connection between the monastery and the tomb named after the tribal chief and religious scholar, Sheikh Yassin, and the name 'Shaul's Hill'? Who knows. Usually, it's easy to trace back to the real names, even when the new, distorted ones allude to some ancient site, to fool people into thinking the place belonged only to their ancestors. For me, the name Deir Yassin can never be replaced and will never cease being tied to orphanhood, displacement, and the cases that our school specialised in sheltering and caring for.

I had to go and collect a package of books that had been sent by my London-based friend, the artist Mai Ghoussoub, as a gift to Jerusalem's libraries. I had to receive it specifically from the Deir Yassin Post Office, nowhere else would do. The package was addressed to my relatives in Jerusalem and could only be processed at the central post office in Giv'at Shaul, that is to say Deir Yassin, because, at that time, every package first had to arrive at this centre and undergo a strict security inspection. Even the Palestinian Authority's postal service was not allowed to send or receive parcels, because it remains forever accused of vague, undisclosed charges that it can never appeal against.

I headed towards that post office with one of the boarding school's long-serving drivers. We drove up the road, crossing West Jerusalem towards Deir Yassin, leaving behind us the hillside where the remains of what was once the charming village of Lifta lay, and going up to the top of the hill that overlooked Ein Karem, all the while taking in the breathtaking mountain views.

As soon as we reached Deir Yassin, I felt my body clench. These people did not even bother to cover the traces of their crimes.

The place had remained as it was, in its sad, dreary state, with only a few old houses and no public spaces. It felt like the backyard of a giant prison. There was nothing more than a handful of run-down homes. Even the fields seemed to have packed up and gone, leaving behind only meaningless mud.

There were no people there, no inhabitants. The place seemed cursed, worn down by destruction and catastrophe. I wanted to understand what it was about this forsaken place that evoked such dread in me and messed with my head each time its name was mentioned.

I never imagined I would ever visit it. It was the site of a notorious massacre, where whole families had been slaughtered – a great horror that the settler gangs had celebrated and used to terrorise tens of thousands of families into fleeing. The very name of the place spread panic.

In vain, I tried to unpack the secret of this damned place and see what remained of it. To understand why the settlers chose to uproot it from the natural memory of a land where ordinary people just wanted to live in peace.

Now, it was a place emptied of its native inhabitants, those in whose hands springtime had once blossomed. But the colonisers who had replaced them could not ignore the lingering stench of death, nor could they tolerate its state of misery. They found no use in it except to establish a large psychiatric hospital there, as if the killers themselves now needed a facility to care for their own. They even built a park there and named it 'Zacharov', as a cover.

This was not the only place they transformed into a psychiatric hospital. Following the Qareena principle, other buildings were transformed into their darker doppelgangers. For example, there was that agriculture high school in the early 1940s in the village of Bani Amr, on the road between Jerusalem and Yaffa. It had been established by the renowned educator Ahmad Sameh Al-Khalidi in 1939, for the orphaned children of the martyrs of the 1936 Revolt – under the auspices of 'The Arab Orphan Committee'. It included a dormitory housing 60 students, and they had begun constructing a girls' school alongside it. But then the Zionist gangs stormed it and turned it into a psychiatric hospital – Eitanim.

I SWEAR, THIS ALL HAPPENED

Love... and its Stories

A year after my return, entering Jerusalem once again became an impossibility. The settlers had established permanent checkpoints and demanded permits with conditions that were impossible for any of us to meet. I was categorised as a West Bank citizen, a classification that meant I was prohibited from entering Jerusalem – although Jerusalem was my birthplace and my extended family still lived there.

To add insult to injury, my official identification documents now gave Israel *in general* as my birthplace. To obscure the fact that some of us were born in Jerusalem before it was occupied, they removed all mention of my actual birthplace from my paperwork.

At that time, I still occasionally found ways of sneaking into Jerusalem; for instance, if I rode one of the minibuses that were always packed with passengers, the guards would overlook me. Being more focused on checking the permits of the male passengers, they often turned a blind eye to the women. Perhaps, in their eyes, my gentle appearance placed me in the category of 'quiet, harmless woman' who wouldn't dare enter Jerusalem without authorisation.

Could they possibly have understood how thirsty Farida and I were to meet again, to talk about everything that had happened through all the long years we'd been separated? Could they have imagined that we were just looking for a chance to exchange some of those little secrets we had been kept from telling each other? Because Farida, too, had never got a chance to tell me everything.

She told me the story of how she had once been determined to marry a fellow student who went with her to Germany on a scholarship program. Then she told me how she left him, or maybe he left her, after the briefest of affairs, and how she went on to marry her current husband. There was so much we needed to talk about and evaluate, or maybe just gossip over during our rare reunions, that never came by easily.

Our conversations usually began with Farida bursting out laughing, as she recalled my first major panic attack – when I came to her, my face pale, after seeing my period for the first time. I had come looking for her early that morning, almost fainting from fear, to tell her how terrified I was that I was actually bleeding coffee, having found a brown stain in my underwear.

'Coffee?!' I had said. 'There's coffee on my clothes.'

Farida checked my underwear gently, almost maternally, and said: 'You silly girl. That's called a menstrual period, not tea or coffee.' She reassured me that the colour didn't matter in this case, and that the blood didn't always have to appear fresh red.

This then became a running joke between us, one we brought up repeatedly in our conversations.

I seized every opportunity possible to visit Farida, after her shift at the boarding school finished, as there was still so much that we hadn't yet told each other, so many funny stories and memories that were still waiting to be shared.

Sometime in 1995

Yes! There were so many stories and secrets we shared between us during those brief exchanges before I had to rush back to Ramallah before the patrols found me and evicted me from my own city by force. All citizens of the West Bank and Gaza were forbidden from staying overnight in Jerusalem, even if they were born and bred there.

We whispered the secrets to one another like dewdrops brought by the summer dawn to ripen the figs. There was an irresistible urge between us to observe the differences and similarities in our lives, perhaps to bridge the lost years of our friendship. We even found ourselves recalling the names of films whose heroes we admired, dances that we never forgot, books that went on to shape our lives, and the people we learned from. We remembered lines from Sir Walter Scott's famous poem 'Ivanhoe', and how Miss Samia had us perform parts of it on the school stage.

But...

1995, WHEN THEY SET UP THAT TENT

Then came that day when, on my way to meet Farida, I was surprised to find the school's iron gate shut, with a note indicating the gate was permanently locked. The shouting of dozens of people huddled inside a big tent opposite the gate alarmed me. I didn't know who they were or where they had come from in the first place.

I called the school on my mobile, and Farida said it was impossible now to open the main gate. She asked that I go to the back door near the Colony hotel, where one of the girls would let me in.

I didn't understand what was happening on that street facing the Orient House, but I noticed one of the girls had opened the back door just for me. Only then did I realise the purpose of the tent that had been set up by the settlers on the pavement in front of the Orient House. It was to block all entry and exit to the entire street.

Their presence was shocking and incomprehensible. Their shouting through loudspeakers, the beating of their drums and their screams into handheld microphones in Hebrew were beyond disturbing. As usual, they were demanding their government give them the Orient House.

'What? Just like that?' I asked.

As usual, they believed that simply laying their eyes on something of ours, conveyed automatic ownership to them.

What justification could they possibly have for seizing what didn't belong to them? Of course, they had got used to being able to strip any Palestinian of their property, with impunity and under the full protection of their army. And everyone around them helped make it easier for them to complain about their fate, as if fate was to blame for not magically transferring our properties into their hands. Their logic was always the same: everything that was ours had to become theirs.

The next day, one tent became two. The people inside wore identical outfits to the extent that their features started to become indistinguishable. The middle-aged women were dressed in black, and the elderly men wore long grey beards. The darkness inside the now expanded tent, which grew each time I came by, also made it impossible to see their faces clearly or decipher their expressions. Screaming into the microphones seemed to be the foundation of their entire presence.

Eventually, I noticed that many of the men inside there resembled the men who lived nearby, in the ultra-orthodox neighbourhood 'Mea She'arim'. The woman's wrinkled faces and the bearded faces of the men were both blurred by the intensity of hatred in their expressions. It was almost impossible to discern any other emotions.

Inside the high school, the playground remained completely empty of students. Loud songs and aggressive slogans howled from behind the curtains of the big tent. This situation persisted for at least a month and a half.

Their campaign focused on conveying the settler's rage as well as manifesting their claim that Jerusalem must be theirs, all while they repeatedly threatened to storm the Orient House if it wasn't handed over to them, the beautiful house that was built by Ismail Musa Al-Husseini in 1897.

It was in this house that he had once hosted a grand reception in honour of the German Emperor, Kaiser Wilhelm, together with his wife, Princess Augusta Victoria, during their visit to Jerusalem in 1898. Later, he welcomed the Habesha

Emperor Haile Selassie of Ethiopia, who resided there with his wife after being exiled by the Italians between 1936 and 1937, in addition to many other international dignitaries over the years. Much later, the place was known to host global figures who sympathised with the Palestinians, especially during the First Intifada.

The loud slogans from the tent continued. Threats to the school rained down, mixed with the aggressive melodies of ritualistic songs blasted at full volume; voices raised their pitch with each new assertion of their claim to the place. The schoolyard remained empty, with the girls continuing to sneak in through the back door.

All of this continued for about two months.

Until one day, the Orient House was completely shut down. A court order was issued later banning entry entirely, but the deranged wars against us continued in various new forms.

Then one day, it happened that I came across the book *Interpretation of Dreams* by Ibn Sirin. I started reading it to understand whether one's Qareen might become visible in sleep, during the hours when our eyes are closed. Ibn Sirin, the classical Arab dream specialist said that, to this day, no one had ever seen their Qareen, not even in their dreams. He claimed that the sole purpose of the Qareen was to whisper to people, tempting them into harmful or destructive actions.

At this point I found myself asking: Was the Deir Yassin Massacre, where 245 Palestinians were killed, half of them women and children, somehow the result of these mysterious words, whispered in the settlers' ears as they slept? The massacre where 55 fighters from Irgun and another 45 from the Stern Gang had attacked the village with machine guns, mortars, and Sten rifles, despite the signing of a non-aggression pact by all parties to protect both sides.

Could all that have come from the whispers of a strange, invisible being?

Of course not. I had grown up now and I stopped believing in tales of mythical creatures, although I continued to feel pity for the ogress in one particular story. The one who was cooking a meal for her children one day when a human stumbled in and greeted her, to which she replied: 'If your greeting hadn't come before your speaking, I would have crushed your bones.'

Then she would invite the man to stay the night, lifting her long breast over her shoulder in a motherly gesture of welcome. The hero would wash her hair, trim and file her long nails, sprinkle her with cool, fresh water, and by morning, he would go on his way feeling safe, honourable, and uplifted.

This was the least and best thing the ogress could have done – at least according to the countless stories that filled our childhood.

From Now Until Tomorrow…

Now, as we live through the genocide of Gaza where – they have murdered tens of thousands of our people and destroyed homes, hospitals, schools, and community centres with their horrific weapons, hoping to take the land for free – we recall the words of Mahmoud Darwish:

'Oh you, who live beneath the earth, rise,
for the spirit of those who live above it has already died.'

Did the poet think that the Qareena'a could transcend their nature to compensate for the lost lives? What is a Qareen anyway? I don't understand whether it is some inner, mystical being, expressing a drive towards self-destruction and the destruction of others, as various schools of psychology suggest, or whether it is the shadow of a human being so desperate to escape something that it kills everything in its path? Was it the Qareen who whispered destruction, killing and annihilation into the minds of those IDF gangs, or was the Qareen merely a myth with unknown origins?

Media sources say that, following the massacre of Deir Yassin, a *New York Times*[5] correspondent happened to be sitting in the new Giv'at Shaul settlement, having a cup of tea and eating ka'ek with officers who described to him, in great detail, the success of their military operation.

I still visit the school every year, whenever I get a chance to enter Jerusalem during the month of Ramadan – just to breathe in the scent of the ancient pine and cypress trees. I wander through the playground I once believed to be as vast as the plaza of a beautiful town, only to find it narrow and small, like the story of a tragedy that now seems minor next to what is unfolding today. I try to remember the settlers' lorries in which they loaded the wounded villagers, parading them though the streets of Jerusalem in a mock victory amid the cheers of their supporters, to display them as a sign of their 'glorious triumph', before returning them to the execution ground to finish them off at the original site of the massacre.

I still remember how we queued in the mornings at school to sing anthems and recite words that glorified the places we dreamt of returning to, hoping to grow up and find freedom and justice. I smile inwardly at the memory of my younger self holding a piece of a paper in my hand, preparing to read it in the morning assembly, in honour of the heroic guest who was meant to visit our school that day. Her name was Djamila Bouhired.[6]

Our guest was running late but I still held up that paper and I read it, at the request of our great principal, who urged me to go ahead so that the guests' absence wouldn't delay the moment.

I held it up and I read the scattered paragraphs I had written, welcoming the guest, and telling her that we love our homeland no less than she loves hers.

Our important guest never arrived, but the headmistress who founded our school had taught us that some things cannot be postponed, especially those that concern our lives.

Since then, I have continued to read and read, never waiting for the right time to come for this story, knowing it would find its way into the world on its own. By itself. And knowing it would forever carry its scent with it, like the pine and cypress trees of our old school.

Notes

1. According to Islam, a Qareen(a) is a djinni companion assigned to each person from birth, acting as a shadow or companion that can steer a person toward good or evil.
2. A copper or silver bowl, engraved with certain Quranic verses, which when filled with water and drank from, is believed to calm a child's nerves.
3. Imtiyaz was considered to be one of the youngest infants to be found abandoned in the streets of the old city of Jerusalem, without family or relatives. No one ever knew if she was a survivor of the the Deir Yassin massacre or from another nearby village, such as Abu Shusha.
4. The Buraq (meaning 'lightning') is a mythical, supernatural steed in Islamic tradition (often depicted with wings) that carried the Islamic prophet Muhammad during his Night Journey (Isra and Mi'raj) from Mecca to Jerusalem.
5. '200 Arabs Killed, Stronghold Taken; Irgun and Stern Groups Unite to Win Deir Yasin – Kastel is Recaptured by Haganah,' Dana Adams Schmidt, *New York Time,* 10/4/1948.
6. Djamila Bouhired is an Algerian nationalist freedom fighter who opposed the French colonial rule of Algeria as a member of the National Liberation Front.

Flood

George Abraham

as told to the author by Yehuda Dajaj, via broken Hebrew voice memos, which have subsequently been untranslated back into his native English.

> *They come from the lower world and therefore we meet them generally in places which have direct connection with the lower regions: trees whose roots go down into the interior of the earth; cracks, caves, springs, and wells which have a direct or indirect connection with the above-named original abode of the demons. It is therefore not at all accidental that the oriental believes every one of the above-named places to be inhabited.'*
> – Tawfiq Canaan, *Haunted Springs and Water Demons in Palestine*

> *'I wish for you what you wish for Palestinians'*
> – Contemporary Palestinian Proverb

I.

I WAKE UP, DRENCHED in sweat, to discover half a dozen lines of unsnorted coke on my nightstand. Jolting upwards from my empty bed, my ass cheeks tell the story of clinging sheets. *Piss or night sweats?* I ask my seventh PTSD diagnosis.

In the distance of the open window overlooking the sea,

I hear a woman singing opera. Polish? Or is it Russian? Who can know. I'm from a suburb of Tampa and so the citizens of Tel Aviv think me equal parts edgy and illiterate.

I put on electronic music and close the window to drown out the singing. I check my phone and ignore the tenth alarm I've already snoozed through. As if by instinct, I pull open my *Monday* dashboard to see what fires I'm already behind in putting out at work – tech, boring work – before the app reminds me it's the Friday I took off.

Finally! A day of rest and relaxation!

When my last therapist asked me to consider how my relationship with my father might make me set unrealistic day-to-day work expectations, I fired her on the spot. What is a father if not a backhand to the face or palm to an ass? What is a father if not work? I don't need another bitch who charges 500 shekels an hour to give me yet another PTSD diagnosis…

But today, I wake up wet. My skin is moist with want and sick motion. My wanting makes me large. I am engorged and so I matter.

I succumb to the flood.

II.

I came to Israel because I thought it would be a nice addition to my already long and impressive résumé. Summa cum tech whore that I was, a part of me always knew that life would take me further than Florida.

I remember scrolling on Grindr one Friday evening, back in a time before the 'saved phrases' function, when all the gays and theys had to copy and paste their *hello hi what's up you dtf* messages manually one by one. The sea of familiar Floridian small town ghost-faces was interrupted by an ad: a VISIT TEL AVIV THE GAY CAPITAL OF THE MIDDLE EAST banner splayed across a man with curly hair, a freshly shaved six-pack, and tan lines leading my eyes downwards, downwards… Needless to say, my panties were on the floor instantly.

Listen. I'm not saying I'm a catch, but I have standards. Sure, I'm a little stocky – who doesn't like a little chunk, the Gays^{TM} apparently! I'm hairy enough to shine in tasteful nudes, but just thin-spread enough to the point where, whenever I shave, I don't *not* look like a slightly overweight naked mole rat… I look slightly younger than my actual age, but not in a Nice Jewish Boy kind of way. I was raised in a household of vague, unseasoned conservatism – not quite religious, not brave enough to claim atheism with their whole chest. Culturally Jewish at best, maybe. But hey, one grandparent is enough to become Israeli, or so I'm told.

All to say, yes, maybe it was equal parts boredom and horniness that brought me to Tel Aviv. Or maybe this was the only way I knew how to love myself.

III.

Needless to say, Israel wasn't exactly what I expected it to be… Israeli gays are the kind who will feign interest on apps only to ghost once a more attractive option pops up. The kind who post Instagram stories at secret, invite-only underground raves they definitely didn't text you about – the kind who lace their cigarettes with coke and call it their personality. The kind who identify as 'more Israeli than Jewish really', who had names like Chadrick Smith before they came to The New Country and gave themselves different names. Some resembled Sith Lords – in the stories of dates after failed dates that I text my home friends, I've given up and started naming the men Obi-Wan Kenobi no 1, 2, 3, and so forth before they become Darth Sidious no 1, 2, 3, and so forth… At times, their vaguely ethnic names almost feel like catfishing. The jump scare, for instance, of first meeting my boss Amir and finding myself face-to-face with an old, bald, white, Polish man…

All to say – I came to Israel to love myself and found only people even more incapable of loving themselves…

But none of that matters today, on my day of rest and

relaxation – the one-year anniversary of my immigration! Today, I honour the self I was who knew he deserved better than white, conservative, middle-of-nowhere Florida. Moves like this never come without terms and conditions. I mean, think about the first pilgrims who came over to America! The cost of expanding the frontiers of one's own life was always steep, never without risk of completely and earth-shatteringly unravelling.

To begin my day, I skip the elaborate sunblock portion of my skin care routine, praising the arrival of fall, finally, after an impossible summer. 10:07am. I walk down to the Arabic coffee shop down the block from my apartment (see, we're not *that* racist! Co-existence!). I text Adam, my one work friend who isn't really my work friend any more – on leave, technically, for military service.

Me: wyd bitchhhhhhhhh
A: finishing at the gym, u?
Me: on your one and only precious day off?!
A: haha
Me: meet me for iced coffee at the angry camel?
A: sure gimme 20.

'Excuse me,' I look up, interrupted from my phone by a curly-haired brown boy with eyes the colour of well water. 'Your order, sir?'

'Sorry!' I put my phone away, avoiding his gaze. 'Let me have...' Indecisive! Libra season and I'm already blushing!

The barista is unfazed, not even unimpressed, simply blank-stared and blinking.

'An iced Americano, black?' I settle on this, not being able to read most of the menu's Hebrew, let alone Arabic.

'Do you want it Arabic style?' The boy asks.

I decide to be adventurous! It is, after all, my day! Of rest! And relaxation!

I grab a seat at the bar, in clear view of the barista cutie, stealing glances between my mindless phone scrolling. He grabs a small, worn, bronze pot, fills it with some primordial fluid, and his biceps bulge as he nurses it over an open flame.

'Sorry,' his expression doesn't break, fixed as stone, 'ready in ten.'

'I have time,' I smile and he doesn't reciprocate.

Something about semi-cunty men who work in service turns me on unlike anything else. The horrors of capitalism! What it does to the body! Equal parts gorgeous and tragic! Eventually, my charade is up as the barista catches me staring at him, darts an unmoving look back in my direction… Maybe he likes being watched? He's probably straight, I must remind myself. No more getting my hopes up. The DL bro hookups were a figment of my Floridian past, not my Israeli present in the gay capital of the Middle East! But what if he isn't straight? He is, after all, here… Thank heavens he's not in Gaza, where they throw faggots off buildings…

I open one gay dating app, scanning for faceless profiles near me. None within a 0.5 mile radius. I check my other apps and they are equally unsuccessful. I look back at him, taking the coffee off the flame and stirring it gently as he holds it close to his bulging chest. I fix my look, wanting him to look me back in the eye. That will be my test. I'll know what he is if he looks at me, I just need a second, I just…

And then, something like the sound of metal cutting metal erupts between us. The Arab boy doesn't react. I look around and notice, for the first time since my arrival, that the shop is empty. Its details, ancient. Where I would normally expect curly-script live laugh love wall art, I notice empty stone. Where my mind would place brutalist-adjacent bisexual seating – humble stools of brown wood and hay. Had it always been like this, or am I just now noticing? The Arab boy's eyes, fixed to the coffee pot, glow with grey light. The whirr of gas beneath the open flame. The spoon clicking against the rim of the coffee pot. As if by instinct, I look away from the boy at the exact moment he glances over to me. A chill descends my spine. In the reflection of my unlit phone screen, I see the Arab approach me, eyes flooding with grey light, curly hair expanding, rising, as if snakes.

'Harr ou barid? Li qahwatek?' The Arabic escapes him like ancient history, primordial as the light leaking from his eyes.

I click my phone screen on. 10:37am – had 30 minutes really passed in my gazing? And no Adam? In the corner, just as the screen dims itself, I think I see the year flicker back and forth, back and forth between several numbers: 35, 47, 66, 81, too many to count…

'How much longer will this take?' I ask the boy's reflection in my phone screen.

'Sorry,' the metallic cutting stops, the whirr of cars and busy streets resume around us. I meet his eyes which have gone back to their normal lightless well-water hue. 'Hot or iced?'

'Is it weird to have coffee like this iced?' I ask, inhaling the scent like a country I once could fall in love with.

'Of course not,' he smiles lightly and pours the liquid over a cup of ice. 'Have a nice day.'

The coffee still burns on its way down.

IV.

I need to address the elephant in the room. The one question about moving to Israel that everyone thinks about but very few have the gumption to ask about: military service.

After making my move and settling into my apartment, a few months into my time here, I eventually got my summons in the mail. I took the opposite of a relaxing day off work to travel to the nearest base, which was not far – Israel is more a military outpost than a country, even the most delusional among us know this. We learned to be this way. We had to be this way. Eventually, I was ushered into a crowded waiting room and the only empty seat was next to a hulkish man with thick eyebrows and a heavy East European accent.

'Excited to start your service?' He bumped me with his elbow as if trying to hype me up.

'Not quite the word I'd use, but...' I trailed off, lost in the thought of my gay not-twink but not-quite-bear and nevertheless fragile body holding a gun, failing my way through boot camp, or whatever the most vegan-friendly, cruelty-free army in the world needed of my body...

'I've dreamt of this day since I was a little boy,' he said. 'I don't know which I love more, my country or the thought of killing Arabs for her.'

'So you were born here? Where is your family from?' I asked, trying to change the subject away from military details.

But before the man could answer *Ukraine* or whatever, an officer called my government name and motioned me through a doorway. I followed him for what felt like ten minutes, snaking through labyrinthine bureaucratic hallways, passing closed doors that muffled shouts and gut punches and rough Hebrew and occasionally music. Eventually, we arrived at our destination: 'Send him in, lieutenant,' said a voice from inside.

A square-faced man in full army uniform, medaled and all, sat behind a metal desk. He ordered me to sit, and I obeyed.

'Let's cut to the chase,' the man said, before I had a chance to introduce myself, 'I don't think you are fit for typical combat military service.'

Thank heavens, I thought but did not say aloud.

'I have a proposition for you instead. Something more... suitable for your skill set.'

What might that mean? My thoughts raced, wondering if he was complementing or insulting me.

'Being in the cyber security industry, I'm sure you are aware of Israel's need for technological literacy in our military ranks, correct?'

'Yes, back in Florida, I was a technology consultant for

various Jewish American–'

'I've seen your resume,' he interrupted. 'We have a need that's quite… Unique, shall we say.'

'How so?'

'We are aware, too, of your proclivities towards…'

'Men,' I finish. 'How I am a homosexual. No need to beat around the bush,' I say, thinking something about the gay capital of the Middle East.

'Yes, you said it, not me. As you know, Israel has the most homosexual-friendly military in the world, let alone the Middle East. Now tell me, how familiar are you with the popular dating apps here in our region?'

'Not much different from the US, no?'

'Indeed,' he paused. 'The Arabs, especially the resistance, are getting harder and harder to surveil with the standard practices – purchased data, cell phone and internet records. They've gotten better at hiding their digital footprints. As a result, we have the need to get, shall we say, *creative* about how we spy on our enemy, who wants nothing more than to bring death to the Jewish state and our good citizens. You wouldn't want that, now, would you?'

'No, sir.' My heartbeat accelerated with some new-found force.

'And you don't want to waste your time or that of our good officers with combat training to fail at killing the Arabs, no?'

'No, sir.'

'Then tell me,' he smirked. 'Have you heard of… What's that show in America, directed by one of our former soldiers… *Catfish*?'

V.

The thing about that cunt-a-saurus rex Adam… He's flaky as fuck. These gym bros all think they can start disrespecting people's time, especially us regular shmegular six-on-a-good-day gays, once they hit a certain level of buff...

A block away from the coffee shop, I throw my spicy Americano away, watch it flood the bin, and continue about my day of rest and relaxation sans Adam. I walk to the small playground in front of my apartment building – it's where I go to have a cigarette and get my life together when I'm not off terrorising some poor service worker. It's usually empty, especially on a weekday morning, but today there are gaggles of little gits running amok like a minor plague. As I find a bench to sit and type a mentally ill message to Adam, I overhear one child shouting to all the rest: 'MEET AT THE SWINGS IF YOU WANNA PLAY HUMANS VERSUS TERRORISTS.'

I begin typing, *Adam you bitch-whore where the fuck are you* before promptly deleting it, distracted by the children's noise. All but one congregate before the swing sets as their pack leader prosthelatyses like a Baptist preacher:

'The rules are simple: team human, your base is the top of the orange slide. Team terrorist, your base is beneath the jungle gym across from it because it's the closest thing we have to tunnels.' The children cackle maniacally – one even starts to chant *death death to the Arabs* but is drowned out by the laughter.

It is at this point I notice the one child who doesn't join their game, sitting on a seesaw by himself, kicking himself up off the ground before the gravity returns him back down. He has long, curly hair that flaps in the wind as he goes up and down and up and down, content in his own little world beyond the humans and terrorists.

'Humans, your job is to defend your country...'

As the child leader explains the rules of the game, something about terrorists crawling on all fours like the animals they are, I return to texting my real-life manchild: *you bitch... I left, lmk if you wanna meet up later or–*

One child raises his hand. 'How do terrorists kill humans?'

'They don't. They can only win by stealing the flag. It's an all-or-nothing operation. They have to flood the base completely, by...'

The children are distracting me. I untype my message and start retyping again, but the sound of metallic cutting erupts in the sky before I can finish deleting my message. The children are unfazed, off in their respective countries plotting their strategies. I look to the seesaw and notice the long-haired child missing. Beyond the gate of the playground, a patch of green earth in an ocean of gravel.

Thinking nothing of it, I return to my phone: *Hii! So I'll probably either be at home or go to the spa if you can't hang, just let me know what you're–*

A water droplet. Two. A small stream. Then, a flood. The sprinklers have come on and all the children are running, screaming, soaked, crying *KHAMAS!* or some other form of *BLOODY MURDER!* I run, drenched in something other than my own sweat for once.

As I walk back to my apartment to change, I hear laughter. Just beyond the park's gates, the long-haired child, eyes aglow with stone-coloured light, closing the sprinkler's control panel. I walk towards him, and he fades before my eyes.

I check my phone. 11:00am. Adam leaves my messages on *seen*.

This isn't turning out to be a day of rest *or* relaxation...

I decide not to dry off... Spa day it is!

VI.

The first time I visited the baths, I had no ulterior motives: the baths were simply my place of rest and relaxation! It was the perfect set-up: a large single open room where half the walls were mirrors, where the lockers snaked into the showers, which opened out into four concentric circular pools, a wet sauna, and a dry sauna. The pools ranged in water temperature from ice cold to lukewarm to hot to scalding, where even less than a minute left my skin bright red up to whatever water line I could bear to sink myself into. The law of the land was also, importantly, mandatory nudity. The cleaning staff, mostly jaded (which is to say, Arab) barely came around except at specific cleaning hours throughout the day.

I was still new to this country, not yet conscripted into my instead-of-military service. Hebrew was a language that sat rough on my tongue – dry, mechanical, distant from any other language I had known. *It's not antisemitic if I, a semite, call Hebrew ugly*, I convinced myself eventually. But the world I had known before this was the world of English: the world of my dreams and failures. I could never imagine loving someone in Hebrew. I could never imagine delivering hard news to someone in Hebrew. I could never imagine summoning any language but obedience.

Needless to say, the main languages of the bath house clientele were Hebrew and Arabic, the former being the language of the rich and ruling elite who could afford to frequent such places, the latter being an attempt at flying under the radar of the former.

On an ordinary Wednesday, early into my time in Israel, I remember the way language had interrupted my usual bathtime reverie. Cutting around the corner, a rumble of Hebrew and spitting. In the backdrop, a chorus of running water. I looked into a mirror which gave me a gaze right from the pool and into the showers where a man, gripping the engorged length of himself, jerked back and forth, faster than I thought possible. I had never seen anything like this, not in the bath house, but perhaps I wasn't paying attention.

I walked over to join him and, immediately, both him and the man across the steams, who was obscured from the angle of my view in the mirror, stopped abruptly, and turned their tent posts around, just out of sight. I showered three faucets to the left of them, letting the awkwardly cool water trickle down my half-hairy chest. Before I could summon language like, *Go ahead*, or *Can I watch*, the men scurried off back to their respective lockers, avoiding eye contact. I looked towards them, from my gaze in the mirror, but they would not glance back. They simply dressed and left, one after the other, separated by a healthy couple of minutes.

That day at the baths changed my whole world, or at least, how I conceptualised that space, where I looked and did not look. Here, in this country of mirrors, I experienced so many of my naked firsts:

The first time I got lucky in this country, a dark-skinned man, who I came to learn was from Ethiopia, let me jerk him off in the medium hot tub while he fingered my hole under water. I attempted to give him my number on the way out. He never called, but we did see each other there again from time to time.

The first time I forcibly rejected a man, in this country, happened in the wet sauna. The man was white, tall, a bit more heavyset than me, several decades older, but carried himself in a way that implied he was a hunk once in a past life. When it came down to just the two of us, he gave his dick a not-subtle tug. That was his cue, an invitation. I wasn't enthusiastic, but I didn't want to close the door just yet, so I left the sauna with my semi-hard dick and headed back to the tubs. Not only did the man follow me, he parked himself at the hot tub jet immediately to my left, spread his cheeks wide open in front of it, and let chunks from the inside of his hole dissipate into the bath waters. I was so disgusted that, for the rest of my time at the spa, I refused to enter that tub, and gave him a dirty look every time he tried to conjure up small talk.

All of which is to say no, the bath house wasn't a utopia, far from it. Like the country's dating landscape itself, there was a pecking order. Being young and pale-skinned and fat put me exactly on the precipice, most days: I was desired by most but rarely by the ones I wanted most. I was the convenient second choice for some rare young and hungs in the case that an older fit, or fellow hot and young, wasn't there. I was liked by 90 per cent of the elders, who would run their fingers through my sparse chest hair like one would a wounded animal. It was here, in a language of touch, that I learned to become the self I could never become in Hebrew. It was here I first learned how to language my wanting.

VII.

Needless to say, the bath house has become a familiar habitat for me. The workers know me on a first-name basis, and today, like all days of rest and relaxation, they would roll out the red carpet and prepare my special oversized robe and comfy XL slippers – the ones I'd slip my feet into like a fetish – before leading me to my special, full-sized locker, number 47, where I would get out of my clothes immediately. I would shower and enter the grey-tiled room, starting with the lukewarm bath, watching the water slightly overflow the pool's rim.

Israel, in my experience, is a country of time: a country in which time is always in the room, hovering at the margins of every social interaction. For a country whose largest national hobby is archaeology, time is not merely the ground we walk on, it structures every room we move through. The baths, on the other hand, are the exact opposite: they are the only place I can escape time, give my mind permission to wander. It's easy to forget I have a *self* in this country, buried beneath the rubble of my daily multilingual clowning, this corporate circuit act that is my working life…

Across the room, an Arab emerges from the showers. The pink tip of his cock hangs just below his sac, flopping up and down as he walks, with the casual recklessness of living in a country you're only half committed to. I want him, which is to say, it. Just a tip to taste.

I follow him into the sauna, the steam so thick the room feels infinite. I walk forward and do not see the Arab, nor the usual terraced wall of men sitting in their small hierarchies of dick and mouth.

'HELLO?!' I shout. My English betrays me.

I turn back towards the door only to realise there is no door. The floor beneath me, not the grey tile spreading out like a gentrification (sorry, *development*) project, but a slick limestone. *Fuck it*, I think, *this is the most interesting thing to happen all year*, as I walk onwards into the mist. I try not to think too hard about it all. As I walk, I dream of wandering into an Arab, no two, no a whole country of them, in a never-ending orgy to which I'm invited. I dream of parting their sea of hands, of being touched and tongued at every orifice by a different man. In the dream, the men are wearing nothing but head scarves. Their eyes are stone, their fingers half-curled in their primordial want. I get hard in my dreaming, I get closer, closer, closer, until…

That noise. There it comes again, like metal cutting through the TraumCom of my daydreaming. The steam begins to spiral around me, the particles condensing, coalescing into a small vortex. For the first time, visibility: I am not in the room of the bath house sauna, I am nowhere. The floor is stone and the walls are nonexistent. There is just me and the vortex, growing, growing, as my boner exsanguinates itself. I look down at my smart watch, rub the steam off, and the year is stuck on 1947 and the time is unmoving. As the vortex absorbs more and more steam, it begins to whisper. The whisper becomes an airy roar, its tone descending to the depths of some hell.

Off about 100 yards behind me, the steam has cleared enough for me to see a door, modern and upright, connected to no walls. A glitch in the ancient landscape. I run towards it and the vortex descends unto me, wailing, cutting the air between us. I can almost feel it reaching, as if it, too, had hands that wanted to unmake me.

I barrel into the door and fling it open, only to fall face first into the floor of the bath house. Across the room, the Arab, who has become two Arabs, shift their gaze to me for the first time. I get myself up, wondering if my face plant has caused a nosebleed, and the Arabs turn their gaze away, perhaps out of compassion to not engage whatever spectacle I have become, perhaps out of utter indifference. I turn back to the sauna door, still open and leaking steam. The room has assumed its normal form of terraced walls, completely empty.

I brush it off, decide that this steam-induced fever dream won't ruin my day of rest and relaxation. I walk into the pool where the one Arab that had become two Arabs are sitting. I try to meet their gaze, but their eyes are stone, and fixed perpetually away from my direction. Their dicks are half-mast, one pointed towards the other, beneath the water. I touch myself and they do not look. I clear my throat and they stand, in unison, and walk together to the next pool. I follow, and they leave to the next pool. By the third time, I take the hint, as they walk into the shower room, together, and I swear I can see their hands inching closer to each other.

I leave, skipping the showers and heading back to my locker. Finally, a text back from that smegma-whore Adam: *sup bro, srry got distracted. A few of us are thinking of going to this tonight.* Below the text, a link to a pop-up rave, location TBA as the night approaches.

Behind me, I glance in the mirror wall, which is perfectly angled into the showers, with a full and generous view of the Arabs, showering together, hard as rocks. The left one squeezes soap into his hand and begins touching himself. The right one follows suit.

I turn back to my phone, text back, *I'll be there*, before opening my camera app, positioning it into the grating of my locker as if it were instinct by now, and pressing *record*.

VIII.

The arrangement was this: instead of a compulsory military service that would require me to take a leave from work and likely give me yet another PTSD diagnosis, I would work as a catfish informant in my off-time. I was told to gather information by any means necessary. Anything could be useful – screenshots of M4M conversations, details of cruising sites that could be bugged and infiltrated, nudes of course were the best as they could be used to blackmail Arabs into becoming informants themselves.

 Obviously none of the Arabs would fall for an Israeli gay like myself, so I had to get creative about my dating profile designs. Facelessness was the perfect 'paranoid 4 paranoid' situation – the Arabs are a deeply and perpetually suspicious people. My backstory was some permutation of Arab American, on vacation or visiting the holy land or studying abroad. I was always closeted. I was usually from Florida, Orlando has a lot of Arabs from what I hear. My name was Ahmed or Abdullah or if I was feeling spicy, Mahmoud like the poet. I sourced my pictures from gym bro influencers, sometimes Latino or South Asian ones.

 I was a convincing Arab American for a while, but eventually, my conversations would dead-end at the inevitable meet-up or video chat ultimatum. I had to get creative. I had to up the risk if I wanted something juicy. Around that time, I had begun to discover the other world of cruising that happened at the bath houses, or as the Arabs call them, the *hamams*. Whereas the top cruising spot for Israelis was the remnants of the destroyed villages littering the hillsides, the Arabs lived out their cruisiest DL bro fantasies in the baths. I would also, inevitably, find new faceless profiles on dating apps with each bathhouse visit, so it was a double win. It was the perfect *kill three drones with one stone* situation: I would go to the baths and satisfy, at once, my work needs, my horniness, and my eternal longing for rest and relaxation.

IX.

After capturing the Arabs – let's be honest, for work as much as personal pleasure – I dry off and change back into my clothes. I head home to get ready for the rave, only to find out that the location has been announced: the middle of the fucking desert…

I call Adam and he doesn't pick up. I text him, *how tf are you getting to this place?!* And after a few more calls and non-responses, I decide to call a taxi and beg they won't cancel on me or abandon me midway through the ride in the middle of nowhere. The taxi driver is, of course, an Arab, meaning he's desperate enough to accept the ride.

We sit silently on the long, dark ride – the usual for me with Arab taxi drivers. I pull up Google Maps, the drive will take one hour and twenty minutes without traffic, so maybe even two hours given the size of this thing. The more I research it, the more I see that it isn't just some dingy underground rave, but a whole coordinated festival that will continue all weekend. I want to walk into it like the endless steam, losing myself in the crowd. I want to upgrade myself from not just a day but a whole weekend of rest and relaxation!

I open my Arab American cosplay dating apps to try and find new profiles from areas I frequent less. The Arabs are everywhere, in my experience, even in the margins of the Jewish neighborhoods and cities. There's always a DL janitor, driver, dish washer, mechanic – it reminds me of the way the US economy needs undocumented workers, a truth I have tried and failed to tell my racist relatives who, even in a place like Florida, cannot help but invest their anxieties in US-Mexico border crossings.

An hour passes without bites. It is then I realise it's Friday, meaning it's a holy day for a lot of Muslim Arabs – maybe that's what's keeping them off the dating apps? I refresh my app and nearly a dozen faceless profiles pop up. I look at the Google

Maps of my taxi driver and notice that we're nearing the border of the Gaza Strip. *Juicy*, I think but do not say aloud.

Someone messages me in Arabic, what Grindr auto-translates to: *how are you dear?* I do my usual back and forth, saying that I don't know much Arabic because I'm from the States and need to use Google Translate. The man begins to text back in broken English, wondering about where I'm from. He gets excited when I tell him of my invented Palestinian American family in Florida. He calls me beautiful. I text him a picture of a blonde-haired blue-eyed Arab boy and he says he wishes he could take me on a date and spoil me while showing me his Palestine. He says we likely can never meet, because he is in Gaza, which he calls a 'concentration camp' and says it's not easy for US citizens to enter. I say, *Why don't we video-chat sometime instead?* He sends me a broken heart emoji before blocking me. Somewhere inside me, I feel a sting, but it feels like a distant stab, a baby insect trying to bite but failing to break my skin.

'Is this good, sir?' The driver asks in perfect English. We have arrived: tents as far as I can see, lines of cars parked off on the side of the road in both directions, in the far distance, what looks like a massive stage waiting to be lit up.

'Yes, thank you.' I exit the car, tip 5% on the app since it was an expensive ride to begin with, and walk towards the noise.

A buzz.

Adam: *srry broseph, I was called back in for emergency service on my day off. Happens a lot these days… I hope you enjoy the festival, Ben will be there, tell that psycho I say wassup!*

Alone. Again. But this time, in the middle of the fucking desert. Just me and nothing to my name but some guy named Ben who I can barely remember among Adam's gay bro friends. I have half a mind to run back to the car, apologise for the rude tip, and beg for a ride back then and there. But the car is nowhere to be found.

I have nowhere to go. I have nowhere to go, except…

X.

I must talk about the real reason I left my comfortable but boring middle-class suburban life in America. It is the story of my sexuality's awakening as much as it is the story of my Israeli identity's awakening.

The story begins where it ends: the locker room.

The first time I ever saw another person's penis was in the sixth grade. Every day before swim team practice, I'd wrap my mole-like body with a towel over half the size of my whole body to change into my swimsuit. All the older guys would just let it hang out, stripping completely naked, showing off their body hair coming in, making fun of those of us who hadn't quite gotten our pubes yet. It wasn't even the cocks and balls as much as the bushes that turned me on – that which I did not yet have, that which I might never have, my younger self feared!

Ever since, I've become obsessed with locker rooms. The banter, the horsing around, the casual naked comradery, the men with bodies hairier, fitter, slenderer and more toned than mine. It wasn't creepy at first, no, just a young and growing curiosity – the traces of a life I could never live, being lived out before my eyes. As I aged – less like fine wine, more like bleu cheese – this life appeared to me in continuous glimpses, at these liminal zones of lockers, showers, and pools, and never seemed to get any closer to the life I was actually living.

Tired of being ignored on dating apps throughout my teenage years, I decided to make a catfish profile of the man I could never be. He was a tall, hunky, brown-skinned, not immediately recognisably famous content creator I found. I gave him a generic first name and vaguely ethnic-sounding last name: Nick Abudajaj. While other people my age wrote fan fictions, I was living one, each night, seducing the hottest gays around me just for the rush of it. I wanted nothing more than the seduction, I knew not to go too far with anyone, dare

I say, fall in love. It was just for shits and giggles…

Until the nudes started coming in. I always found porn to be too boringly predictable, too performative. I craved something more immersive; if the intimacy of the life I wanted was perpetually being denied to me, maybe the universe could meet me at some halfway point, some fucked-up version of edging the life I wanted. Nothing would turn me on like those stolen, catfished nudes would – even if the guy himself wasn't particularly attractive.

I had morals, of course. I never went for guys I actually knew. That was my limit… Until it became the first border I broke.

Florida was Florida, which is to say, it got repetitive, boring, and disastrous all at once. At that point, I was attending a large state university where most of the guys were straight, and the others weren't even faceless dating app flavoured DL gay. But the showers at the locker room, those were open, without stall doors to border us. I couldn't catfish these bros on dating apps, sure, but I could sneak peaks in the locker rooms.

Eventually, I was able to secure a locker directly in the line of sight of the shower room. The possibilities were limitless, I thought – I could grow my own personal spank bank, stolen from the bodies who never looked twice at me! Only, the tiny-holed grates of my locker door didn't allow my full camera to peep through, so one day, at the earliest hour of the morning when literally no one was swimming, I arrived with a knife and got to work, jamming it in and out, attempting to open the hole of my locker grate ever so slightly to let my camera record, but not large enough to be noticed. It was harder than I imagined, as I cut and cut, metal to metal, trying not to stab myself or not to mess up the locker too visibly. The sound of cutting metal was so grating, I decided to chip away at it, little by little, to not attract attention. Eventually, the hole was just wide enough to allow my camera to see the showers unobstructed.

I could have spiralled off so much worse. I could have

made a decent side income, selling my videos to the Pervs of America. But I refused to monetise it – there was something more attractive about the privacy of this archive, the fact that it was mine and mine alone. Eventually, as the years passed and I graduated but stayed in the area, maintaining my membership and gym locker through the university's alumni discount, I recorded more and more jocks every day, every year bringing in a new batch of fresh meat.

I wish there wasn't a *but* to this story. I wish I wasn't forced to take this plunge, in my new Israeli life. I could have survived America, I think. I could have lived off my job and my desire alone. I could have performed happiness, maybe married a nice Jewish woman, and had a few children myself to keep me happy, all the while satisfying my urges with my little secret. But it wasn't meant to be.

I was discovered, to say the least. A student complained about me, I think it was an Arab one – the one who, one day while towelling off in a recording, made direct, stone-cold eye contact with the camera, and began positioning himself out of the frame's view thereafter. It isn't often, in these recordings, that a subject looks directly into the camera. It is a hard thing to have your secret subject looking you right in the eyes, and it is also a thing that made me unbelievably hard. I wanted more. I wanted to capture him from a different angle, to see him in a new light, to one-up him in this game of cat and mouse he was initiating. My cockiness got the better of me, as the administration heard reports of a man tampering suspiciously with his locker.

It happened when I was naked, having just dried off after a swim. A row of cops were waiting for me at my second locker – the one I used to attempt installing a 24/7 surveillance set-up. They asked me to open it. I asked for a warrant. The cop tried to cut the metal lock but it resisted. He clipped and clipped away at it, as the metal screeched, and eventually, it gave way, only to reveal an empty locker.

To this day, I will never forget the sound of cutting metal, the sound of my own handiwork and the police's – how had I been less careful, the evidence that I tampered with the locker could have incriminated me indirectly. How, I had gotten away with it by accident: my goals to install a more ambitious system had failed, and the videos were not uploading properly, so the night before the cops came, I had removed the camera and taken it home to try and fix it. Were it not for my own incompetent camera set-up, I could have been caught and imprisoned.

I escaped that day, sure. But the eyes were all over me, now. The whispers were whispered. Florida was Florida, which is to say, I knew everyone and no one all at once. I couldn't bear it – the paranoia, knowing that around any corner, there could be someone who had heard even the faintest insinuation of what I was. I never returned to that gym again, never attempted to find a suitable replacement. I needed out and fast.

And then: a Grindr ad telling me to come to a gay oasis in the Middle East, designed just for me. Somewhere I could actually live the life I had broken all laws and morals attempting to touch, in traces. Somewhere I could actually escape the orbit of my abusive father without arousing too much suspicion – he, too, once considered moving to Israel, apparently. Somewhere I could reinvent myself from the ground up.

XI.

If I'm alone, I can't do this sober, I think as I move onwards, through the tents of coke-sniffers and barefoot college students and tie-dye wearers. In the middle of a circle that feels almost cult-like, a white woman with dreads dances to herself, bluetooth speaker in hand. *Perfect*, I think.

'Excuse me,' I interrupt. 'Where can a gay find something to get lit?'

The woman, still bouncing at the hips, reaches out for my shoulders. 'Oh honey, if you're not already lit, go take a nap, it's gonna be a long night!'

I look down at my smartwatch. 10:39pm dominating the centre of the screen, with a small 10.6.2023 at the corner. 'I wasn't thinking of staying too long, maybe seeing a few acts then heading back tonight.'

'First time at a rave?' She still clings to my shoulders, trying to rope me into her dance.

'How could you tell?' Sweat begins to bead down my forehead.

'This is the pre-game, hun. The best acts all start around 4-6am. All the party girlies time their high to drop right at sunrise.'

'My friend left me here all by myself,' I say, trying to escape her grip. 'I'm just trying to have a day of rest and relaxation, that I thought would become a weekend of rest and relaxation, but here I am, abandoned in the middle of the fucking desert…'

'Oh sweetie, look around you! You're not alone! You have this, you have us, all of us! You have the whole fucking world right here, in the palm of your hand.' She slips two blue pills into my right hand and closes my fist around them.

'What is this?'

'You wouldn't believe me if I told you.'

'When should I take them? To get my peak high at sunrise?'

'Take the first pill now, it'll help you go off and make some new friends!' She holds my arm and slides my watch right off.

'What are you –'

'Setting a timer for 2am for your second pill. Here we go! 2am, October 7, 2023. All set!' She slips the watch back onto my wrist.

I take the first pill.

'Let the party begin!'

★

The first few hours are a blur. I dance a bit with my new white woman dreadhead friend, who tells me her name is 'Regina, like Spektor'. Shuffling between beats, our fragmented dialogue goes like:

Me: I can't believe the tickets were so cheap, I mean the taxi down from Tel Aviv costed more!
Regina: I drove down with my lovely humans. You should come to our tent and meet them, you can crash with us if you need!
Me: Thanks for covering me with, I mean, whatever this is, I forgot my own stash back at my house, in the rush to grab the taxi.
Regina: So you're from Tel Aviv?
Me: No, I'm from the States.
Regina: Oh like New York City?! I'm from Brooklyn!
Me: Not exactly… Let's just say… I needed to escape to a little gay haven, if you get my drift.
Regina: [gasps] Shut! Up! Oh my GOD, I've always wanted to be a fag hag! All my lovely human friends are straight! I've always wanted a GBF!
Me: [awkward, chuckling, changing the subject] So how long have you lived in, uh, where are you living again?
Regina: Oh my family lives, you know… In the territories.
Me: I mean, don't we all live in a territory?
Regina: No, I mean like… Judea and Samaria…
Me: Oh, got it! I haven't had a chance to go out to the West Bank, too complicated to figure out!
Regina: Festivals like this are my little escape, you know. I live with my strict father who's all like, *we're a decent Polish family*, meaning I always have to sneak out, even though I'm a [screaming at the top of her lungs] FULLY GROWN FUCKING ADULT! Jeffrey Yehuda is the worst, I'm telling

you! But anyways, back in the US when I lived with my mom in Brooklyn, she'd always take me to raves like, ever since I was a little girl.
Me: Woah, that's so wild. My family sounds more like your father.
Regina: I know, fathers are the WORST! I wish I was still living with my mom, I kinda hate Israel sometimes? Like isn't it the fucking worst?
Me: I mean, totally, here we are partying, and you know what, on the way here I matched with a guy on Grindr… In Gaza… He called it a concentration camp, it was kinda sad…
Regina: Ugh, that is disgusting! How anti-semitic!
Me: Oh… Yeah, I mean, I didn't really think of it like that, but…
Regina: It's like, my mother is a fun Jew who insists on staying in the US… And my dad is not a fun Jew who insists on coming to Israel… Like why can't they just swap places? I feel like my mom is more Israeli and my dad is more Jewish, you know?
Me: So do you split your time between here and the States?
Regina: Yeah, my dad makes me visit for half of the year…
Me: So what do you do for work?
Regina: I help my father run his store. He makes his living selling overpriced shit to tourists visiting the Dead Sea.
Me: Oh nice, is that why your face is glowing? All the skincare products?
Regina: No, it's from all the Arab babies I behead and drink the blood from! Or that's probably what your man in Gaza thinks!
Me: [nervous laughing]

Neither of us know where to go from here, so we just hold each other and dance a little longer, trying to avoid eye contact, and failing. And as soon as I meet Regina's gaze, my high begins to set in. And before I know it, I'm making out with her, I'm closing my eyes and picturing Adam or the faceless man from Gaza or the Arab who became two Arabs from the bath house. She reaches into my pants and grabs me and, not letting go, leads me back to her tent.

*

Is it homophobic if I say, my first time with a woman is the best sex I've ever had in my life? I mean, surely this is more the drugs' doing than anything, I couldn't keep my eyes open for 95% of it, of course. I swear, even when I was inside of her, she still told me to call her my fag hag...

Speaking of, I wonder where Adam is right now, what he's doing, why he got called back onto duty tonight. It feels like it's been so quiet here in Israel, not nearly the war-torn country I expected to walk into, and yet Adam's been summoned back to work from his off days more often than not.

I decide to go for a walk to enjoy my high while Regina tends to her lovely humans. The whole world, I remind myself, is in the palm of my fucking hand. The whole night feels like a kaleidoscopic blur, some slant rhyme between some 'hippies in the wood' type shit but translated to the desert, and Coachella. Around me, I hear clips of everyone's conversations: 'I don't remember the last time something this big happened in Israel or It feels like I'm in Europe, finally or Trance isn't just music, Samantha, it's a state of mind.'

I pass a man pushing his daughter towards the main stage in a wheelchair, the girl decorated in glow sticks, and remember Regina's story of going to raves since she was seven years old. *What kind of parent...* I begin to think before killing the thought in my head: there's no room for judgment in my day, no, weekend of relaxation!

And then, my wrist buzzes. 2am, time for pill number two. Time to go to the main stage.

*

Past the encampments, the bonfires, the tables of paint for live artmaking, the main stage peaks outward on the horizon. The pavilion leading up to it is completely lit up in triangular blue, pink, and black banners, like a flock of dismembered kites cutting through the sky. I'm not usually well-behaved at parties. I simply do not know what to do with my body. I feel like I am always awkwardly in the way. I'm too sheepish to dance alone, and I'm not the kind of boy who gets invited out to raves with the Gays. But this, all of this, feels different somehow. Maybe it's the second pill setting in, but I feel at one with the earth and the humans around me. My sweat is flowing, pounding, flooding out of me. I dance like a river, joining the sea of us – every single molecule of me joins the collective of sweat. I kiss a stranger, two, maybe seventeen. A man places a glow stick around my neck like a fallen halo. When the man with the mic says jump, I jump. I am as obedient as my Hebrew. I become something more than language. I become body and body mine and body his and body hers and body ours. And then, at that moment of peak body, sunrise.

★

I don't know how I feel or hear it, but something is terribly wrong. There is a shake in the earth. A tremor. I look down at my watch, 6:29am. I feel it in my feet though no one around me changes a thing. The sky shrieks with the sound of cutting metal, as it has all day but a thousand-fold. I collapse to my knees, cover my ears, but the metal keeps shrieking, shrieking. A pair of hands that becomes two pairs of hands tries to help me up but I swat them away. The nosebleed I should have had earlier, after my fall in the sauna, finally arrives, streams down my face. Then, a soft hand at my cheek. A cloth beneath my nostrils. I look up and lock eyes with Ben, Adam's friend, finally!

As he helps me up, he says: 'That bitch-whore Adam told me to keep an eye on you because he thought you were too much of a pussy to last all night here.'

I collect myself and follow.

*

On the way to the bathroom, Ben and I pass small crowds of people looking up at the sky.

'Fireworks!' A curly-haired woman shouts, 'Look, they're doing fireworks for us to celebrate the festival!'

'I think those are rockets, babe,' her boyfriend says back.

Another group of college kids take a selfie with the rocket fire in the background, all of them smiling and cracking jokes about how the terrorists of Gaza couldn't touch us, even if they wanted to.

In the bathroom, Ben leaves me be at the sink while I clean my face up. 'I look like bloody murder, don't I?'

'Nah, I've seen worse.' He chuckles. 'You should have seen our boy Adam, that one night some homophobic fuck called us faggots. He fucked that boy's face up like I've never seen. That's the thing about Adam, he doesn't flinch when it comes down to it.'

Perhaps because of the pills, or maybe the overstimulation of it all, or maybe Ben's story was the straw that broke the camel's back, but all at once, I begin to cry for the first time in, well, I can't even remember. The tears break out into sobs as I crumple to the floor again.

'You good bro?' Ben bends down.

'WHY AM I HERE, BEN?' My eyes are redder than my nose at this point.

'Yo, chillax, what did you all take tonight?'

'IT'S MORNING, BENJAMIN! Nearly seven in the fucking morning and that tit-for-brains Adam abandoned BOTH OF US. I mean, dude, we're in the middle of the fucking desert, getting sunburnt to shit, what the fuck are we doing here? I mean, what the fuck are any of us doing here?!?!'

'Uhh… Should I call for some help or?'

'NO, DON'T CALL FOR FUCKING HELP, I CAN HELP MYSELF! I'm just saying,' I begin to choke up. 'Why. The. Fuck. Did. I. Move Here.'

'Calm down, broski,' Ben taps me. 'Deep breaths, one step at a time, this is probably just a bad trip.'

I sniffle. 'You're right, I'm sorry, I just… Sometimes I think I moved to Israel more because I hate my father than because I love it here, you know?'

'Real shit, dude. The first year I moved here, bro, you wouldn't believe it! My allergies went to shit from all the olive trees! I was breaking out in rashes every single day, I became bed-ridden it was so bad.'

'But you seem so… Well-adjusted?'

'It's fake dude. Typical gays from Tel Aviv shit. We all fake it till we make it here, because at least we're here and not, well, wherever the hell we came from.'

A lightness, for the first time all day. I step down from the counter and hug him like I've never hugged him before. 'Thanks for this.'

'Let's go back to the music, yeah?'

★

As soon as we step outside, we notice the entire vibe has changed. The music has stopped, some people are running back to their cars, others are forming little jam groups around guitars and small speakers.

Ben stops one of the women, running frantically with her tent all packed up. 'Yo, what's going on? Everything okay?'

'You didn't hear? People are saying there are terrorist attacks happening, we need to make for a bomb shelter and get the fuck out of here!'

'She's overreacting!' A man in a tie-dye shirt shouts from about ten feet away. 'Dude, the terrorists can't TOUCH us!

This will be over in thirty minutes, my guys, just chill the fuck out.'

'Then why aren't any of the police picking up? Where is the army? Why are emergency services offline? Why are people live streaming with the sound of gunshots in the background? I'm getting the fuck out of here!' She storms off, not needing to be convinced.

'Dude, she's probably just gonna get in her car and be stuck down 232 with all the traffic of drugged-up paranoid motherfuckers trying to get the fuck away, I mean… We should just chill out, stay put, we'll be safe here if we lie low.'

A conundrum emerges, one which my drugged state won't allow me to think too deeply about.

Ben pulls out his phone and finds the nearest bomb shelter. 'It's just over a mile away, up the road. We can walk and make it, I think.'

God, I'm gonna kill Adam if we make it out of this alive…

*

The next thing I remember is waking up with blood on my hands. In my lap, the upper half of Ben's body, legs completely blown off. *It must have been the grenade*, I think to myself. I search my memories and all I can see is light, a flood… We were running along the road, watching the cars zigzag and crash into each other… We were hiding behind a car lined with bullet holes to hide from a gang of terrorists who passed by us on motorcycles, unknowing. But where am I and how did we get here?

'UP, UP!' A man shouts in an accent I barely recognise. He's standing just yards away, holding a rifle aimed right at me, talking into a radio. From the fragments I can understand, something about how it took a half dozen grenades to break through because the dead boy kept throwing them back, live.

'I'm unarmed, I swear, I'll cooperate,' I say back, raising my hands above my head, hoping my English will save me.

The man comes over, ties my hands together, and blindfolds me. He presses his gun to my back and leads me into what feels like a vehicle – we're driving before I know it. I nod off.

★

Like a slap to the face, I wake up, sweat staining the air around me where the man's hand reverberated. My hands are still tied, but my blindfold has been removed. I look around the room – windows boarded up, barely anything visible besides the chair I'm sitting in, the official with a Hamas logo on his arm standing before me, and a table with my smartwatch reading 10:40am and a tiny 10.7.2023 in the corner – and ask, 'Where am I?'

Another slap. 'We'll ask the questions, not you.'

I look up. The watch reads 10:41am, 6.5.1967. The man is now wearing a red scarf around his face.

'But what are you–'

Another slap. I look up. The watch reads 10:42am, 11.30.1947. The man is now wearing a white scarf with a headband securing it to his head.

'What do you want with–'

Another slap. The edges of my vision are beginning to blur. 10:42am. 4.15.1936. The man is hazy, a stone-coloured outline of a man. An idea. A metaphor.

'Am I going to surv–'

Another slap. Something tells me I won't survive many more of these. I'm losing water and blood and fast. I can no longer raise my head, can no longer look the man, the idea, in the eye. In the distant background, the sound of chanting. It's Arabic, I think, but older, unrecognisable to me aside from the refrain *Nebi Musa*, which I recognised from a religious studies class I took years ago. Out of the corner of my vision, I can only see the edge of the watch, the year reading 1920.

'What am I doing here?'

No slap comes. The story is happening, I think, and it's happening around me. My body is the furthest thing from protagonist.

'What am I doing?'

Silence. The air, thick with sweat and moisture. And, for the first time, an honest question surfaces.

'What am I –'

A man kicks down the door. The Hamas official runs behind me, wraps his arm around me, and holds a gun to my head. He props me up like a rag doll. I let the weight of my whole body fall backwards onto his body, which feels like stone. He's probably 6'3", I can smell the cigarette smoke from his breath against my neck. In my delirium, in what little blood I have left, I begin to get hard.

He shoves me right and my head follows. I turn to make eyes with the man at the door: a soldier in an IDF uniform, whose gun is also aimed at my head. I squint, I look harder. I recognise those blue eyes, that tuft of hair sticking out at the left.

Adam, I do not have the energy to say, though my mouth falls open.

An eternity passes between us. The man at my front spitting words I do not recognise. The man at my back gripping me tighter than I've ever been held. The warmth of him, my warmth. The moisture of him, my moisture. A trickle runs down my leg and I can't tell which fluid, or whose, I'm wet with. I'm close, I'm close, I'm so close to –

The sound of bullets.

The man's grip only tightens as Adam's bullets penetrate me, and eventually, him, but only through my body.

The man clamps down on the gun, sends me singing from ear to ear.

And for the first time in this pathetic thing I call a life, I feel…

Love?

Glossary

Abu – 'father of' (followed by the name of the eldest son, or occasionally daughter).
Amaanah – the entrusted.
Baba – Father (in Palestinian Arabic, it can also be used by a father to refer to his children).
Adthaan – Call to prayer
Al-balad – the homeland.
Ba'ullac & *Bakullatch* (Gazan/West Bank) – I'm telling you.
Beit – house or home.
Eleblad – homelands.
Ghul & *Ghulla/Ghulleh* – monster, ghoul (m & f) (Gazan/West Bank).
Habibi/khabibi & *habibti/khabibti* (Gazan/West Bank) – a term of endearment (m & f).
Hajja – Old woman.
Hatta – keffiyeh (traditional, patterned headscarf).
Ilabad – forever.
I'qaal – traditional thick, black rope used to affix the i'qaal.
Al-Khalil – Hebron.
Mactoob & *Matchtoob* (Gazan/West Bank) – it is written.
Mar – Saint (preceding the name).
Meshi/Mashi – OK.
Mihrab – A niche on the mosque wall, on the side pointing towards Mecca, that the congregation prey towards.
Mukhtar – villager, tribal or family leader.
Qumbaz – a traditional, loose-fitting shirt.
Sabra – prickly pear.
Al-shataat – the diaspora.
Umm – 'mother of' (followed by the name of the eldest son,

or occasionally daughter)
Ustaaz – sir.
Ultellu & *K*ultellu (Gazan/West Bank) – I told him.
Yaba – Father (in Palestinian Arabic, it can also be used by a father to refer to his children).
Yalla - come on.
Yamma (or *Yumma*) – mum.
Zalameh – mate.

About the Authors

Geroge Abraham is a Palestinian poet who is currently living as a settler in the US project. They teach English for a living.

Ibtisam Azem is a Palestinian novelist and journalist, based in New York. She has published two novels in Arabic: *Sariq al-Nawm* (*The Sleep Thief*, 2011) and *Sifr al-Ikhtifaa* (*The Book of Disappearance*, 2014), both by Dar al-Jamal. The latter is translated to English by Sinan Antoon and published by Syracuse University Press and And Other Stories.

Liana Badr is a novelist, short story writer, journalist, and poet. Raised in Jericho, she obtained a BA in philosophy and psychology from the Beirut Arab University, but was not able to complete her MA due to the Lebanese Civil War. She has worked as a volunteer in various Palestinian women's organisations, and as an editor in the Al Hurriyya review cultural section. After 1982, she moved to Damascus, then Tunis, and Amman. She returned to Palestine in 1994. Since her first novel *A Compass for the Sunflower*, in 1979, she has since published three collection so of short stories (*Stories of Love and Pursuit, Golden Hell, I Want the Day*), a collection of novellas (*Balcony Over the Fakahani*), two further novels, a biography of the poet Fadwa Touqan and five children's books.

Selma Dabbagh (born 1970) is a British Palestinian writer of fiction, living in London. She grew up between the UK, Saudi Arabia and Kuwait and has also lived in Bahrain, Egypt, the West Bank and France. Her first novel, *Out of It* (2012), was a Guardian Book of the Year. Several of Selma's short stories and plays have won, or been nominated for awards. Her writing has been published by *Granta, The Guardian*, International PEN, the *London Review of Books*, the British Council and Saqi Books. Her radio plays have been produced by the BBC and WDR. Her father's family is from Jaffa.

Yehuda Dajaj is your worst nightmare.

Yara El-Ghadban (born 1976) is a Palestinian-Canadian novelist and anthropologist. She is the author of four novels. *La danse des flamants roses* (2024) won the Mare Nostrum Prize, the Prix du 3e Poulpe and was shortlisted for the Prix Frontières in France. Her third novel *Je suis Ariel Sharon* (2018) has been translated into English, Arabic and German. She lives and writes in Montreal.

Basma Ghalayini (born 1983) is the editor of *Palestine + 100: Stories from a Century After the Nakba*. She is an occasional translator from the Arabic and is the Productions Manager at Comma Press. She was born in Khan Younis, and grew up in the Gaza Strip.

Anwar Hamed (born 1957) is a Palestinian novelist, poet, literary critic, and former BBC employee living in London. He has published ten novels in Arabic, and a number of other works in Hungarian, as well as contributed to several non-fiction titles, most recently: *Being Palestinian: Personal Reflections on Palestinian Identity in the Diaspora*, edited by Yasir Suleiman. His novel *Jaffa Makes the Morning Coffee* was longlisted for the International Prize for Arabic Fiction (IPAF). His most recent novels are *Outsider* and *Ghosts*. He was born in Anabta in the West Bank near Tulkarm, where his family is from.

ABOUT THE AUTHORS

Ahmed Jaber holds a PhD in Transportation Engineering. He won the Abdul Mohsen Qattan Foundation Young Writer Award in 2017 for his short story collection *Mr. Azraq in the Cinema*, and his work has appeared in Comma Press's *The Book of Ramallah* as well as in local and regional newspapers and websites. He also serves on the editorial board of several academic journals and continues to publish both academic and literary writing.

Mazen Maarouf (born 1978) is a writer, poet, translator and journalist. He holds a bachelor degree in General Chemistry from the Lebanese University. He has published two collections of short stories *Jokes for the Gunmen* (translated into English by Jonathan Wright, and winner of the inaugural Al-Multaqa Prize for the Arabic Short Story), and *Rats that Licked the Karate Champion's Ear*. He has also published three collections of poetry: T*he Camera Doesn't Capture Birds, Our Grief Resembles Bread and An Angel Suspended On a Clothesline* (2012). In 1948, all four of his grandparents (as well as his father, who was six years old at the time) fled the village of Deir al-Qasi in the mountains of Galilee and travelled on foot to Lebanon. His parents lived in Tel El-Zaatar refugee camp until the late seventies when they had to flee again at the start of the Lebanese civil war.

Abdalmuti Maqboul (born 1987) is a Palestinian writer, novelist, and visual artist. He holds an MA in International Relations and Public Administration from Ankara University (2016) and a BA in Graphic Design from An-Najah National University (2009). He participated in the International Writing Program at the University of Iowa. He recently received the A. M. Qattan Foundation's First Book Grant for his short story collection *Thatun Okhra (Other Selves)*, recently published by Al-Ahlia. He was born and lives in Nablus.

ABOUT THE AUTHORS

Lina Meruane is a Chilean writer and scholar of Palestinian descent. She has authored two collections of short stories and five novels translated into twelve languages. Meruane has written several non-fiction books, including her memoir *Palestine in Pieces*. She has received awards such as the prestigious Premio Iberoamericano de Letras José Donoso (Chile 2023), Blue Metropolis (Canada 2023), Cálamo (Spain 2021), Sor Juana Inés de la Cruz Novel Prize (Mexico 2012), and Anna Seghers Prize (Germany 2011) as well as grants from the Guggenheim Foundation, the National Endowment for the Arts, and DAAD Writer in Residence in Berlin.

Mahmoud Shukair (born Jerusalem, 1941) is one of the Arab world's best-known short-story writers, with translations of his work into numerous languages. He has published over 85 books, including thirteen short story collections, five novels, and 50 children's titles. He has also written extensively for television, theatre, print, and online media. In 2011 he received the Mahmoud Darwish Prize for Freedom and Creativity. His 2016 novel *Praise for the Women of the Family* was shortlisted for the International Prize for Arabic Fiction (IPAF). He previously served as editor-in-chief of the weekly Jerusalem newspaper *Al-Taliah*.

Sonia Sulaiman writes short speculative fiction inspired by Palestinian folklore. Her work has appeared in *Arab Lit Quarterly, Beladi, FANTASY, FIYAH Magazine, Xenocultivars: Stories of Queer Growth, Seize the Press, Lackington's Magazine* and *Ask the Night for a Dream*. Her works have been nominated for Pushcart, Lammy, Locus, Ignyte, Ember and Best New Weird awards. In her spare time, she curates the Read Palestinian Spec Fic Reading list. She is the author of *Muneera and the Moon: Stories Inspired by Palestinian Folklore* (2023), and the editor of *Thyme Travellers: An Anthology of Palestinian Speculative Fiction* (2024).

About the Translators

Maisa Almanasreh is a Palestinian translator based in Portugal. She has an MA in Interpreting and Translation from Leeds University and has previously translated fiction for *Egypt + 100: Stories from a Century After Tahrir* and *The Book of Sana'a* (both Comma Press).

Rana Asfour is the Managing Editor at *The Markaz Review*, as well as a freelance writer, book critic and translator. Her work has appeared in such publications as *Madame Magazine*, *The Guardian* and *The National*. She chairs the TMR English-language BookGroup.

Helen Constantine is an author and translator from the French. She has published two volumes of translated short stories, *Paris Tales* (2004), and *French Tales* (2008) and edits a series of *City Tales* for Oxford University Press. She has translated *Mademoiselle de Maupin* by Théophile Gautier and *Dangerous Liaisons* by Choderlos de Laclos and Balzac's *La Peau de Chagrin* for OUP. With her husband, David Constantine, she edited *Modern Poetry in Translation* for many years.

Raph Cormack is a translator and researcher in modern Arabic literature, and author of *Midnight in Cairo: The Female Stars of Egypt's Roaring `20s* (Saqi, 2021) and the forthcoming *Holy Men of the Electronic Age: A Forgotten History of the Occult* (Hurst, 2025). He is Assistant Professor in the Arabic

ABOUT THE TRANSLATORS

Department at the University of Durham and is an editor of *The Book of Khartoum* and *The Book of Cairo* (both Comma, 2016 and 2019).

Mohammed Ghalayini worked for two years as a reporter for New York-based Free Speech Radio News in Gaza and as a presenter on the Palestine Satellite Channel. His translations have appeared in *The Book of Khartoum, Palestine + 100, The Book of Ramallah*, and *Egypt + 100* (all with Comma). He works as an air quality scientist and, in late 2023, offered extensive first-hand reporting on the genocide being conducted in Gaza.

Andrew Leber is an assistant professor at Tulane University's Department of Political Science, where he researches the politics of the Middle East and North Africa. His translations have appeared in outlets such as *AGNI* online, *The New Statesman, The Brooklyn Rail, Jadaliyya* and *Guernica*.

Andrea Rosenberg is a translator from Spanish and Portuguese. Her full-length translations include novels and graphic narrative by Manuel Vilas, Tomás González, Inês Pedrosa, Aura Xilonen, Juan Gómez Bárcena, Paco Roca, and Marcelo D'Salete. Her translation of D'Salete's graphic novel *Run for It: Stories of Slaves Who Fought for Their Freedom* (Fantagraphics, 2017) won an Eisner Award in July 2018. She holds an MFA in literary translation and an MA in Spanish from the University of Iowa, and she has been the recipient of awards and grants from the Fulbright Program, the American Literary Translators Association, and the Banff International Literary Translation Centre.

Adam Talib is the translator of Fatma Qandil's *Empty Cages* (Hoopoe, 2025) and associate professor of classical Arabic literature at the American University in Cairo.

ABOUT THE TRANSLATORS

Jonathan Wright is a translator and former Reuters journalist. His previous translations from the Arabic include Khaled Al Khamissi's *Taxi*, Youssef Ziedan's *Azazeel* (Winner of the IPAF, 2009), Saud Alsanousi's *The Bamboo Stalk* (Winner of the IPAF, 2013), Hammour Ziada's *The Longing of the Dervish* (Winner of the Naguib Mahfouz Prize), Ahmed Saadawi's *Frankenstein in Baghdad* (shortlisted for the Man Booker International), Mazen Maarouf's *Jokes for the Gunmen* (shortlisted for the Man Booker International), and Hassan Blasim's *The Madman of Freedom Square* and *The Iraqi Christ* (winner of the 2014 Independent Foreign Fiction Prize).

ALSO AVAILABLE IN THIS SERIES

Palestine + 100
Stories from a Century after the Nakba

Edited by Basma Ghalayini
ISBN: 9781910974445

Featuring: Talal Abu Shawish, Anwar Hamed, Tasnim Abutabikh, Selma Dabbagh, Emad El-Din Aysha, Samir El-Youssef, Saleem Haddad, Majd Kayyal, Mazen Maarouf, Abdalmuti Maqboul, Ahmed Masoud & Rawan Yaghi

Palestine + 100 poses a question to twelve Palestinian writers: what might your country look like in the year 2048 – a century after the tragedies and trauma of what has come to be called the Nakba. How might this event – which, in 1948, saw the expulsion of over 750,000 Palestinian Arabs from their homes – reach across a century of occupation, oppression, and political isolation, to shape the country and its people? Will a lasting peace finally have been reached, or will future technology only amplify the suffering and mistreatment of Palestinians?

'This rich and varied anthology offers thoughtful insight into the hopes, fears and traumas of people whose suffering has been wilfully ignored by the mainstream media for decades. It's also a timely and entertaining reminder of the potential of SF as a literature that reframes perceptions and challenges assumptions.' – Morning Star

FUTURES' PAST

Iraq + 100:
Stories from a Century Aftre the Invasion
Edited by Hassan Blasim

Palestine + 100:
Stories from a Century Aftre the Nakba
Edited by Basma Ghalayini

Kurdistan + 100:
Stories from a Future Republic
Edited by Orsola Casagrande & Mustafa Gundogdu

Egypt + 100:
Stories from a Century After Tahrir
Edited by Ahmed Naji

Iran + 100:
Stories from a Century After the Coup
Edited by Fereshteh Ahmadi, Leila Elder & Peter Adrian Behravesh